This Land

*A Cross-Country Anthology of
Canadian Fiction for Young Readers*

KIT PEARSON

VIKING

VIKING
Published by the Penguin Group
Penguin Books Canada Ltd, 10 Alcorn Avenue, Toronto, Ontario, Canada M4V 3B2
Penguin Books Ltd, 27 Wrights Lane, London W8 5TZ, England
Penguin Putnam Inc., 375 Hudson Street, New York, New York 10014, U.S.A.
Penguin Books Australia Ltd, Ringwood, Victoria, Australia
Penguin Books (NZ) Ltd, cnr Rosedale and Airborne Roads, Albany, Auckland
1310, New Zealand

Penguin Books Ltd, Registered Offices: Harmondsworth, Middlesex, England

First published 1998
2 4 6 8 10 9 7 5 3 1

Printed and bound in Canada on acid free paper ∞

CANADIAN CATALOGUING IN PUBLICATION DATA

This land: an anthology of Canadian stories for young readers

ISBN 0-670-87896-0

1. Children's stories, Canadian (English).* I. Pearson, Kit, 1947– .

PS8321.T44 1998   jC813'.01089289   C98-930714-X
PZ5.Th 1998

Visit Penguin Canada's web site at www.penguin.ca

*For Sheila Egoff, the first cartographer
of this land's literature for children*

Contents

Introduction

This land is far more important than we are. To know it is to be young and ancient all at once.

> *Hugh MacLennan,* The Colour of Canada

When I was a child growing up in Alberta and B.C., fiction was something that happened elsewhere. Almost all the stories I read or that were read to me took place in American small towns or the English countryside. I was totally familiar with the places where the Moffats or the Little Women lived; and I was even more intimate with the "enchanted place" on top of the forest where Christopher Robin sits with Pooh.

The most potent region of all for me was the English Lake District. I was first introduced to it through the misty watercolours in the Beatrix Potter books, and was later suffused with the area through reading and rereading what are still my favourite children's novels, Arthur Ransome's "Swallows and Amazons" series.

When I grew up, these fictional settings had such a powerful grip on me that I began to go on pilgrimages to find the real places. I visited Orchard House in Concord and saw where Meg, Jo, Beth and Amy hung their curtain for their plays; and Ashdown Forest in Sussex, where I found Galleons Lap, the real enchanted place. I spent several blissful holidays in the Lake District, exploring the fells and lakes that Mrs. Tiggy-Winkle and Squirrel Nutkin inhabit, and looking for the real Wildcat Island and the real Kanchenjunga from Ransome's books. When I found these places I always felt the same delicious shock of recognition. The author or illustrator had portrayed its essence so well that I already knew it.

There were so few books published for children in my own country when I was young that I encountered only two Canadian authors: Farley Mowat and L.M. Montgomery. As a prairie child, discovering Mowat's *The Dog Who Wouldn't Be* was a revelation. Reading about such utterly familiar things as gophers and sloughs and saskatoon berries, I felt almost embarrassed, as if I'd just finished a book about my own family. Conversely, the tidy landscape of Montgomery's Anne and Emily books was so different from my own setting that Prince Edward Island seemed as exotic as the other places I had read about.

Canadian children can now have a very different experience from mine. Their own country provides them with a wealth of fiction to make many areas of Canada come as alive to them as Mary Lennox's secret garden or Ramona the Pest's Klickitat Street.

The intention of this anthology is to create a tapestry of Canada, a living map composed of only a small portion of the vast literature we now enjoy. Choosing just twenty-two selections was a very difficult task. I didn't use the texts of illustrated books, except in a few cases where the words seemed able to stand alone; I hope readers will look for the originals of these, however, with their wonderful accompanying pictures. The number of selections for each province reflects both its population and how many authors have written about it. Newfoundland, for example, has inspired a remarkable number of writers, and separate anthologies could easily be made of Ontario and B.C. writing. I tried to vary the age groups, balance the male and female protagonists, and include selections from the past as well as the present, modern as well as classic, fantasy as well as reality, and to represent as many different cultures as possible. In the case of the novel excerpts, I hope the selections will encourage readers to seek out the books. My main criterion was good writing, and that was where selection was the hardest; I could have chosen dozens of other pieces that are just as well written.

These authors use setting in many different ways, but all of them give it an important role in the story. Sometimes the characters are so emotionally involved with their place that it affects the plot. Emily's passion for the house and community around New Moon is what inspires her to be a writer; Mary's awe of her new land gives Janet Lunn's *Shadow in Hawthorn Bay* its intensity; and the ambitions of the young narrator in Budge Wilson's "Dreams" are both inspired and thwarted by his surroundings. In several books the young use their environment like a huge playground: Tim Wynne-Jones's, Brian Doyle's and Farley Mowat's characters happily *own* rural Ontario or Ottawa or the Saskatchewan prairie as only the roaming young can. It is often said that place is another character in a story; the Arctic in *Tikta'liktak* and the lake in *Who Is Frances Rain?* are especially strong examples of this. A setting can shape its young inhabitants by its climate, such as the long winters in *Ticket to Curlew* and *Baseball Bats for Christmas*. Place is often a healer: Norah in *Looking at the Moon* and the protagonist of *Jasmin* are both soothed by their surroundings. Sometimes that healing place gives characters the strength to survive newer, alien places, as in *My Name Is Seepeetza* or *Hold Fast*. Place often comprises the community living there: both Roch Carrier and Mary Alice Downie evoke Quebec village life in their stories. Place also includes its non-human inhabitants: Sir Charles G.D. Roberts and George Clutesi view the natural world through the eyes of animals, one with realism, the other with legend. Finally, as Hugh MacLennan says, to know a place is to know the ancient, the past that is hidden in our landscape. Joan Clark, Janet McNaughton and Julie Lawson take us both imaginatively and literally back in time, in re-creating Viking Newfoundland, Toronto in the twenties and nineteenth-century B.C. Paul Yee does the same thing through myth in "Spirits of the Railway."

Of course place in fiction plays a much lesser role than character and story. But a strong sense of setting makes the book more real. If the place is so specific that the reader can inhabit it in his or her mind, then the characters and story spring to life as well. Just as the particular evokes the universal, the details—from the street names in *Angel Square* to the rivers and mountains in "Spirits of the Railway" or the horses thundering on the prairie in *Ticket to Curlew*—are the threads in a shimmering tapestry. Our literature for children is still young, but we are slowly beginning to create a fictional map of Canada. In a time of political and cultural identity crisis, perhaps it's this sense of the land we all share that brings us together. A child living in downtown Toronto has a very different life from a child living in the Arctic. But because both those children can read about each other's settings, their imaginative experience is expanded. Modern Canadian children are still as imbued with distant places as I was, not only in their reading but through television and pop culture. Therefore it's even more important for them to know their own land as well, which, in MacLennan's words, is "far more important than we are."

In memorable fiction an author mythologizes the setting of the story, gives it a sheen, an otherness, that makes it magic—that makes you want to go there. Perhaps the magical settings of these and of a myriad other stories will inspire not only young Canadians but readers from other countries to go on quests such as I did. They have always made literary pilgrimages to Prince Edward Island; now they might visit the land of no trees where Arvaarluk lives, or the B.C. ranching country that Seepeetza longs for, or the main street of Saskatoon where Billy and Bruce participate in the pet parade. But of course readers don't have to go there because they've already been, through the enchanted worlds that all of these authors have created.

This
LAND

Ko-ishin-mit Invites Chims-meet to Dinner

by

GEORGE CLUTESI

This is a Tse-Shaht fable featuring the greedy prankster Ko-ishin-mit, Son of Raven, and his long-suffering squirrel wife, Pash-hook. It is illustrated with black-and-white pictures by the author.

> *When kook-sim the geese fly high in the sky,*
> *When red leaves flutter in the gusty wind,*
> *When Chims-meet swats his salmon ashore,*
> *Blue smoke from the alder will fill the air.*
> *'Tis the cutting season for the folk*
> *And the salmon will be smoked,*
> *Done to their taste.*

Red leaves sailed down the ever-increasing currents of the streams. The mist rose from the waters to meet the fresh nip in the chill of the morning air. It was late fall. The moon of the cutting and smoking season was drawing to a close.

Every household in the village was busy putting in the last of their winter's supply of dried salmon, preparing to pack it away in huge cedar food chests. Rows and rows of filleted salmon hung from the sleek cedar poles to be smoked and cured so it would keep throughout the long winter moons.

Ko-ishin-mit sat by his own little fire poking at the embers with his fire stick and wishing he could have some of the newly smoked salmon for his next meal. He had been to every household in the village too many times, he told himself. Where could he go for his next free meal? Suddenly he thought—the bears. Chims-meet the bear. That's where he would go.

"Why didn't I think of this before," he chided himself. His excitement at the prospect of yet another free meal was overwhelming.

"Nah, my dear," he called to his little mate, "I'm going into the woods to hunt," he lied. "I may be gone for some time so do not wait to have dinner with me."

Pash-hook, his little wife, never questioned her husband's wishes and always did everything he asked of her. She loved her husband very much.

All the womenfolk in the village felt sorry for Pash-hook because they knew Ko-ishin-mit never brought any food to their house. That was the reason Pash-hook was so skinny, they all said. Normally some kind woman would find the time to bring her something good to eat but since the moon of cutting season had arrived few indeed came to offer her any food. At this time of year poor Pash-hook looked thinner than ever.

Chims-meet and Mamma Bear were big people. They were kind and thoughtful and so very generous at heart. They welcomed all people or travellers that came their way and always had a bountiful supply of food, especially during the winter moons.

Chims-meet was the best fisherman in all the land. He loved

to wade into the streams when the salmon season was on. Whenever he saw Sah-tsup, the king of all salmon, he would swat it onto the beach with his great left hand. Mamma Bear would then flop it into her big cedar root basket that she carried over her plump shoulders suspended by a tump-line that ran across her broad forehead. When the basket was full of the fattest salmon she would tote it to their smoke-house, to be cut up and spread to dry on the long slender cedar poles. This was their winter food.

Mamma Bear had a heart as large as she was and always before leaving the river to smoke the salmon she would remind her husband not to catch any of the mother salmon. Indian people never molest the mother fish because they come up the streams to lay their eggs in the gravel for more and more fish to come back in other years.

During the berry season Mamma Bear would pick berries with her left hand. It is said that all bears are left handed. They do everything with their left hands. She would spread the berries on the hot rocks in the sun and when they were thoroughly cured she would store them away. At that time of year Chims-meet loved to go out and look for wild honey which Mamma Bear would store in airtight salmon bladders.

The house where the Bears lived was built beside a stream where the cohoe and chum salmon went up to spawn. It was deep inside the heart of the woods a long distance from the village but Ko-ishin-mit did not mind the long walk. He was so greedy he would go any distance for a free meal.

"Well, well, well, Son of Raven. The weather is fine. Come in, come in," invited Chims-meet when Ko-ishin-mit arrived at the door of his house. "Sit down, do sit down and we shall have a bite to eat," the friendly Chims-meet said in his great rumbling voice. Chims-meet was at home because his work was done and all his food-stuff for the winter was carefully packed away in the big cedar chests.

Ko-ishin-mit saw the great boxes lined along the walls and he knew that they were filled with dried salmon, berries and wild honey. His mouth slobbered at the thought of that bounteous supply of food.

"I wonder where he keeps his oils," he thought, for no matter how much food was offered to him he always wanted more. Ko-ishin-mit was never content. He was shamefully greedy. "Best of all, I would like some oil with my broiled salmon," he kept saying to himself.

Ko-ishin-mit had not visited the Bears before and he was a little shy at first. "Ah yes, it is indeed a fine morning. I have been out hunting. The weather is too still and the creeping things are wary."

The sly one pretended not to be too anxious to stay, but all the while his beady little eyes were busy looking around the huge room for any sign of the oils he loved so well. He pretended to be very tired and he sighed and stumbled a little as he finally said he would stay for a short while.

Mamma Bear came into the room with a big fat salmon in her left hand. She stoked up the live coals and began roasting the large fish. The aroma of the salmon cooking smelled very sweet to the greedy Ko-ishin-mit.

"I wish I could have some oil with my salmon. I wonder where they keep their oils," Ko-ishin-mit kept asking himself.

At last the smoked salmon was ready. Mamma Bear wrapped it in some cedar matting and put it to steam for a while and then reached for two of the largest clam shells Ko-ishin-mit had ever seen. Setting the shells down by the hot coals Mamma Bear called to her mate, "There you are. All ready for you."

Big fat Chims-meet chuckled at his wife and then turned to Ko-ishin-mit. "Sit away from the fire while I draw the oil," and so saying he faced the live coals and spread his great hands directly over the two clam shells, all the while chanting a little rhyme:

Clear oil run smooth, good oil flow well, rich oil come now
Fill ah-meek, both ah-meek I say
Clear oil run smooth, good oil flow well, rich oil come now
Fill ah-meek, both ah-meek I say.

Chims-meet sang his ditty in a low, rich, powerful voice and before Ko-ishin-mit's very eyes the clearest and richest oil began to flow from the bear's hands into the two waiting clam shells. Soon both shells were full to the brim.

"Tu-shack, tu-shack? What has happened?" was all Ko-ishin-mit could say. "Tu-shack, tu-shack?" His beady little eyes almost popped out of their sockets with surprise. Ko-ishin-mit had seen a lot of strange things in his lifetime but this was something new to him.

As was his habit Ko-ishin-mit ate with no regard to his hosts. He gobbled up the roast salmon with greed, pushing his whole hand into the oil and into his mouth without stopping. He had no manners whatever when he was eating.

Mamma Bear watched secretly as Ko-ishin-mit made a glutton of himself, since it was not polite to watch another person eating. "Oh, how the poor man can eat," she thought to herself.

As usual Ko-ishin-mit ate too much and got too full. As a result he went to sleep beside the fire and snored and snored. The good Bears kept quiet and let him sleep. At long last he roused himself and mumbled that he must be getting home. While he was dusting the white fly ash off his coat he very politely asked the Bears to have lunch with him and his little mate, Pash-hook, the very next day.

"We shall be delighted and honoured to have lunch with you," Chims-meet replied.

When the Bears arrived on the following day, Ko-ishin-mit was very excited. He hopped and flitted about his little house ordering Pash-hook about. "Bring in more wood. Stoke the fire. Make ready the salmon for the coals. Get out my clam shell, no, make it two."

Poor little Pash-hook was agitated because of their very important guests. She was determined to please them. She scurried and bounded about doing everything her husband asked of her. She brought out their only dried salmon and then burned it by trying to roast it too near the red-hot coals. She wondered what her husband wanted the clam shells for, but she got them anyway. It was said Pash-hook was light-minded but she was a good and obedient wife to Ko-ishin-mit and that was really all that mattered to both of them.

"Stand aside while I draw the oil," Ko-ishin-mit announced with a great flourish as he went up to the freshly stoked fire clutching the glistening ah-meek. "Stand aside while I draw the oil," he repeated as loud as he could in his croaky voice.

Pash-hook's whole married life had been spent in wondering and marvelling at her husband's continual attempts, no matter how fruitless, to do anything and everything as well as any other person. Wishing above all to please her guests and her husband she poked at the fire again with the fire stick.

Ko-ishin-mit strutted to the flaming fire and squatted on his little backside. With a flourish he very deliberately spread his scrawny little hands before the hot fire directly above the waiting clam shells. He sat for several minutes before the roaring fire with hands outspread, but nothing happened.

He sat before the fire for a very long time, but still nothing happened. No oil flowed into the two clam shells. Ko-ishin-mit sat there until his whole little body was burned black—his beak, his eyes, his whole coat and especially his scrawny little hands. They were burned until they curled up into claws.

It is said by the old people that this is why all ravens, to this day, are all black, because Ko-ishin-mit, the Son of Raven, burned himself while trying to copy the fat Chims-meet in drawing oil from his hands.

The guests all agreed it was not good to try to copy other people. Chims-meet and Mamma Bear went back home without any dinner.

from

White Jade Tiger

by

JULIE LAWSON

After the death of her mother, Jasmine is sent to stay with her Aunt Val in Victoria while her father is in China. Withdrawn and angry, Jasmine takes refuge in the compelling dreams she has been having about a girl called Bright Jade.

When Val came to say good night, Jasmine remembered. "We're going on a field trip to Chinatown tomorrow, so I'll meet my class there and you won't have to drive me to school. Did Dad tell you?"

Her aunt nodded. "I'll drop you off at eleven."

"We can wear something Chinese if we like, but I don't have anything."

Val grinned. "I've got just the thing."

In a minute she was back holding a dark bundle and a wide-brimmed hat. "What do you think?" she asked, placing the hat on Jasmine's head.

Jasmine looked in the mirror. "Great!"

"Now this." She held a jacket against Jasmine's chest. "Looks like it might even fit. Try it on."

The jacket was lined inside, heavily padded with cotton. It had wide sleeves and hung loosely over her jeans. Jasmine did up the frog fastenings, closing herself in from neck to hem. "It fits perfectly."

"It's what the Chinese coolies wore when they came to work on the railroad. Try on the pants."

Jasmine slipped them on. "A bit long."

"That's OK. We'll just roll them up, like so. Now, the shoes." She handed her a pair of black cotton shoes.

"These fit too."

Val smiled. "You've certainly got the hair for it. One long pigtail, like the Chinese had in those days."

The clothes felt good, well-worn and comfortable. Jasmine grinned at her reflection. "I look just like a Chinese coolie."

Val's face suddenly fell. "What's wrong?" Jasmine asked, surprised at her aunt's reaction.

"Nothing," Val said, laughing it off. "It's the way you looked just then, as if—have you ever had the feeling that something has happened before? *Déjà vu*, it's called. When your mom was about your age, she went to a Halloween party. She didn't know what to wear, so I suggested the coolie clothes. She put them on, stood in front of the mirror and said exactly what you said."

"Did she wear them to the party?"

"Yes, and had a horrible time. The kids teased her and called her names. She came home in tears, tore off the clothes and kicked them out of the room. This is the first time they've been worn since then." Seeing the look on Jasmine's face, Val said, "Don't worry. I'm sure the kids in your class are more enlightened."

* * *

It was raining the day of the Chinatown trip, a heavy rain that splashed the pavement with neon reflections and made the street shimmer. "I'll meet you at Fan Tan Alley at 2:00," Val said as the school bus arrived. "Here's a note for your teacher." She gave Jasmine's braid a tug. "You look terrific," she said. "Have fun."

The class spilled off the bus and gathered in excited clusters in front of the restaurant. A spattering of red sweaters brightened the sidewalk, along with shirts emblazoned with dragons and Chinese writing.

"Hi Jasmine," said Krista, giving her a friendly wave. "Where did you get the clothes?"

"From my aunt. It's what the Chinese wore when they came to build the railroad."

"I didn't know that," said Becky. "You look great. But don't you feel like, *weird?*"

"No," Jasmine replied. The question surprised her. "I feel right at home."

"Figures," Becky said with a grin. "You always like to be different. But you can sit with us anyway, ok?"

"Sure." Becky's words stung. Was there an edge to them she hadn't noticed before? Was she hearing things differently, or was she just too sensitive?

They're still my friends, she thought as they trooped up the stairs. Even though I've gone quiet on them. But something was missing—the easy warmth, the feeling of being accepted. She paused by the aquarium at the top of the stairs. Was she really so different? And if she was, so what? It didn't matter.

"Fish for abundance and prosperity," Becky said. "Right, Jasmine?"

"I think so." There were so many symbols: a chicken for happiness, a cricket for good luck, a tortoise for long life. It was because of the language, Mrs. Butler had explained. If a word had the same sound as another word, then it took on the same meaning. Like the word for pear. Don't share a pear with a friend, because pear has the same sound as the word for departure. Had she shared a pear with her dad? No, neither of them liked pears anyway.

And red was supposed to bring good luck. She had tied a red ribbon around her braid, hoping her dad's flight would be cancelled. Or maybe he'd have an accident—just a little one, just enough for him to be sent home.

No sooner had they sat at the round table than the waiters began bringing food. Deep fried egg rolls, steamed dumplings stuffed with pork. Chop suey with water chestnuts, bamboo shoots and beef. Bite-sized portions of pork drenched in sweet and sour sauce. A plate of chow mein, heaped with diced chicken, fried noodles and vegetables.

"This is hard to eat," Jasmine said, as the beansprouts slipped from her chopsticks.

"You can come here with your aunt," Krista said. "You'll get lots of practice."

"Oh, I almost forgot." Jasmine took out the note and handed it to her teacher. "My aunt's meeting me at Fan Tan Alley at 2:00, wherever that is."

"It's one of the stops on your scavenger hunt," said Mrs. Butler. "You'll find it easily enough."

At the end of the meal, the fortune cookies arrived. Becky read, "*You will travel a great distance.* You should've got this one, Jasmine, since your aunt's driving you to Sooke every day. What does yours say?"

"*Someone from your past will soon re-enter your life.*" Good, she thought. Maybe Dad won't stay in China after all.

Mrs. Butler was handing out the scavenger hunt lists. "Mark

off the items as you find them. I'll meet everyone in front of the restaurant at 2:00."

By the time they left the restaurant the rain had turned into a thick fog, enveloping them in the exotic atmosphere of Chinatown. On both sides of the street, shops displayed huge earthenware jars and vases painted with phoenixes or dragons. Outdoor stands offered a variety of fruits and vegetables, from lemon grass and winter melon to long stalks of sugar cane. Red posts topped with pagoda-shaped lanterns lined the street; even the telephone booth had a pagoda-like roof. At the end of the block was the gate Jasmine had seen the night before, a brilliantly painted structure flanked by two stone lions. She checked it on her list: the *Gate of Harmonious Interest*.

Every doorway opened into a different world. "Look at this," Krista said. She held up a bulky packet of paper money, used for burning on ancestors' graves. "When it burns, the smoke rises to heaven. Then the ancestors have money to spend."

They checked off pickled jellyfish, bins of white rice and black rice, tins of shark fin soup, fluttery black mushrooms, fish dried and flattened as thin as parchment.

In the herb shop they gasped at the overpowering smell of dried fish and lizards, animal parts and strange plants used to treat ailments and allergies. "How do people eat them?" Jasmine wondered.

"Put them in stew or soup, or boil them in water and drink like tea," the herbalist said. He held up a dried sea-horse. "You want to try?"

"No thanks," they said.

In another store they found ink sticks and chopsticks, a poster showing the Great Wall covered with snow, and jade figures in all shades of green. But no white jade, Jasmine noticed. And no jade tigers.

"Here it is," Becky said suddenly, pointing to a signpost. "Fan Tan Alley. Isn't this where you're supposed to meet your aunt?"

"Yes, but I've still got 15 minutes. I haven't even bought anything yet."

"Come on, you guys," Krista said excitedly. "This store is really neat."

The entrance was jammed with paper chains and streamers cascading from the ceiling like papery pagodas, brightly coloured in red, turquoise, green and gold. Jars and boxes crowded the shelves, stuffed with little toys and gadgets, from panda pencil sharpeners and tin whistles to Chinese dolls.

Krista led the way down a narrow passageway crowded with blue and white porcelain, Chinese junks, statues of Buddha. It opened into another room, a jumble of cotton slippers, wicker baskets, straw hats and slippery silk robes. "Hurry up," she called. "There's *another* room in this never-ending store."

They followed her along a dark and twisting passage into a larger room. "It's a kind of museum," she said. "See that guy in there? Doesn't he look real?" A mannequin dressed in a long black gown stood behind a wicket, counting out money. "This used to be a gambling den." She bounded over to a display case. "Where's the list? Check off the tiles for playing Mah Jong, then we'll go down the alley."

"Hey, look." Jasmine pointed to a pile of buttons and a brass cup. "It's a fan-tan game," she said, reading the label. "That's how the alley got its name. See, the banker divides a pile of buttons into fours, and the players bet on how many will be left over."

"Too much like math," said Becky. "Now let's go. There's only one store left."

"Wait a minute," Jasmine said. A row of dragons leaping along a dusty shelf caught her eye. "I want to look at these."

"Catch up to us then." Krista and Becky headed back to the main entrance, while Jasmine turned her attention to the dragons. As she was reaching for the blue one, her eye flicked over to the mannequin. It seemed as though he were watching her.

"You like the dragon?" An old man appeared through a curtained doorway. "Brings good luck, the dragon. *Lung*, we call him. Come, I'll take your money. For you, that dragon is ten dollars. Very special."

Jasmine thought for a moment. Ten dollars was more than she wanted to spend, but... "OK," she said impulsively, and handed him a ten-dollar bill. "No tax?"

The man laughed. "Not today!" he said. He wrapped the dragon carefully and placed it in a bag. "You want more luck?" He picked up a red envelope lying on the counter and placed a coin inside. "Here," he said. "*Lai see*, just for you."

"Thanks." Jasmine smiled. "This is lucky money, right?" She traced her fingers around the Chinese characters printed in gold on the envelope. "*Gung hey fat choy!*" she said.

"Yes, yes! Happy New Year!" He studied her closely, smiling and nodding his head as if pleased with what he saw. "Happy New Year, Dragon Girl!"

How does he know I'm a Dragon Girl? And why does he keep staring at me? Must be the clothes, she decided. That's all.

As she was turning to go she noticed another small room that opened onto an alley. "Isn't that Fan Tan Alley?" She pointed to the *No Exit* sign hanging from the glass door. "Can I go out that way?"

"Yes, Fan Tan Alley!" He rubbed his hands together gleefully. "For you, door open. Exit, for good luck dragon." He took a key from his pocket and unlocked the door. "Goodbye, Dragon Girl."

Then he bowed to Jasmine as she walked through the door and into the alley.

*   *   *

Something had changed. Jasmine knew it the instant the door closed behind her. The sounds were different. No traffic. No brakes, no horns, no whish of tires. And no people. No footsteps, no voices. A silence so heavy she could almost touch it.

She looked at her watch. Almost 2:00, time to go. But which way? Mist curled around her like a cocoon, shutting out her surroundings. She had no sense of space, no sense of direction. What's more, the doorway she had passed through had disappeared. There was no way back.

With fumbling fingers she opened the *lai see* envelope. What had the old man put inside? A silver coin, the size of a quarter. On one side was the portrait of a queen with the words VICTORIA DEI GRATIA REGINA CANADA. OK, she thought. Victoria is in Canada. She turned the coin over. There were maple boughs etched along the edges, tied at the bottom with a ribbon and separated at the top by a crown. Beneath the crown were three lines: 25 CENTS 1881.

1881? Then Victoria must refer to the queen, not the place at all. But what did it mean? What had happened?

She sank to the ground and hugged herself tightly, thinking, don't panic, concentrate on your breathing. Tai chi breathing, from deep down...

It was the smell that roused her, the stink of rotting garbage and raw sewage. And something else, a sweet, cloying smell like boiled potatoes. She found herself in an alley, hemmed in by buildings on either side. She was sitting on the ground, leaning against a wall, surrounded by wooden boxes, crates and piles of refuse. Overhead she could see a patch of sky, bright with stars. I must have slept, she thought, looking at her watch. It still said five minutes to two.

She was about to stand up when she heard footsteps. She crouched down, making herself as small as possible. Groups of men passed by. Some disappeared along narrow passages leading off the alley, others ducked through doorways. A thought struck her. *When you are a stranger, be invisible.* She took the red ribbon out of her hair and pulled down the brim of her hat. Then she slipped her watch inside her fluorescent backpack and stashed it behind a pile of crates.

Think, she told herself. If this really is 1881 then the glass door won't be there. But it could be the same building. All you have to do is find the right doorway and—

A sudden shattering broke into her thoughts. Angry voices rocked the alley. She froze as three men tore out a doorway just ahead of her. With pigtails flying, they rushed past and vanished in the shadows.

"Worthless sons of dogs!" a man shouted after them. "Don't come back until you've found it!"

What are they looking for? she wondered. Then stopped short. She could have sworn the man had spoken a Chinese dialect, but she had understood the words. How could that be? She didn't know any Chinese, apart from the New Year's greeting. She must have imagined it.

But she hadn't imagined the doorway. Cautiously, she peered inside. The dimly lit room reeked with the smell of smoke, sweat, liquor and kerosene. Men of all ages crowded together, talking, laughing, throwing dice and clacking dominoes. Fan-tan players noisily placed their bets as dealers swept up piles of buttons. Mah Jong tiles clattered with the chatter of voices.

Through the smoky haze Jasmine saw several men clustered around a wicket. As one stepped back, she caught a glimpse of the cashier. Her eyes widened. Surely that wasn't—No. That other cashier was a dummy. This one was real. But the room in the never-ending store had been a gambling den. This must be the same place. And somewhere, there was a way back.

Unnoticed, she crept past a boy sweeping up bits of debris and broken glass. No, not glass. China. One green piece looked like the curling tail of a dragon.

"Come on, Useless. Sweep it all up."

This time there was no mistake. It was the voice she'd heard in the alley, speaking the same Chinese dialect. And she could understand the words.

The scar-faced man shook his fist at the boy and scowled. Like the others, he wore his hair in one long pigtail. But instead of the dark pants and quilted jacket worn by the others, this man wore an embroidered robe, along with an air of arrogance and authority. He consulted with the cashier from time to time and strutted from table to table overseeing the various games. Jasmine noticed how the players cowered under his scrutiny, and breathed more easily when he moved on.

Suddenly, without warning, he grabbed an old fellow by his jacket and lifted him out of his chair. "Take this message to your worthless son," he snarled. "No one tries to trick Blue-Scar Wong. He has three days to pay his debt. Hear that, old man? Three days."

"Leave him alone!" The boy gripped the broom and boldly faced the older man.

Blue-Scar spun around, his face contorted with anger. "Do

not interfere with me," he said, his voice hard as steel. He drew a knife from the folds of his sleeve and waved it at the boy. "Your time is running out, too."

Unflinching, the boy stared back. In his eyes, Jasmine recognized something familiar. Or was it someone? She remembered the boy in her dream, standing alone on the crowded ship. Remembered, too, how his eyes had seemed to pull her in. Was this the boy? And if so, was she *meant* to be here? She slid to the floor, frightened without knowing why.

"Bah!" Blue-Scar spat with contempt. "Get back to your work."

As he stormed away, Jasmine looked up and found the boy gazing at her with an incredulous look on his face, a look that clearly said: *I know you.* Then he shook his head as if clearing it of dreams and went back to his sweeping.

The swell of voices rose steadily as the night wore on. Shouts of joy mingled with cries of despair as winners and losers continued to play.

But the presence of Blue-Scar Wong clouded the room. Once, Jasmine felt his eyes burning into her. She buried her face in her arms, terrified that he would expose her as the stranger she was. *Maybe he'll think I'm asleep and leave me alone. Or he'll throw me out. Or make me get up and gamble.* But before he could confront her a fight broke out, demanding his attention. She breathed a sigh of relief and shifted to a pile of crates. Half-hidden, she trembled alone in the dingy room, trying to think of a way out.

When she opened her eyes, the room was quiet and cold. Lamps had been extinguished, leaving behind a thick pall of smoke. Light filtered through the open doorway. Only the boy remained.

He stood in the doorway staring at her, rubbing his eyes in disbelief. Wasn't this the face he'd seen in his dreams? And if so, it was a *girl* crouching there on the floor, not another coolie. But how could that be? The face in his dreams belonged to Bright Jade, a spirit from another time. This girl was real. And she was *here*, in *his* time. I'll put her to the test, he decided. Turning abruptly, he bolted into the alley.

Jasmine leaped up and followed. Down the alley, through passageways and courtyards, twisting through a maze enclosed by huts, crudely built sheds and tumbledown fences. Weathered shacks tottered on pilings or on top of each other, leaning crazily this way and that in a desperate attempt to stay upright. They reminded her of tattered people, supporting each other as they peered warily at the world through tiny, grime-streaked windows.

She kept the boy in sight as he dashed between pilings, over rickety bridges held up by stilts, over muddy ground soaked with rain and waste water, over narrow passages clogged with garbage and reeking with the stench of sewage.

How will I ever find my way out of here? she wondered, wishing she'd left a trail of crumbs like Hansel and Gretel. And where is he going, to the witch? Or worse? She felt a prickle of fear, but there was no question of turning back. Something was pulling her, some force she couldn't explain.

The boy darted into another courtyard, with a chicken coop and a patch of dirt for growing vegetables. A rooster crowed and hens began clucking. Somewhere a dog barked. Someone shouted. Jasmine ducked under several lines of laundry and followed the boy up a staircase that snaked its way along the back of a wooden building. Up one flight, then another and another, until finally he stopped in front of a red door, panting and out of breath.

"Whew!" Jasmine gasped. She brushed past him and leaned

against the door. Two faded posters partially hid the peeling red paint. "Door Guardians," she said, recognizing the fierce warriors she'd seen in a book. "To keep away evil spirits and unwanted guests."

Then she smiled, her eyes bright with wonder. For the words sliding over her tongue were Cantonese, and she was speaking it as easily as if she'd spoken it all her life.

The boy gaped, his thoughts in a turmoil. She had passed the test, had followed him around all sorts of sharp angles and curves when everyone knows spirits can only travel in straight lines. So, she wasn't a spirit. But if she wasn't Bright Jade, who was she? How was it she could speak his dialect? And where had she come from? Perhaps Dragon Maker would know. He opened the door and stepped in.

Jasmine followed, her nerves tingling with excitement. The room smelled of incense. A pot-bellied stove stood in one corner, its crooked chimney climbing precariously through a hole in the ceiling. Dragons danced along the shelves and tumbled across the battered table. A man stood with his back to her, bent over—

Déjà vu. Her aunt's words came back. She knew the man was old, knew his skin was burnished the colour of copper. She knew he held three lighted sticks of incense, knew he would place them in a cup of earth before a small altar. And so he did. Then he turned and said, "Welcome, Jasmine. Welcome, Dragon Girl. I am the one they call Dragon Maker, as you can see." His weather-beaten face cracked in a slow smile.

Jasmine drew back, puzzled. "How did you know my name?"

His eyes pierced deep inside her, as if looking for something. "I have known you in another time," he said, his voice warm as velvet. "And you have been expected."

"Expected for what?"

"You will know in time." He turned to the boy. "Keung, give her some soup. She needs to eat something and rest awhile."

Jasmine breathed in the aroma of herbs, surprised at how hungry she felt. When she finished the soup, Dragon Maker handed her a cup of fragrant tea. Delicate white petals floated on top. She took a sip, remembering the first time she had tasted it, the night before her father went away. "I bought some jasmine tea for you," he said, "so when you drink it you'll think of me in China." She refused to speak or even look at him. As soon as he left the room, she'd poured it down the sink.

A wave of exhaustion washed over her. Had the boy put a sleeping potion in her soup? Some herbs caused drowsiness. Maybe powdered crickets were in the soup, or worse. Maybe Dragon Maker's voice had hypnotized her, put her in a trance. Her head drooped. Her eyelids felt unbearably heavy.

The boy took her arm and led her into a room no bigger than a closet. A mat lay on the plank floor. She curled up on it as the boy covered her with a quilt. "Who are you?" she asked sleepily. "Why are you here?"

"I'm Chan Tai Keung. I've come to find my father."

"I've lost my father, too," she said. "And my mother." Her face crumpled and she felt the sting of tears. She closed her eyes and drifted off to sleep.

*   *   *

"Here she is! Jasmine, what happened?" Voices floated through the fog. Voices coming closer, calling her back.

She looked up to find a group of classmates standing over her, their faces creased with worry. "What happened?" asked Becky. "Did you fall or something?"

"Get up, Jasmine," said Krista. "It's 2:00, time to go."

"2:00? It can't be. There wasn't time for all that to happen. I couldn't have spent the night—" Their bewildered looks made her stop abruptly.

"What are you talking about? What night? For all what to happen?"

"Nothing." She tried to stand, steadying herself against the brick wall, but fell back, overcome by dizziness.

"Are you OK?" Becky leaned over and helped her up. "You look like you're going to pass out."

"My head feels funny, that's all." She blinked a few times, trying to focus on her surroundings. She was definitely in Fan Tan Alley. There was the glass doorway. And there was a passage leading off the alley. Was that where she had gone? "My backpack," she remembered suddenly. "I left it behind some crates, but—"

"Relax, it's right here," Krista said, handing it to her. "You must have dropped it when you fell. Now come on. Your aunt's waiting."

Jasmine took one last look around, hoping to see—what? She wasn't sure. But before leaving the alley she thought she heard a voice calling her name. She glanced over her shoulder just in time to see a dark figure staring in her direction. Although it was partially hidden by mist, she couldn't help but notice the outstretched arm entreating her to stay.

from

My Name Is Seepeetza

by

SHIRLEY STERLING

In 1958 twelve-year-old Martha Stone—whose Salish name is Seepeetza—is required by law to attend the Kalamak Indian Residential School in the interior of B.C. Her diary records her misery and homesickness in heart-rending detail.

Thursday, April 2, 1959 K.I.R.S.

Father Sloane came to the girls' rec yesterday to tease us about April Fool's Day. He said you can't choose your own face but you can pick your own nose. I don't know why that is so funny. He comes every day almost, for a few minutes. Once he told me that my name Martha comes from the Bible. Martha was a friend of Jesus. I don't like my white name much. It's not very pretty.

My dad gave me my Indian name, Seepeetza. I was named after an old lady who died a long time ago. My dad laughs sometimes when he says my name, because it means White Skin or Scared Hide. It's a good name for me because I get scared of things, like devils.

My dad called me Tootie first, when I was really small. We were sitting at the table having tea, and he was teaching me some words. Say pass the spoon, he said to me. I said pass the spoot, and he laughed and laughed. Then he started calling me Toot McSpoot, and everybody at home calls me Toot or Tootie now. My dad still calls me McSpoot. He's the only one.

We all have Indian names but we're not allowed to use them at school. Jimmy is Kyep-kin, Coyote Head, because he sings a lot. Dorothy is Qwileen meaning Birch Tree because she worries about the trees. Missy is Kekkix meaning Mouse Hands and Benny is Hop-o-lox-kin. I don't know what that means. We don't use our Indian names much. My parents know we would get in trouble at school if we used them there.

Benny got his name from an old lady called Mathilda. She asked Mum what she was going to call that little boy. Mum said she was going to call him Toy-ax-kin, because he runs all over the hills. Old Mathilda said she should call him Hop-o-lox-kin after her grandfather, because my dad is her relative. Then she took a quarter out of her pocket. She said she was going to give that quarter to Benny and if he took it then his name was going to be Hop-o-lox-kin. Sure enough he took it and then he got his name.

All the old Indian people know our Indian names, our white names and our nicknames. They know all about us.

The old timers call my little sister Missy Poison. When she was a little girl she used to mix all her food in one bowl, then turn it upside down over her head. She almost ate a spider once too. It was a popcorn spider that came down from the ceiling in the veranda onto her baby walker. Mum came out and saw the legs in her hand and washed it off.

Yah-yah says not to kill spiders or there will be a thunderstorm. She said a long time ago it was Skokki the Spider who travelled to the moon and learned from the sky dwellers how to weave.

That's why our people have baskets. My mum's grandmother used to make baskets out of cedar roots and choke-cherry bark. Mum doesn't make baskets. She collects medicine tea from the mountains, and Yah-yah makes things like moccasins out of buckskin. Moccasins are like slippers.

Thursday, April 9, 1959 K.I.R.S.

I went to see the dentist. He looked at my teeth and said I needed seven fillings. I got really scared. Cookie said that fillings are the worst because you sometimes have to get a needle in your mouth. It's called freezing. She said it hurts worse if you don't get the needle. The dentist doesn't believe in freezing, but if kids start screaming he gives it to them in their gums.

Mr. Oiko sent some of us to the nurse's room. We sat on chairs outside and listened to the kids crying and screaming in there, and something that sounded like a sewing machine. We could hear a man's voice snarling. One of the kids whispered that he slapped a grade five girl because she turned her head away and broke the needle in her mouth. One of the grade twos came out holding her mouth with blood seeping through a white bandage and rolling down her chin. She was crying, and she wouldn't look at us.

Then it was my turn, and I felt like I had a bellyache. The dentist looked at me and told me to sit in this big chair that moved up and down. He was holding a needle. He put it down and made me open my mouth. He looked around my mouth with a little mirror on a little silver handle. He poked at my teeth with a silver tool. His hand smelled like soap. He had on thick glasses, and he was really big. He growled, "Get your TONGUE out of the way." Everything he said was like a growl. Move your HEAD back. Don't close your MOUTH. Keep STILL. OPEN YOUR MOUTH!

When he said I had to get seven fillings I thought I was going to get them done right away, and I felt like my blood was draining from my body.

Then he told me to leave and come back the next day. I had a bellyache all night. I couldn't sleep. I didn't want to eat. It reminded me of a book I read called *A Tale of Two Cities*. This guy Charles Darnay knew he was going to the guillotine the next day to get his head chopped off. That's how I felt.

This time when I went to the dentist at least I was ready. I sat in the chair and held onto the chair sides until my hands and arms and neck ached while he drilled my teeth. That drill sounded like a scream. At first it didn't hurt. Then it felt like a hot knife, and I started to groan and he pulled the drill out. Then he heated up some metal and pushed it into the hole he made. He made big ones, and now my teeth are all ugly.

I couldn't believe I needed seven fillings because they said you only have to get fillings if your teeth are partly rotten or have black dots on them. Mine were all white, except for one small dot. Cookie says the dentist gets so much money for each filling and each tooth he pulls. He takes them out with a tool that looks like a pair of pliers.

Thursday, April 16, 1959 K.I.R.S.

Sister Theo always gets cranky on Monday, laundry day. Every other Monday we have to take our bottom sheets, pillowcases, towels, facecloths, bloomers and undershirts and put them into baskets to be taken to the laundry in the basement.

We have to work on laundry day too. The older girls handle the washers and dryers and mangle which presses the sheets. Two of us stand at the end and fold sheets as they come off the mangle.

Sometimes I press clothes or fold clothes as they come out of the dryers. Later we darn socks.

One thing I like is that two of us get to carry the basket of clean socks to the boys' side. It's the only time we're allowed to go there. It looks just like the girls' side. We like to see which boys are around, and whether they smile at us.

In the afternoon we go to class but before we do Sister lines us up and tells us that she has been slaving like a black in the laundry room for us for thirteen years. She calls us ungrateful wretches and sly-puss, boy crazy, amathons. I don't know what amathon means, maybe like female warriors along the Amazon River.

Sister Theo must get tired. She is the supervisor for ninety-nine intermediate girls, the biggest group in school. That means she has to get us up and ready for Mass, line us up for breakfast, give us all jobs to do after breakfast, make sure we get to class on time, make us change into smocks after school, hand out apples. She has to make sure we do our homework, take our baths, brush our teeth and change our sheets. She's also in charge of the dancers, the costumes, the out-of-town trips. I heard Father Sloane say once that Sister is like a sergeant major, always yelling orders. She told Father he was a scream. Those Irish talk to each other like that. They insult each other, then laugh and laugh.

I told Dorothy I hated Sister Theo because she gave me the strap for forgetting my towel downstairs. My mum and dad never hit us. Then Dorothy told me all those things Sister has to do. She said the Sisters have to get up at five o'clock in the morning to say prayers. I wasn't mad any more.

I still don't like Sister Theo, though. Once she came into my tub room when I was going to have my bath. She told me to get my clothes off and get in the water. I wouldn't. I will not let anyone see me without my clothes on. When she yelled at me to take my bloomers off and get in the tub I looked at the DANGER sign up where the electricity switches are. She saw it too. I was thinking if she made me do it I would wait till she left, climb up on the pipe, touch the switch and get electrocuted. We stared at each other. Then she opened the door and went out.

I took my bloomers off and climbed in the tub. My hands were shaking for a long time. We're not supposed to look at the Sisters like that.

Thursday, April 23, 1959 K.I.R.S.

I saw St. Joseph last night. I think it was him because he wore a brown robe like St. Joseph in the holy picture of Baby Jesus and the Virgin Mary. That St. Joseph was old with white hair but the one I talked to last night had long dark hair and looked younger.

At first when I woke up it was dark, and I couldn't see him very well. I woke up when he put his hand on my arm. It was warm. It felt like he knew me, like we were best friends. He smiled and said my real name, Seepeetza.

I asked him how come I had to get into trouble so much. In class I get in trouble for daydreaming. In the rec Edna wants to beat me up because I have green eyes. White people don't like us because our clothes are old. Sister clobbers me for making dancing mistakes. The worst is that I get scared to walk to the bathroom in the dark. In the morning I feel just sick when Sister yells at me and hits me and makes me wear my wet sheet over my head in front of everybody.

St. Joseph looked right into my eyes and told me that I had

to learn humility, that it was really important. He held me close, and I fell asleep.

When I woke up again, Sister was ringing the bell. I checked my bed. It was dry. I was so happy. I slid off the bed onto my knees. We all said our morning prayers, the Our Father, Hail Mary and Glory Be. I didn't tell anyone about my dream, but I was happy all day.

Sister told us about St. Joseph. He was humble because he looked after Mary and Jesus even though Jesus wasn't his own son. He was a carpenter. I think that's true because his hand was calloused like my dad's. My dad works hard on the ranch.

I'm not very humble. I know this because my mum said I have a temper like my dad. Once we were walking in front of the boys on our way to class when Father Sloane came along and picked me up, laughing. When he threw me over his shoulder, my skirt flew up and the whole class saw my bloomers. My bloomers were inside out because Sister made us hurry too fast in the morning. All the boys except Charlie laughed at me. I got so mad that I decided to sharpen my pencil and stab Father Sloane with it if he did that again.

If I was humble I wouldn't have been so mad. I think St. Joseph knows that. That's why he came. I guess what I want most in the world is for someone to like me, to be my best friend. Nobody wants to be friends with someone who looks like a shamah. Even Cookie avoids me most of the time. I miss my mum. I miss her all the time. When St. Joseph came he showed me lots of friends, maybe a million that I will have one day. They were reaching out to shake my hand. The trouble is I was really old. Over twenty, I think.

Thursday, April 30, 1959 K.I.R.S.

I keep thinking about my dream of St. Joseph. You can tell he likes children. He understands about things. Like what Sister told us about devils dragging us into hell if we sin.

During the day I'm not afraid of devils but at night when the lights go out an awful thing happens. I feel like I'm falling into a huge black hole where the devils are waiting, laughing. They are really horrible. Big. I feel sweat on my face but I'm cold. I take tiny breaths so they won't hear me. They stay under my bed all night waiting for me to make a mistake or breathe too loud. I stay awake sometimes until it starts getting light outside.

After I saw St. Joseph I felt like someone was looking out for me. I was still scared of the devils but I got up anyway and tiptoed to the bathroom really quiet. I kept hearing creaks behind me but I wouldn't look. The hair at the back of my head prickled. When I got to the bathroom I switched the light on really fast. It took me a long time to go back to bed because I was scared to turn off the bathroom light again.

I'm still scared of the devils. I still can't sleep for a long time at night or let my hands or feet go over the edge of the bed, but at least now my bed is dry.

Sister told us about sin in catechism class. She said we sin when we lie or cheat or steal or skip Mass on Sunday, eat meat on Friday, kill, curse, or argue, or call names, or even think bad thoughts. She said everybody sins every day, at least seven times. If we die without confessing small sins, then we will go to purgatory. If we die in a state of mortal sin we go to hell. You can pray people out of purgatory but never out of hell.

But what about Sister? She's not nice. I don't think St. Joseph liked it that I was so angry at Sister. He said Sisters are poor things sometimes too. He said to keep my eyes on my own heart. What a funny thing to say.

Once I stole a pair of socks from Edna. Somebody stole my socks and I think it was her because she hates me. She holds her fist up to my nose all the time. Edna told Sister Theo that I stole her socks but Sister didn't believe her.

We have to wash our socks every night before we go to bed and hang them on the iron bar above our pillows beside our towels and facecloths. Next morning my socks were gone, and there was an ugly pair there instead. Somebody usually steals my comb and my toothpaste, probably Edna. Then I have to borrow a comb and brush my teeth with baking soda. It tastes ugly. Sometimes Cookie and I get so hungry at night we eat her toothpaste. It tastes like peppermint candy.

Saturday, May 6, 1959 K.I.R.S.

I never thought I could be happy here at school, but who'd have thought Father Sloane would get us a swimming pool. It's made of cement with a deep end and a shallow end and two diving boards. It's aqua. The water tastes like bleach.

This afternoon after we got our ironing done Sister said we could go swimming. She handed out red bathing suits. I put mine on and went out to the pool with my towel. The water was ice-cold, but I didn't mind. I love swimming as much as I love riding and art.

We just got to stay in the pool for a few minutes. Then we had to go inside, because it was the boys' turn. We looked out the windows and watched them because the pool is just below the girls' side. Sister Delores was watching them too, from one of our dorm windows. Some of the girls snickered about that. A nun watching boys.

At home we go swimming at Big Rock in the Calico River. It's about half a mile from our ranch. We walk or sometimes my dad takes us there on the horses after we get the haying done for the day, or he drives us in his pickup truck. He tells Mum to pack a picnic lunch of sweet tea, tea biscuits, homemade butter, wild strawberry jam or huckleberry jam, and slices of cold roast deer meat, or baloney.

Sometimes my dad takes his spear to catch fish. It has three prongs with a long pole. He watches for a long time where there are logs and branches in the river with the spear ready. Then he plunges the spear into the water. He catches trout that way.

Once Mum made a fish trap out of willow switches and twine. She put it in a place where the fish like to rest, under some branches. Her grandmother, Yetko, taught her how to do this when she was just a little girl. Mum says Yetko taught her everything. She was her friend. Yetko saddled up her little horse and took my mother into the hills to pick wild onions, wild celery, flower tea and all kinds of berries. That's how Mum learned about Indian medicine. They would camp up there alone, sometimes for a week. They never took weapons. My mum said the animals never hurt them.

Mum still knows all about which plants can cure sicknesses. She makes tea out of dried honeysuckle flowers or willow bark to cure headaches. For stomach aches she makes wild strawberry tea. For woman trouble she makes Labrador tea. For really bad sickness she gives a tea made out of deer root. It smells and tastes awful but it cures you. It's strange to think my mum was a little girl, but I saw a picture of her when she was fourteen. She was so tiny.

My mum only went to grade three. She went to Kalamak too. The nuns strapped her all the time for speaking Indian, because she couldn't speak English. She said just when the welts on her hands and arms healed, she got it again. That's why she didn't want us to learn Indian. When Mum and Dad want to talk without us understanding them, they speak Indian. It sounds soft and gentle, like the wind in pines.

Thursday, May 14, 1959 K.I.R.S.
Sometimes the boys climb Osprey Mountain, not far from the school. We can see them from the dorm and hear them whooping like Indians in the movies. The Indians in the movies are not like anyone I know. Real Indians are just people like anyone else except they love the mountains.

At the end of summer at home we pack up our tent, lots of food, warm winter clothes, all our picking baskets, cooking gear and warm quilts. Then we head up into the mountains to Tekameen Summit. The whole family climbs into the pickup truck and away we go.

When we get up there we pitch the tent, and Mum cooks supper over the campfire. Then we sit around the campfire in the dark and tell stories. My dad tells the best ones, about bears, his war stories and funny things that happen to people. One of his favourites is about the bar in England that wouldn't let you in unless you were a Scot and had Mac in front of your name. One guy tried to get in by saying his name was Macaroni. My dad laughed and laughed and thumped his leg when he told that story.

We camp up there until we fill all our baskets with shiny almost black huckleberries, the best berries of all. They taste sweet and tart. Mum calls them medicine food. We serve huckleberries when we have important visitors.

Yah-yah usually comes berry-picking with us or with Uncle Tommy and his family or Uncle Willy and his family. We all camp in the same spot so we can visit each other's campfires or share food if the hunters get a deer. They call it a moweech.

Usually other Indian families come berry-picking too, and camp nearby. They tell us all the news of their families and some funny stories. They discuss serious business sometimes too, but they talk in Indian so I don't understand what they are talking about. But you can tell it's important by their voices, the serious looks and the quietness of the people listening.

There is something really special about being mountain people. It's a feeling like you know who you are, and you know each other. You belong to the mountains.

The old people like Yah-yah smile at you and tell you something about the trail you're following or show you how to cover your berries with leaves so they stay fresh. They know where to find the biggest berries and how to cook delicious food over the campfire. They notice how many berries you pick, who sneaks off to go fishing, and what everybody likes to eat. They tease you around the campfire if you don't pick many berries. Next day you pick lots.

Two or three ladies will pick in one spot together and talk and laugh all day. One time Mum and I were picking some nice big berries on the side of a steep hill. Just as we were heading down to camp I tripped on a tree root and went rolling and tumbling all the way down the hill, still holding on to my basket. I landed on my shoulder with my legs high up in the air. My mum caught up to me, then started to laugh. "You saved ALL your berries," she said. She told everybody about it at the campfire. She said,

"Tootie rolled all the way down a BIG hill, and she didn't spill ANY BERRIES." Yah-yah turned and looked at me with a little smile, and Dad chuckled. "Good for you, McSpoot," he said.

When it rains Yah-yah makes a tiny little fire and practically sits on it to keep warm. Everybody else makes big fires. Once, too many people crowded around Yah-yah's fire so Uncle Tommy had to make her another one.

The men go out with baskets and guns on horseback or on foot. They circle all around the camp and the picking spots to check for bears before they go. Sometimes they come back with lots of berries. Other times they just look the mountain valley over, or do a bit of hunting. They're very quiet in the woods. We look up sometimes when we're picking berries and there they are looking at us, and we never heard them come.

When they hunt, they get up before dawn to bathe in a deep pool in the mountain stream. When they come back from the mountains my dad and uncles talk to each other in Indian and tell each other what they saw. There isn't a thing about those mountains they don't know.

Spirits of
the Railway

by

P A U L   Y E E

This is one of the original legends the author has created based on the history and folk traditions of Chinese immigrants to the West in the nineteenth century. Each story is preceded by a stunning illustration by Simon Ng.

One summer many, many years ago, heavy floodwaters suddenly swept through south China again. Farmer Chu and his family fled to high ground and wept as the rising river drowned their rice crops, their chickens and their water buffalo.

With their food and farm gone, Farmer Chu went to town to look for work. But a thousand other starving peasants were already there. So when he heard there was work across the ocean in the New World, he borrowed some money, bought a ticket, and off he sailed.

Long months passed as his family waited to hear from him. Farmer Chu's wife fell ill from worry and weariness. From her hard board bed she called out her husband's name over and over, until at last her eldest son borrowed money to cross the Pacific in search of his father.

For two months, young Chu listened to waves batter the groaning planks of the ship as it crossed the ocean. For two months he dreaded that he might drown at any minute. For two months he thought of nothing but his father and his family.

Finally he arrived in a busy port city. He asked everywhere for his father, but no one in Chinatown had heard the name. There were thousands of Chinese flung throughout the New World, he was told. Gold miners scrabbled along icy rivers, farmers ploughed the long low valleys, and labourers travelled through towns and forests, from job to job. Who could find one single man in this enormous wilderness?

Young Chu was soon penniless. But he was young and strong, and he feared neither danger nor hard labour. He joined a work gang of thirty Chinese, and a steamer ferried them up a river canyon to build the railway.

When the morning mist lifted, Chu's mouth fell open. On both sides of the rushing river, grey mountains rose like walls to block the sky. The rock face dropped into ragged cliffs that only eagles could ascend and jutted out from cracks where scrawny trees clung. Never before had he seen such towering ranges of dark raw rock.

The crew pitched their tents and began to work. They hacked at hills with hand-scoops and shovels to level a pathway for the train. Their hammers and chisels chipped boulders into gravel and fill. Their dynamite and drills thrust tunnels deep into the mountain. At night, the crew would sit around the campfire chewing tobacco, playing cards and talking.

From one camp to another, the men trekked up the rail line, their food and tools dangling from sturdy shoulder poles. When they met other workers, Chu would run ahead and shout his father's name and ask for news. But the workers just shook their heads grimly.

"Search no more, young man!" one grizzled old worker said. "Don't you know that too many have died here? My own brother was buried alive in a mudslide."

"My uncle was killed in a dynamite blast," muttered another. "No one warned him about the fuse."

The angry memories rose and swirled like smoke among the workers.

"The white boss treats us like mules and dogs!"

"They need a railway to tie this nation together, but they can't afford to pay decent wages."

"What kind of country is this?"

Chu listened, but still he felt certain that his father was alive.

Then winter came and halted all work. Snows buried everything under a heavy blanket of white. The white boss went to town to live in a warm hotel, but Chu and the workers stayed in camp. The men tied potato sacks around their feet and huddled by the fire, while ice storms howled like wolves through the mountains. Chu thought the winter would never end.

When spring finally arrived, the survivors struggled outside and shook the chill from their bones. They dug graves for two workers who had succumbed to sickness. They watched the river surge alive from the melting snow. Work resumed, and Chu began to search again for his father.

Late one afternoon, the gang reached a mountain with a half-finished tunnel. As usual, Chu ran up to shout his father's name, but before he could say a word, other workers came running out of the tunnel.

"It's haunted!" they cried. "Watch out! There are ghosts inside!"

"Dark figures slide soundlessly through the rocks!" one man whispered. "We hear heavy footsteps approaching but never arriving. We hear sighs and groans coming from corners where no man stands."

Chu's friends dropped their packs and refused to set up camp. But the white boss rode up on his horse and shook his fist at the men. "No work, no pay!" he shouted. "Now get to work!"

Then he galloped off. The workers squatted on the rocks and looked helplessly at one another. They needed the money badly for food and supplies.

Chu stood up. "What is there to fear?" he cried. "The ghosts have no reason to harm us. There is no reason to be afraid. We have hurt no one."

"Do you want to die?" a man called out.

"I will spend the night inside the tunnel," Chu declared as the men muttered unbelievingly. "Tomorrow we can work."

Chu took his bedroll, a lamp, and food and marched into the mountain. He heard the crunch of his boots and water dripping. He knelt to light his lamp. Rocks lay in loose piles everywhere, and the shadowy walls closed in on him.

At the end of the tunnel he sat down and ate his food. He closed his eyes and wondered where his father was. He pictured his mother weeping in her bed and heard her voice calling his father's name. He lay down, pulled his blankets close, and eventually he fell asleep.

Chu awoke gasping for breath. Something heavy was pressing down on his chest. He tried to raise his arms but could not. He clenched his fists and summoned all his strength, but still he was paralyzed. His eyes strained into the darkness, but saw nothing.

Suddenly the pressure eased and Chu groped for the lamp. As the chamber sprang into light, he cried, "What do you want? Who are you?"

Silence greeted him, and then a murmur sounded from behind. Chu spun around and saw a figure in the shadows. He slowly raised the lamp. The flickering light travelled up blood-stained trousers and a mud-encrusted jacket. Then Chu saw his father's face.

"Papa!" he whispered, lunging forward.

"No! Do not come closer!" The figure stopped him. "I am not of your world. Do not embrace me."

Tears rose in Chu's eyes. "So, it's true," he choked. "You . . . you have left us . . ."

His father's voice quivered with rage. "I am gone, but I am not done yet. My son, an accident here killed many men. A fuse exploded before the workers could run. A ton of rock dropped on us and crushed us flat. They buried the whites in a church-yard, but our bodies were thrown into the river, where the current swept us away. We have no final resting place."

Chu fell upon his knees. "What shall I do?"

His father's words filled the tunnel. "Take chopsticks; they shall be our bones. Take straw matting; that can be our flesh. Wrap them together and tie them tightly. Take the bundles to the mountain top high above the nests of eagles, and cover us with soil. Pour tea over our beds. Then we shall sleep in peace."

When Chu looked up, his father had vanished. He stumbled out of the tunnel and blurted the story to his friends. Immediately they prepared the bundles and sent him off with ropes and a shovel to the foot of the cliff, and Chu began to climb.

When he swung himself over the top of the cliff, he was so high up that he thought he could see the distant ocean. He dug the graves deeper than any wild animal could dig, and laid the bundles gently in the earth.

Then Chu brought his fists together above his head and bowed three times. He knelt and touched his forehead to the soil three times. In a loud clear voice he declared, "Three times I bow, three things I vow. Your pain shall stop now, your sleep shall soothe you now, and I will never forget you. Farewell."

Then, hanging onto the rope looped around a tree, Chu slid slowly back down the cliff. When he reached the bottom, he looked back and saw that the rope had turned into a giant snake that was sliding smoothly up the rock face.

"Good," he smiled to himself. "It will guard the graves well." Then he returned to the camp, where he and his fellow workers lit their lamps and headed into the tunnel. And spirits never again disturbed them, nor the long trains that came later.

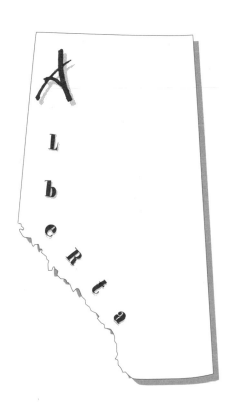

from

Ticket to Curlew

by

CELIA BARKER LOTTRIDGE

Young Sam Ferrier has recently moved to Curlew, Alberta, from Iowa with his family. Starting over on the barren prairies in 1915 isn't easy, but Sam takes great pleasure in his horse, Prince. The book is illustrated with line drawings by Wendy Wolsak-Frith.

The next day Sam worked with Pa to get the barn ready for the winter. Pa covered cracks between the boards with tar-paper while Sam gave the stalls an extra good cleaning.

He was just starting to pitch in fresh bedding straw when Pa said, "You'll only need to take care of two of the horse stalls, Sam. You see, we have a problem."

He laid his hammer on a low beam and turned toward Sam. "We can't afford to feed all the horses all winter. We don't have the money to buy oats, and anyway, we don't have enough hay for five horses. It's a problem lots of folks out here have, but they have a solution."

Sam stood with the pitchfork in his hand and stared at Pa. Was he going to sell Prince?

Pa went on, "People turn the horses loose on the prairie to fend for themselves for the winter. The horses run in herds. They can find grass under the snow to eat and folks build shelters of fencing and straw to make wind breaks for them. They get along all right."

"But you won't put out all the horses," Sam managed to say.

"No, we have to have a couple. We'll need to get into town and there may be some work we can do around the place. I've decided to keep Rabbit and Lady in the barn. They have never faced a prairie winter. The other three have. Why, Prince was probably born out on the range."

"But Prince is small and he's used to being almost a pet," said Sam. He couldn't believe that Pa would turn Prince out.

"The horses look after each other," said Pa. "They choose a leader who keeps them together and finds shelter when they need it. Prince is a tough horse. He'll be fine."

Sam went back to pitching straw. He could hardly see where it was landing because of the tears in his eyes.

Josie was furious when Pa told the rest of the family about the horses.

"Prince will die," she said. "He's used to people who share their lunch with him. The horses will fight and he'll get killed or he'll starve. I know he will."

Matt just said, "I'll miss him, I'll miss him."

"I'm sorry," said Pa, "but facts are facts. We can't afford to feed five horses. Rabbit and Lady are a good team of work horses. We can't run a farm without a team like that. I could sell Prince and Goldie and Pete. But this way they'll be back next summer."

Sam sat feeling miserable. He knew what Pa was saying. If they had to lose a horse it would be better to lose Prince than a good plough horse. There was no use arguing about it.

All that night Sam dreamed about blizzards. He was searching for Prince in the swirling snow. Again and again he saw a shape in the blinding whiteness, but each time he got near, it disappeared. He woke up exhausted.

At breakfast Pa said, "Ride out with me, son, to set the horses loose. You'll see that they accept it. I'm sure it's happened to all three of them before."

So Sam got Prince from the barn. Pa rode on Rabbit leading Pete and Goldie. Rabbit would bring both Pa and Sam back. As they left the farmyard, Sam could see Matt and Josie standing at the front window. He knew they were crying.

They rode about five miles to the north. Pa said that a number of settlers had agreed to set their horses loose in the same area so they could form a herd.

After that they didn't talk much. Sam was feeling Prince's muscles move beneath his hide and watching his mane blow in the cold wind. He wished he could tell him that this was not his idea.

The place they stopped was no different from any other part of the prairie except there was a U-shaped structure built of posts and wire with straw heaped inside it. Pa said it was a shelter. Sam didn't believe that loose straw would even cut the icy wind, but he couldn't say anything.

He slid off Prince's back and went around to his head. He held out a piece of biscuit he had saved from breakfast. It had apple butter on it. Prince took it with his soft mouth and munched it. Sam rubbed his long nose.

"Take care of yourself, boy," he whispered. "I'll be waiting for you."

Pa reached a hand down so that Sam could swing up behind him. Then he turned Rabbit and urged him to a gallop. Sam looked back. Pete and Goldie were already nosing the snow, hunting for grass. But Prince was gazing after Sam and Pa. He followed them with his black eyes until Sam couldn't see him any more.

The next morning Josie got up from the breakfast table and began to clear the dishes away. Suddenly she stepped over to the window.

"Look," she said. "I knew Prince wasn't a range horse."

They all looked. Prince was standing at the farm gate. Pa got up.

"You children stay here," he said. "I'll take him out alone this time."

But before he left he went into the bedroom and they heard him pull the storage box from under the bed. When he came through the kitchen he was carrying the rifle. Josie gasped and Matt's eyes were big and round.

Sam took two steps toward the door, but Pa held up his hand.

"I'm not going to shoot anything," he said. "But I have to drive Prince away or he'll keep coming back. A shot in the air will do it, I hope."

He pulled on his boots and his heavy jacket and went out with the gun in the crook of his arm.

The children sat glumly around the table. Mama cleared away the dishes, poured hot water from the kettle into the dishpan and began to wash the bowls. She didn't ask anyone to dry. Sam thought of the cold empty land where Prince would have to live through the coldest emptiest months. He hated the prairie. He hated it for Prince and for himself. Without Prince the prairie seemed like a prison.

Once the dishes were done, Mama must have thought that they had brooded long enough.

"It's just two weeks to Christmas," she said. "I'm counting on you children to decorate the house."

They would not have a Christmas tree or evergreen branches, of course, but Mama had been saving paper. Some was coloured and some was white.

"Paper chains will make the house look festive," she said. Josie and Matt cheered up immediately. Josie mixed up some flour-and-water paste and Matt began cutting sheets of paper into strips.

"Pa left me some work to do," said Sam, and he went out to the barn where he spent the morning fiercely nailing strips of tarpaper over every tiny crack in the walls. By the time Pa came back he was hot and the job was nearly done.

Pa looked around and said, "Good work, Sam. Stop pounding a minute. Prince will be all right. He trotted off in the direction of some other horses. He's not alone."

Sam said, "Yes, Pa," and went back into the house. There he was swept up in preparations for Christmas whether he liked it or not.

That's the way it was every day. If he didn't want to make paper chains or cut snowflakes from the pages Matt had torn out of his old scribbler, he had to go out to the barn where Prince's empty stall made him feel sad and angry.

Jabbing the pitchfork into the stacked-up hay and tossing it hard into the stall helped some. At least Rabbit and Lady didn't try to cheer him up. Sam thought they missed the other horses. And they probably hated staying in the barn as much as he hated staying in the house.

He was so gloomy for the first few days after Prince was gone that Mama finally said, "Sam, the only help for you is work." She gave him a little blank notebook and set him to planning the crops they might plant next year and the yield they might expect. "Who knows what will come to pass," she said, "but if you draw the plans neatly and do the calculations properly, it may help your pa."

Pa looked at Sam's figures about the yield of wheat and barley they might expect if the weather was perfect. "If we're that lucky we'll buy a Model T Ford," he said. "What do you think about that, Sam?"

A Model T! It was the first interesting thing Sam had thought about since the school concert. A few people in Curlew had automobiles. It was wonderful to watch them wheeling down the street all by themselves. But there were hardly any roads that wouldn't shake a car to bits or get it stuck in the mud depending on the season. A horse, now, could go almost anywhere. And there he was, thinking about Prince again.

Mama saw his face change. "Sam," she said, "it does no good to mope. Prince will either survive the winter or he won't. He's lived his whole life on these prairies. I think he has a good chance."

Sam didn't know why, but Mama's blunt words made him feel better. He still worried, but he stopped moping and began to think about Christmas. The next time Pa drove Rabbit and Lady to town, Sam went along.

He took the few dollars he had earned helping Adam build a fence and went into Pratt's store. There he picked out a photograph album for Mama and Pa. Pa took pictures sometimes but they were all jumbled loose in a box. He knew Mama would like sorting through them and sticking them on the handsome black pages of the album. He looked at hair ribbons for Josie but in the end he got her a wooden top. She would like it better. He really wanted to get a jack-knife for Matt, but they cost too much so he settled for a bag of marbles. He didn't see why they couldn't play marbles in the house or in the barn instead of waiting for spring.

So Sam was ready for Christmas in spite of everything. The house was strung with paper chains and hung with snowflakes, and a frozen turkey, ordered from Edmonton through Mr. Pratt, was thawing in the coolest corner of the house. Sam went to sleep on Christmas Eve with the happy feeling that Christmas, at least, could be counted upon.

He was right. The only thing missing was the smell of the Christmas tree. The biggest surprise was a sleigh. Pa called it a cutter, and as soon as there was enough snow they would all go for a ride.

But Sam liked Pa's present even better than the cutter. It came in a thin flat package. Sam felt it carefully through the paper. "It feels like a picture."

Pa looked mysterious. "Ah, but what picture? That is the question." Sam tore open the package.

It was a picture of Sam standing by the house holding up the two ducks he had shot. Looking over his shoulder was Prince.

Sam was amazed. He had forgotten that Pa had taken a picture that day. Looking at it he remembered how Prince had waited patiently for him while he waited for the ducks. Then they had come home together, triumphantly.

"Where are you going to put it, Sam?" asked Pa after Sam had thanked him several times.

Sam looked around. "Not in the bedroom," he said. "It's too cold in there. Could I put it right here beside the window? Then we can all see it whenever we want to."

"Good," said Pa, and he got a hammer and drove in a nail. Sam hung the picture and they all looked at it and thought of Prince.

"He's fine," said Mama. "I'm sure of it. Look what a smart horse he is."

Sam looked at the picture for one more moment. Prince was smart. He just hoped he was lucky, too, out there on the prairie. He turned away from the picture.

"That turkey sure smells good," he said.

*   *   *

February began with a five-day storm. The ordinary rush of the wind changed to a howl that started as a low moan, rose to a high screech and sank again to a moan but never stopped. The wind carried snow with it until the bedroom windows were nearly covered. Then it changed its mind and angrily blew the great heap of snow clean away.

In those five days the sun was lost. Daytime was faintly grey and nighttime was black dark. Mama kept the lamp burning all day. Every morning Sam watched her tilt the kerosene can to see how much was left in it.

Once she saw him looking and said, "Don't worry, Sam. There's enough here for more days than this storm is likely to last. Anyway, we have candles. And there's plenty of coal. That's the most important thing."

Sam knew she was right, but he felt that the circle of yellow light around the lamp helped hold the storm outside the thin walls of their house. All day long they sat around the table with the lamp in the middle, reading or sewing or playing dominoes. Sam always sat with his back to the stove. From there he could look up and see the white shape of Prince in the photograph beside the window. The horse almost seemed to be in the lamp-lit circle with the family.

Pa had strung a rope to the barn just as he had been advised to do many months before. On the first day of the storm he said to Sam, "I'll do the morning chores, but I'd like your help in the afternoon."

Sam spent the day close to the stove. He played games with Josie and Matt and mended some harness. Pa was teaching him how to make holes with the awl and draw the waxed thread through. The day passed slowly. By chore time he was glad to put on his jacket and boots. The circle of lamplight seemed more like a prison than a haven.

Pa eased the door open just far enough for Sam to slip out, but even so the cold blast of wind filled the little house. Sam got a good grip on the rope. Then Pa came out behind him and pulled the door shut firmly.

Once Sam was away from the shelter of the house, it seemed that there was nothing in the world but wind and icy snow. He knew Pa was behind him, but he could not see him if he looked back or hear him if he shouted. It was fifty steps to the barn. By the time Sam got the barn door open, his face was numb and his fingers were stiff inside his heavy mitts.

Once they got inside, Sam and Pa stood for a minute getting their breath. The still air and the warm smell of the animals made the barn seem less cold than it was.

"It's a good thing we covered up every crack," said Pa. "And it's a good thing we have five animals in here, plus the chickens, of course. They keep each other warm."

Sam thought for just a moment of the horses out in the storm. Were they huddled together to keep from freezing? Then he got on with the milking.

The cows weren't giving much milk these days and he wasn't sure they could get the little bit there was safely to the house, but the animals still had to be milked.

When all the chores were done, Sam and Pa wrapped themselves up again. Pa put the lid on the milk pail and they went back into the storm. By the time they made it to the kitchen, Sam was grateful to be back in the circle of lamplight.

That night and every night of the storm, the howling came into Sam's dreams. He saw Prince trying to outrun the bitter wind, running from wolves, always running. He woke in the mornings as tired as if he had been running all night himself.

By the fourth day of the storm, everyone in the family came to breakfast with heavy eyes. Pa looked at the plateful of biscuit Mama put on the table and said, "It's been days since we've had bread, Clara."

"Exactly how do you expect me to make bread?" said Mama crossly. "I have to keep the stove hot so that we won't freeze, but a foot from the stove it's too cold for bread to rise. We're lucky to have biscuit."

Everyone stared at Mama. Pa looked a little ashamed. Suddenly Matt said, "I know. You can put the bread in Josie's bed. It's the warmest place in the house. It's not fair but it is."

"How could you put bread in my bed," said Josie scornfully.

"I could, you know," said Mama. "If I had it ready, all wrapped up in towels and put it in your bed as soon as you got up, I think it would be warm enough to rise. Matt, thank you. This wind has paralyzed my brain and my manners."

On the fifth morning of the storm Mama did exactly as she had planned. By noon the bread was baking and they ate it straight from the oven, spread with apple butter. Matt got all the end crusts, his favourite part.

On the sixth morning Sam woke up with a strange feeling. Something was missing. He lay in bed listening.

It was the wind. The moaning and shrieking were gone. The

storm had blown itself out. Frost covered the windows, but the light that glowed through it was pale pink.

Pa was already in the barn. "I'll help him, Mama," said Sam. "I'll eat breakfast later."

He put on his coat, hat, boots and mitts and stepped out the door. The world was quiet, and the sun was rising red in the east.

By the time the chores were done the sky was pale blue. Sam ran from the barn to the house. The air was so cold he could feel it burning as he gulped it down his throat. In spite of that he felt like running straight out onto the prairie. But he went into the house instead. He needed hot oatmeal inside him before he did any such thing.

Pa was already sitting at the table. "I'm going to take the cutter and go into town, Sam. Want to come?"

It was tempting to think of town and people to see and talk to, but Sam's legs wanted to run, not ride in a cutter. He looked away from Pa and saw Josie's face, shining and eager. "Take Josie, Pa. I'd rather go for a walk."

Everyone stared at him. "Take a walk in this terrible cold?" said Mama. "Don't you think it's too dangerous, James?"

Pa considered. Then he said, "You've been cooped up all this time, Sam. No wonder you need to run. If you use your common sense you should be all right. That means wrap up well and don't go out of sight of the house. If you see even one single cloud, head for home. This weather won't last and a storm can come up fast. I'm told there is usually a lull of at least a day or two between storms, but you can't be sure."

"What about you, James?" said Mama.

"Josie and I will use common sense, too. We won't linger, will we, Josie? And if we see a cloud we'll head for home. Even if snow starts, Rabbit and Lady know the way."

"What about me?" said Matt. "Can I go with Sam?"

Sam's heart sank. Just for an hour he wanted to be alone. Just for half an hour.

"No, Matt," said Mama. "I need you with me. We'll play some games."

"Outside games," said Matt firmly.

"Of course," said Mama. "I'm tired of this house, too, but, unlike Sam, I'd rather not be alone. We'll play Fox and Geese."

After breakfast they cleared the table in double-quick time. "You three run along," said Mama. "I'll do these up later. We don't want to waste the sun."

They all put on their warmest clothes. Sam had two thick sweaters and he wore them both, as well as three pairs of socks. He turned the flap of his cap down over his ears and even tied the strings under his chin, something he ordinarily scorned to do. Then Mama wound his scarf around him so that it covered his mouth and nose.

"Now remember what your father said," she reminded him a little anxiously. His mouth was so muffled up that he could only nod in reply, but he nodded hard. He had no intention of freezing to death on the prairie.

He decided to walk straight north. That direction the land rose a little and he could see the house from farther off. That was what he told himself, but really it was because Prince had been set loose to the north, and that made his feet want to walk that direction. Of course, there was no telling where the horses were now. Prince could be fifty miles away. Or more.

Sam started to feel gloomy thinking of Prince so far away, but then the glory of the sun shining on the snow and the great sense of space around him wiped everything out of his mind except the wish to run. So he ran. The earth under his boots was as hard as bare rock, and the snow was thin and dry.

When he could run no more he suddenly remembered his promise to Pa and he turned around. The house was still well in view, though small in the distance. The scarf over his mouth was damp with his breath. He tried to shift it to a dry spot with his clumsy mittened hand. Then he turned around slowly.

As on the very first day when he walked out on the prairie, he was in the middle of a great tilting circle with an arching blue sky overhead. But now the blue of the sky was cold and pale and the tops of the taller golden prairie grasses showed above the gleaming white snow. He was in the centre of a blue, white and gold world. He began to run again, partly from exhilaration and partly from the need to keep warm.

Suddenly he heard a great rumbling sound. Thunder. He stopped. Fear made his bones feel weak. Thunder in such cold weather must mean a storm coming fast.

Sam looked up at the sky. The high blue was clear. No clouds. But the thunder rolled on.

Then Sam realized he was hearing the thunder partly through his feet. The frozen ground was shaking. He turned around again slowly, squinting against the dazzle of the sun on the snow.

He saw horses galloping toward him. A whole herd of them running fast, their manes and tails flying in the frosty air.

Sam could not move. Maybe the horses would gallop over him, but he could not move.

He could see their colours now, black and brown and spotted. One that must be Goldie, a dark one that was surely Pete. But where was Prince? There must be a white horse among the others. He scanned the moving mass of bodies anxiously.

Then he saw that the herd had an order to it. That black horse was always in the rear and at the front was a white horse, like a shadow against the white snow. A white horse galloping straight toward him.

As the herd came closer Sam kept his eyes on that white horse. Surely he was smaller than the others. Surely it was Prince.

It was. Prince was galloping straight toward him.

But when the horses were so close that Sam could see Prince's black eyes looking at him, the whole herd suddenly veered away. All the horses followed Prince and he led them in a great circle around Sam. Three times they circled. Then Prince tossed his head and neighed. All the other horses neighed, too, and Prince led them away, straight away from Sam toward the north.

Sam watched them until they were out of sight. Once again he was alone in the middle of that great expanse of white and gold under the arching sky. He stood until a tingle in his right big toe told him he had stood long enough. Then suddenly he was running again, running toward home.

It was a long run. Sam was surprised at how far he had gone. He reached the farmyard just as Pa was leading Lady and Rabbit into the barn. They had been to town and back while he was out on the prairie.

Sam rushed panting into the barn. It was a few minutes before he could speak. Pa stood waiting. Finally Sam took a deep, steadying breath.

"Pa," he said. "Pa, Prince is the king of the horses!" And he told Pa all that had happened.

When he was finished, Pa held up both hands as if he was going to say something very important.

"Sam," he said, "if Prince is the king of the horses, we'll have to change his name."

"Change his name?"

"Yes, Sam Ferrier. From now on the horse once known as Prince will be called King."

For a long moment Sam thought about it.

"King," he said to himself, and then out loud. "King. It sounds right to me, Pa. It sounds true."

from

Jasmin

by

J A N   T R U S S

Jasmin is weary of the demands of being the oldest child in her large family, and she is failing grade six. She decides to run away and live as freely as "Old Meg" in her favourite poem. Hiding out in the foothills of the Rockies, she is like a modern female Crusoe.

A mist of silver dew had settled on the brilliant reds, blues, and yellows of the curled up patchwork cocoon among the willows below a spruce tree. Springy branches bounced and swayed as agile brown squirrels chased along them chattering noisily.

The cocoon stirred, stretched itself out, surprising the squirrels who scurried to the topmost branches to carry on their noisy grumbling.

With one finger, Jasmin pushed the snug goose feather warmth from one eye and looked warily up through the patterns of leaves and twigs and spreading branches. Far away at the top of the pattern she saw bits of a very blue sky. She breathed contentedly. Her first morning, and she was snug, comfortable and safe. Luxuriously she stretched her legs, wriggled her toes that were stiff but warm inside her sneakers. Then she lifted her entire face out into the morning.

"Ooh," she gasped, for the air was chill. She sniffed in the scent of the forest air that was like honey and Christmas trees. She took in a full breath of the freshness and then breathed out a long sigh of contentment. Besides the argumentative squirrels, birds were calling and twittering everywhere. A vivid blue jay landed on a branch almost by her nose, then flashed away.

Jasmin snuggled in the warmth of her quilt and thought happily, *Her bed it was the brown heath turf. Her house was out of doors.* This outdoor waking-up was even better than waking up had been when the sun shone through the leaves of her plants on the window ledge, making trembly shadows on her bed and sometimes on Leroy's face and pillow, while she lay thinking before all the little kids woke up.

She decided that waking up in the forest morning was the best thing she'd ever done in her life. She didn't have to get up because nobody needed her. She relaxed into the lovely warmth, lay back to look upwards through the patterns of the branches. She watched the soft, pale undersides of squirrels and twittering, flitting groups of tiny chickadees.

What an interesting way to see things, she thought, looking up.

Perhaps she would stay all day just watching the underside view of things with the sky shining blue as jewels through the quivering branches. This morning she could *live as she did please.* It was the first morning in the first day of her new life. This morning she didn't have to wash little faces, tie up shoe laces, or fix lunch pails. Nobody was yelling, "Jasmin do this, Jasmin do that."

Today there would be no tests to fail.

Already, she was glad she had run away. It was a very special feeling to be alone and free in the forest morning.

Her thoughts were interrupted. Somewhere, just off to the right of where she lay, there was a crunching and a rustling in the pine-needled underbrush.

She lay quite still, only moving her face slightly to see what it was, but her heart did not beat with fear as it had in the darkness. In the morning light the menace of the forest seemed to have gone away.

Very slowly, the rustling drew near her, then nearer until she saw a lurching, fat ball of a porcupine, crossing the bright dapples of sunshine. Its bristles, touched by the sun, were amber. From down where she was, Jasmin looked up into its sad little grey face with its dim, mild eyes.

For some unknown reason, that face reminded her of Leroy, merrily lurching and shining in the sunshine. Jasmin shivered. It was terrible to get Leroy mixed up with the porcupine in her thoughts. She hated it when her father had to shoot porcupines because they slung their spines into the cattle. The porcupine faces were so sad and hopeless when they looked down from trees they had climbed. Her father would raise his gun. Bang. The porcupine would drop down dead. No shine left, just a dead hunk of prickles. Her father would skin off the spines and her mother would cook the meat. It tasted like chicken.

She studied the porcupine as its little feet brought its armed body closer and closer. Maybe, she speculated, she would have to kill and eat porcupine now she was a fugitive.

No sooner did she think of food than she began to feel hungry. She sat up to scrutinize the forest floor, startling the porcupine who moved just a little quicker, turning away from her. Its movement, even as it hurried, was still so slow that Jasmin thought, Well, I could easily catch a porcupine. But how would I kill it? The thought repelled her.

Clearly, she might have to kill things to eat. The forest floor didn't look any too promising; mostly old dry pine needles, a bit dampened on the top layer by the morning dew. Not a thing in sight to nibble on—except the porcupine.

"Um," Jasmin said to herself, "you had better start facing up to the day's problems. You can't just lie here enjoying yourself. You, my girl, are going to get hungry."

And with the wide-awake thought of hunger there came the thought that somebody could already be looking for her because, by now, they would have found out that her bed was empty and the quilt missing.

"See," she said sorrowfully to herself, "you can't lie late in bed until you've found a place to hide. And it's got to be a place where nobody will find you. Nobody, see. So, get moving," she ended up sternly, adding her voice to the other chattering and twittering creatures in the tree. Talking to herself was beginning to seem quite normal.

Shiveringly, she made herself get out of her snug cocoon and shake out her quilt, which was wet with dew. Her splendid red gown was a crumpled mess because she had used it as a pillow. She rolled the damp quilt and the creased gown together as quickly as she could. Then, with her pack on her back, chewing on a juicy red potato, she started off again on her journey down the narrow deer trail.

Soon she was humming and thinking that this was how explorers must have walked through the land looking for places to settle. She laughed and began to say over to herself things she had learned in social studies about settlements.

"It must be near water for drinking and washing."

"It must be near a source of food."

"It must provide a dry place for sleeping, safe from enemies and wild animals."

She couldn't remember if the last two were really in the social studies lessons or whether she was making those up to suit her own needs. She began to hurry as the thought of finding her own hiding-home excited her.

"I can't remember going anywhere by myself—except to the outhouse," she said and giggled happily. Even as she enjoyed her happiness, she thought of Leroy lurching along by her side. He'd stop to watch a beetle or a caterpillar, kneel behind it, following it with his thick finger, making strange noises of conversation.

Suddenly Jasmin felt awful for not bringing Leroy with her. She could hear her mother's voice crying out, "Don't be so selfish, Jasmin. Take Marigold. Take Carmen Miranda. Take Nathaniel. Take Merron." Her mother never had to yell, "Take Leroy." Leroy always followed her—sometimes to the outhouse.

"I should have brought him with me," she said aloud, but her mind was thinking it wasn't fair. I could never have a friend, or stay overnight. Eglantine had a friend because she wasn't always dragging little kids around with her.

"I ought to have made a pack to carry the babies," she said as she thought how much easier the pack on her back was than her usual load of a heavy baby in her arms.

"If ever I have children, I'll have just one so there won't be an oldest." She marched to the sound of her own voice.

"Or maybe I'll have twins, then there won't be an oldest." As her voice spoke those words she wondered if Leroy would have been like a friend if he hadn't been retarded. Leroy was always coming into her mind. Even in the forest, she couldn't stop worrying about him. In fact, even though she was anxious to find her own hiding-home, she couldn't stop worrying about her family.

"I hope Eglantine is looking after them. She will have to be the oldest now."

Lost in her thoughts, she went on struggling downwards toward the valley on the deer trail that turned and twisted. Twigs and thorns tugged at her jeans and hat and snagged her parka. She moved with urgency because somebody could be searching for her, following her trail.

*　　*　　*

Jasmin lifted her arms and did a graceful dance, twirling around with her potatoes. At last she was out in the bright sunshine, out of the thick bush, hot inside her parka, and her jeans soaked up to the knees in dew. She had reached the margin of the forest where sunlight danced too in the leaves of the quivering aspens. As she whirled and twirled on her way, wild pink roses pulled at her with their thorns reminding Jasmin of precious *Old Meg* inside her lining.

"*Her wine was dew of the wild white rose*," Jasmin sang out, "and mine shall be—dew of the wild pink rose. There's enough dew to get drunk on."

Everywhere dew glistened like jewels on the delicate petals, enchanting Jasmin until she forgot she was in a hurry. She paused to smell a rose, then to taste a dew drop, then to watch a ladybug, then to pick an inchworm off her sleeve and settle it on a rose petal.

"Inchworm, where are you going?" she asked. "Why don't you stay on the petal and keep off the thorns, silly, silly? Oh, I know! Your enemies can't see you, green on green."

Enemies! That reminded her to stop dawdling.

"Goodbye. I've got enemies too. I could be in danger right now." She reminded herself that her father could come riding to find her, urging his horse quickly down the trails where she had struggled so slowly.

"Not exactly enemies. They'll be missing me at home and worrying. Can people who worry about you be your enemies?" she asked herself.

"They are never, never going to find me," she muttered determinedly and put her chin out as she imagined herself caught and taken back like a silly child, everybody knowing she was failing, all the kids at school mocking. She thought wildly that perhaps her father had already got the police out. She remembered that once, when a small plane crashed near the mountains, helicopters had roared and hovered all over the place where she was now, expertly searching.

"Hurry. Must hurry," she urged herself on.

But even her fear and urgency could not take away her sense of happy aloneness. She trailed her fingers through the feathery tops of grasses and touched soft rose petals as she passed, and she hummed to herself. Through the broken brim of her hat, the sun sprinkled gold sparkles that danced on her eyelashes, teased her on her nose, and played on her hand when she tried to catch them. Sometimes she did a little twirl around because she was full of such dancing, singing feelings.

"Hurry. Hurry. Find a hiding-home," she sang to herself. *"Alone with her great family, she lived as she did please. Alone, Alone—"*

When a hawk began to swoop down her pathway, following her, she felt uncomfortable. It swooped over her, then glided off in a wide circle, then swooped back and hovered directly above her. Birds and squirrels, in the thin aspens, called noisy warnings to each other, placing Jasmin right in the middle of a disturbance that would clue in any searcher to the presence of some passing stranger. She realized it wasn't going to be easy to move secretly in the wilderness.

"Go away," she yelled to the crazy hawk. "Go away. You're advertising that I'm here. Please pretend you haven't seen me. You're not being my friend!"

She had yelled up into the sky, her loud voice sounding strange, out of tune with the concert of wild noises. Funny, she thought, all the other noises simply fitted together to make nature's great wide silence.

Funny, too, how bits of school flashed into her thinking. "That's a paradox," she murmured, discovering its real meaning for the first time. "A paradox. All the noises make a silence."

"Go away. Please go away," she called again, but the hawk only teased her, and spread its wings, wide and luxuriously, to glide around her. She swung her potato sack up at it which only made it glide nearer. She heard the echo of her voice. She mustn't run the risk of making such loud sounds. A new thought suddenly struck her.

"Will I forget how to talk when I've lived by myself for a very long time?" she whispered, almost frightened by the idea.

"Can a person think without talking?" She asked the question out loud, and answered firmly, "Leroy does, doesn't he?"

She could hardly bear to think of Leroy, of his pale eyes wild with the thoughts he couldn't make words for. "Oh, go away hawk," she called crossly.

The crossness only lasted a few moments for she saw wild strawberries glinting like rubies down among the grasses. Her mouth watered so hard it brought tears to her eyes.

"I didn't know I was so hungry," she murmured as she went down on her knees among the wet grasses and quickly filled her mouth with the sweet sharp-tasting berries. She crawled along picking and eating, her fingers staining bright strawberry red.

"My first perfect out-of-doors breakfast," she gloated after a while, and still on her knees looked at three berries on the palm of her hand. "So tiny. So sharp tasting. So perfect." She paused with her head on one side to listen to the long sweet silence of nature's morning, down the valley, all the way across to the mountains.

"Oh, stop wasting time, Jasmin," she ordered herself sharply, just as her mother would do if she could see her "daydreaming" —what her mother called thinking. "Get up, Jasmin, and go where you're supposed to be going."

She filled her hand with strawberries, then walked on her way, westwards and downwards, nibbling one tiny berry at a time to make them last. "Strawberries for breakfast, strawberries for breakfast," she chanted in rhythm to her hurrying feet, inwardly deciding that once she was settled in her hiding-home strawberries would be her regular breakfast.

When she'd marched for what seemed a very long time, she came to an edge, a place where the land dropped off almost like a cliff. She must be very near the river. The drop was so sharp that it was difficult to climb down, and made even worse by the pack on her back, and especially by the potato bag in her hand. In places she needed both hands to save herself, as she slipped and slithered grabbing onto branches and roots. It felt as if her potato carrying hand would break. In one place she held the bag in her teeth as she made a daring dive from a stolid tree root to a projecting trunk much lower down. The trees grew sideways out of the earth. Some of them were huge. Everywhere, pale roots, like gnarled ghost fingers, clawed out at the air. As she plunged and slid, Jasmin saw that there were dark places like caves under the twisted bodies of some of the giant trees. She shivered, even though her parka made her warm. There was something creepy in the chill shadow of the steep hillside.

Gobs of slimy brown earth clung to her sneakers, making her feet into heavy weights dragging her legs down. No hawk followed her now. Birds and squirrels had gone silent.

Down in the cleft in the earth, the ghostly roots and dark trees made her think of gnomes and evil spells, thoughts she used to think when she was a little kid. There was the dark smell of old mushrooms.

Her hands felt cold, but Jasmin took a deep breath and tried to keep her chin up as she eased her way along the slippery slimy slope, determined that she would not be scared.

After a while of travelling sideways and downwards she came to a break in the hillside, a rugged sort of red-clay gully, jagged and twisted. It was too wide to jump over. Bright water splashed down at the bottom over rocks and pebbles. Carefully she climbed down and caught a drink of ice-cold water in her cupped hand. Looking around, she thought it was like being inside the body of the earth; grey pine-needled skin, then blood-red insides with bulging roots for veins.

"*A chip hat had she on.*" Jasmin tried her voice to see if the sound made her braver. But she wasn't sure. Her voice sounded so little and sharp and lonely, just a weak thing in a strong and powerful space. Unseen ears seemed to be listening. Unknown eyes seemed to be watching. Uneasily, from deep down in the gully, she looked up and all around her, listening for something. There was nothing. Nothing to feel scared about she told herself sharply and made herself bend and dip into the silvery, icy water for another drink. Just as her hand dipped into the water there was a yelp. A quick thin yelp.

The sudden surprise of the sound made Jasmin's stomach turn a somersault. "Stop it, stop it," she whispered to her thumping heart. She was mad at herself for being so jumpy. "Toughen up," she told herself. She took a deep breath and searched around for the creature that had yelped. The knuckles of her clenched hands were white and strained.

Then, up the opposite slope, she looked right into the yellow eyes and sharp small face of a young coyote. It was just about ten strides up the slope from where she was drinking.

The coyote looked as startled as she felt, as though it had stopped suddenly on its way down to get a drink. Such a little coyote with pricked ears and a shaggy, yellowish coat. Only a poor, shivering, thin little coyote.

As soon as Jasmin moved to straighten up, the coyote darted away, then watched her from higher up the hillside.

A sudden feeling told Jasmin that there was something very interesting about the spot where the coyote had first been standing. A massive jackpine grew thick and sideways out of the earth, then bent upwards at a sharp angle to reach toward the sky. Its heavy bottom branches hung down like a thick, green skirt over some sort of hollow. Maybe it was a hollow where the coyote lived. Maybe its den was behind that heavy curtain of branches. She had to see. As she moved, the coyote stood its ground up the slope, watching her suspiciously. "Don't you worry," she called up to it softly. "I'm only going to investigate. Not going to hurt anything."

She waded through the ice-cold water and scrambled up the slope to the heavily skirted tree. She paused, took a breath for courage, whispered, "Anybody in there?" paused a moment longer then parted the branches and looked behind them. Neat. Oh neato! At about the height of her chest a thick, brownish rock stuck out like a floor in the hillside. It made a wide ledge, and behind it there seemed to be a deep hollow.

Forgetting the coyote, forgetting the gloomy valley and the spooky clawing roots, forgetting everything except the joy of the marvellous discovery, Jasmin took off her pack, her hat, her parka, pushed all her things onto the ledge and hefted herself up. She climbed in through the skirt of branches. Immediately, as soon as she stepped behind the branches, she felt hidden and safe. It was a perfect hiding-home for a fugitive. But, it needed sweeping out. It was scruffy and a bit stinky, with old pine needles, animal hairs and droppings.

"Perfect. Oh perfect!" Jasmin whispered unbelievingly.

The rock ledge was like a balcony with the thick pine branches hanging down like a curtain. The hollow behind went back into the hillside, as though sometime a great hunk of rock had been pushed out to make a little room. It was not very big; not high enough for her to stand in, but with plenty of space for her to sit up, even to kneel up.

She lay down to try it for sleeping size. Just about long enough to stretch out with her toes pointed if she pushed her feet down underneath the rocky wall that jutted out into uneven shelves on the south side.

"And absolutely dry," she rejoiced as she felt around the roof and the walls.

"Coyote, little coyote, you led me to the most perfect place for living in," she murmured with a glance through her green curtain, while she hoped, superstitiously and romantically, that the little coyote had been on the moonlit field with the others last night, and had been watching her ever since on her travels.

"You're crazy, Jasmin." She mocked herself, but liking her story-book thoughts, she stood up on the balcony, looking out through the branches like a princess on her castle wall. "This is the hiding-hollow of Jasmin Marie Antoinette Stalke, wherein she shall dwell—wherein *she shall live as she do please.*

"Shhh," she restrained herself. "Somebody could be looking, listening. Shhhh, nobody is going to find me here. Thank you, coyote."

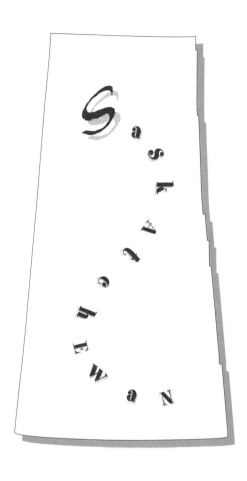

from

Owls in the Family

by

FARLEY MOWAT

The author's famous account of how young Billy finds and tames two owls, Wol and Weeps, is based on his childhood in Saskatoon.

One May morning, my friend Bruce and I went for a hike on the prairie.

Spring was late that year in Saskatoon, Saskatchewan. Snowdrifts still clung along the steep banks of the river, in the shelter of the cottonwood trees. The river was icy with thaw water and, as we crossed over the Railroad Bridge, we could feel a cold breath rising from it. But we felt another breath, a gentle one, blowing across the distant wheat fields and smelling like warm sun shining on soft mud. It was the spring wind, and the smell of it made us walk faster. We were in a hurry to get out of the city and into the real prairie, where you can climb a fence post and see for about a million miles—that's how flat the prairie is.

The great thing about Saskatoon was the way it ended sharp all around its edge. There were no outskirts to Saskatoon. When you stepped off the end of the Railroad Bridge you stepped right onto the prairie and there you were—free as the gophers.

Gophers were the commonest thing on the prairie. The little mounds of yellow dirt around their burrows were so thick, sometimes, it looked as if the fields had yellow measles.

But this day Bruce and I weren't interested in gophers. We were looking for an owl's nest. We had decided that we wanted some pet owls, and if you want pet owls you have to find a nest and get the young ones out of it.

We headed for the nearest of the clumps of cottonwood trees that dot the prairies, and which are called "bluffs" out in Saskatchewan. The ground was spongy under our sneakers, and it squooshed when we hit a wet place. A big jack rabbit bounced up right under my feet, and scared me so much I jumped almost as high as he did. And as we came nearer the bluff, two crows came zooming out of it and swooped down on us, cawing their heads off.

Bluffs are funny places in the spring. The cottonwood trees shed a kind of white fluffy stuff that looks like snow. Sometimes it's so thick it comes right over the top of your sneakers and you get a queer feeling that you really *are* walking through snow, even though the sun on your back is making you sweat right through your shirt.

We walked through this bluff, scuffing our feet in the cottonwood snow and stirring it up in clouds. We kept looking up; and after a while, sure enough, we saw a big mess of twigs high up in a poplar.

"All right," Bruce said to the two crows which were swooping and hollering at us. "If you want me to snitch your eggs—I will!"

With that he handed me his haversack and began to shinny up the tree.

It was an easy climb, because cottonwood poplars always have lots of branches. When he got to the nest and looked into it I yelled up at him: "Any eggs?" Bruce grinned but he wouldn't answer. I could see him doing something with his free hand— the one he wasn't holding on with—and I knew there were eggs there all right. I watched, and sure enough he was popping them into his mouth so he could carry them down out of the tree.

We always carried eggs down out of trees that way. The only thing was, crows' eggs are pretty big and if you have to stuff three or four of them into your mouth it nearly chokes you.

Bruce started to climb down. When he got about ten feet from the ground he stepped on a rotten branch. Poplar branches are always rotten near the ground, and you have to watch out for them. I guess Bruce forgot. Anyway, the branch broke and he slid the rest of the way and lit on his seat with a good hard bump.

All the eggs had broken, and Bruce was spitting out shells and eggs all over the cottonwood snow. I got laughing so hard I couldn't even talk. When Bruce got most of the eggs spat out he came for me and tackled me, and we had a fight. It didn't last long, because it was too hot to really fight, so Bruce ate a sardine sandwich to get the taste of crows' eggs out of his mouth and then we started across the prairie again to search through other bluffs until we found an owl's nest.

I guess we searched about a hundred bluffs that morning, but we never saw an owl. We were getting hungry by then, so we made a sort of nest for ourselves on the ground, out of poplar snow and branches. We curled up in it and opened our haversacks.

Bruce had sandwiches and a lemon in his. He was the only boy I ever knew who liked to eat lemons. He said they were better than oranges, any day of the week.

I had a hard-boiled egg and just for fun I reached over and cracked the shell on Bruce's head. He yelled, and we had another fight, and rolled all over his sardine sandwiches.

We were just finishing our lunch when a wood gopher came snuffling along through the cottonwood snow. Wood gophers are grey and have big bushy tails. This one came right up to us and, when I held a crust out to him, he shuffled up and took it out of my hand.

"Got no sense," said Bruce. "You might have been a coyote, and then where'd he be at?"

"Heck," I said. "He's got more sense than you. Do I look like a coyote?"

The gopher didn't say anything. He just took the crust and scuttled away to his hole somewhere. We picked up our haversacks. The sun was as bright as fireworks and the sky was so clear you could look right through it—like looking through a blue window. We started to walk.

All of a sudden Bruce stopped so fast that I bumped into him.

"Lookee!" he said, and pointed to a bluff about half a mile away. There must have been a million crows around it. It looked as if the bluff was on fire and filling the sky with black smoke—that's how many crows there were.

When you see a bunch of crows all yelling their heads off at something, you can almost bet it's an owl they're after. Crows and owls hate each other, and when a crow spots an owl, he'll call every other crow for miles and they all join in and mob the owl.

We headed for that bluff at a run. The crows saw us coming but they were too excited to pay much attention. We were nearly deaf with their racket by the time we reached the edge of the trees. I was ahead of Bruce when I saw something big and slow go drifting out of one poplar into another. It was a great horned owl, the biggest kind of owl there is, and as soon as it flew, the whole lot of crows came swooping down on it, cawing like fury. I noticed they were careful not to get too close.

Bruce and I started to hunt for the nest. After a while, the owl got more worried about us than about the crows and away he went. He flew low over the fields, almost touching the ground. That way the crows couldn't dive on him. If they tried it they would shoot past him and crash into the dirt.

There wasn't any owl's nest in that bluff after all, but we didn't worry. We knew the nest would have to be in some bluff not too far away. All we had to do was look.

We looked in different bluffs all afternoon. We found seven crows' nests, a red-tailed hawk's nest, and three magpies' nests. I tore the seat out of my trousers climbing to the hawk's-nest, and we both got Russian thistles in our sneakers, so we had sore feet. It got hotter and hotter, and we were so thirsty I could have eaten a lemon myself, except that Bruce didn't have any more.

It was past supper time when we started back toward the railroad. By then we were pretending we were a couple of Arabs lost in the desert. Our camels had died of thirst, and we were going to die too unless we found some water pretty soon.

"Listen," Bruce said. "There's an old well at Haultain Corner. If we cut over past Barney's Slough to the section road, we can get a drink."

"Too late," I told him. "Goodbye old pal, old Sheik. I am doomed. Go on and leave me lay."

"Oh, nuts," said Bruce. "I'm thirsty. C'mon, let's go."

So we cut past Barney's Slough and there were about a thousand mallard ducks on it. They all jumped into the air as we went by and their wings made a sound like a freight train going over a bridge.

"Wish I had my dad's gun!" said Bruce.

But I was wondering why on the prairies they call lakes and ponds "sloughs." I still don't know why. But that's what they're called in Saskatoon.

There was one big bluff between us and Haultain Corner. It was too far to go around it, so we walked right through it. Anyway, it was cooler in among the trees. When we were about halfway through I spotted a crow's-nest in a big old cottonwood.

"Bet it's empty," I said to Bruce. But the truth was that I was just too hot and tired to climb any more trees. Bruce felt the same way, and we walked past. But I took one last look up at it, and there, sticking over the edge of the nest, was the biggest bunch of tail feathers you ever saw. My heart jumped right into my throat and I grabbed Bruce by the shirt and pointed up.

It was a great horned owl all right. We kept as quiet as we could, so as not to scare her, and then we looked around the bottom of the tree. There were bits of rabbits and gophers, and lots of owl pellets. When owls catch something, they eat the whole thing—bones and fur and all. Then, after a while, they burp and spit out a ball of hair and bones. That's an owl pellet.

"By Gang! We found it!" Bruce whispered.

"*I* found it," I said.

"OK," said Bruce. "*You* found it, then. So how about you climbing up and seeing how many young ones are in it?"

"Nothing doing, old pal," I replied. "*I* found the nest. So if *you* want one of the owlets, *you* climb up and have a look."

Neither of us was keen to climb that tree. The old owl was sticking close to her nest, and you can't always tell how fierce an owl is going to be. They can be pretty fierce sometimes.

"Say," said Bruce after a while, "why don't we just leave her be for now? Might scare her into leaving the nest for good if *we* climbed up. What say we get Mr. Miller, and come back tomorrow?"

Mr. Miller was one of our teachers. Bruce and I liked him because he liked the prairie too. He was a great one for taking pictures of birds and things. We knew he would be crazy to get some pictures of the owl—and Mr. Miller never minded climbing trees.

"Sure," I said. "Good idea."

We went off to Haultain Corner and got a drink of water that tasted like old nails, out of the broken pump. Then we walked on home. That night I told Dad about the owl's nest, and he looked at Mother and all he said was:

"Oh NO! Not owls too."

*   *   *

The reason Dad said: "Oh NO! Not owls too" was because I already had some pets.

There was a summerhouse in our backyard and we kept about thirty gophers in it. They belonged to Bruce and me, and to another boy called Murray. We caught them out on the prairie, using snares made of heavy twine.

The way you do it is like this: You walk along until you spot a gopher sitting up beside his hole. Gophers sit straight up, reaching their noses as high as they can, so they can see farther. When you begin to get too close they flick their tails, give a little jump, and whisk down their holes. As soon as they do that, you take a piece of twine that has a noose tied in one end, and you spread the noose over the hole. Then you lie down in the grass holding the other end of the twine in your hand. You can hear the gopher all the while, whistling away to himself somewhere underground. He can hear you, too, and he's wondering what you're up to.

After a while he gets so curious he can't stand it. Out pops his head, and you give a yank on the twine. You have to haul in fast, because if the twine gets loose he'll slip his head out of the noose and zip back down his hole.

We had rats too. Murray's dad was a professor at the university and he got us some white rats from the medical school. We kept them in our garage, which made my dad a little peeved, because he couldn't put the car in the garage for fear the rats would make nests inside the seats. Nobody ever knew how many rats we had because they have so many babies, and they have them so fast. We gave white rats away to all the kids in Saskatoon, but we always seemed to end up with as many as we had at first.

There were the rats and gophers, and then there was a big cardboard box full of garter snakes that we kept under the back porch, because my mother wouldn't let me keep them in the house. Then there were the pigeons. I usually had about ten of them, but they kept bringing their friends and relations for visits, so I never knew how many to expect when I went out to feed them in the mornings. There were some rabbits too, and then there was Mutt, my dog—but he wasn't a pet; he was one of the family.

Sunday morning my father said:

"Billy, I think you have enough pets. I don't think you'd better bring home any owls. In any case, the owls might eat your rats and rabbits and gophers..."

He stopped talking and a queer look came into his face. Then he said:

"On second thought—maybe we *need* an owl around this place!"

So it was all right.

Sunday afternoon Bruce and I met Mr. Miller at his house. He was a big man with a bald head. He wore short pants and carried a great big haversack full of cameras and films. He was excited about the owl's nest, all right, and he was in such a hurry to get to it that Bruce and I had to run most of the way, just to keep up with him.

When we reached the edge of the Owl Bluff Mr. Miller got out his biggest camera and, after he had fussed with it for about half an hour, he said he was ready.

"We'll walk Indian file, boys," he said, "and quiet as mice. Tiptoe... Mustn't scare the owl away."

Well, that sounded all right, only you can't walk quietly in a poplar bluff because of all the dead sticks underfoot. They crack and pop like firecrackers. Under Mr. Miller's feet they sounded like cannon shots. Anyway, when we got to the nest tree there was no sign of the owl.

"Are you sure this is an owl's nest?" Mr. Miller asked us.

"Yes, sir!" Bruce answered. "We seen the owl setting on it!"

Mr. Miller shuddered. "*Saw* the owl *sitting* on it, Bruce... Hmmm... Well—I suppose I'd better climb up and take a peek. But if you ask me, I think it's just an old crow's nest."

He put down his big haversack and the camera, and up he went. He was wearing a big floppy hat to keep his head from getting sunburned and I don't think he could see out from under it very well.

"Boy, has he got knobby knees!" Bruce whispered to me. We both started to giggle and we were still giggling when Mr. Miller began to shout.

"Hoyee!" he yelled. "SCAT—WHOEEE! Hoy, HOY!"

Bruce and I ran around the other side of the tree so we could see up to the nest. Mr. Miller was hanging on to the tree with both arms and he was kicking out with his feet. It looked as if his feet had slipped off the branch and couldn't find a place to get hold of again. Just then there was a swooshing sound and the old owl came diving down right on top of him with her wings spread wide. She looked as big as a house and she didn't miss Mr. Miller by more than an inch. Then she swooped up and away again.

Mr. Miller was yelling some strange things, and good and loud too. He finally got one foot back on a branch but he was in such a hurry to get down that he picked too small a branch. It broke, and he slid about five feet before his belt caught on a stub. While he was trying to get loose, the owl came back for another try. This time she was so close that we could see her big yellow eyes, and both Bruce and I ducked. She had her claws stuck way out in front of her. Just as she dived toward him, Mr. Miller, who couldn't see her coming because of his hat, gave a jump upward to get free of the stub. The result was that the owl couldn't miss him even if she wanted to. There was an awful flapping and yelling and then away went the owl, with Mr. Miller's hat.

I don't think she really wanted that old hat. It was all Mr. Miller's fault for jumping at the wrong time. The owl seemed to be trying to shake the hat loose from her claws, but she couldn't, because her claws were hooked in it. The last we saw of her she was flying out over the prairie and she still had the hat.

When Mr. Miller got down out of the tree he went right to his haversack. He took out a bottle, opened it, and started to drink. His Adam's apple was going in and out like an accordion. After a while he put down the bottle and wiped his mouth. When he saw us staring at him he tried to smile.

"Cold tea," he explained. "Thirsty work—climbing trees in this hot weather."

"It was an owl's nest, wasn't it, sir?" asked Bruce.

Mr. Miller looked at him hard for a moment. Then:

"Yes, Bruce," he said. "I guess it was."

There was one thing about Mr. Miller. You couldn't stop him for long. Now he explained to us that it was probably a bad thing to climb to the nest because it would disturb the owls too much. He had a better idea. He took a hatchet out of his haversack and we set to work building something that he called a "blind." What this was, really, was a little tent fixed on a platform of sticks high up in another tree, but close to the owl tree.

It took a couple of hours to build the blind. Bruce and I went scrounging for pieces of wood and, when we brought them back, Mr. Miller hauled them up the chosen tree with a rope and nailed them into place. When he had a platform built he hauled up the tent. The tent had a round hole, about as big as your fist, in the front of it. That was for the camera. According to Mr. Miller, you could hide in the blind and stay there until the owl thought everything was safe. Then, when the owl came back to her nest, you could take all the pictures you wanted and she would never even know about it.

"He sure must think owls are dumb," Bruce muttered to me when Mr. Miller wasn't near. "She may not see him, but she could see that tent if her eyes were tight shut; and I don't think she's going to like it."

When the blind was finished, Mr. Miller said he was ready to try it.

"You boys go off for a walk," he told us. "Make a lot of noise when you're leaving. The books say birds can't count—so the owl will think all three of us have gone and she'll never guess I've stayed up here in the blind."

"OK, Mr. Miller," I said. "C'mon Brucie, let's get going."

We walked about a mile away to a little slough and started looking for red-winged blackbirds' nests. It was another nice day and we forgot about Mr. Miller until we began to get hungry. Then we went back to the bluff.

Mr. Miller was on the ground. He had just finished the rest of his cold tea, but he didn't look the least bit well. His face was awfully white, and his hands were shaking as he tried to put his camera away. The camera looked as if it had fallen out of a tree. It was all scratched, and covered with dirt.

"Get some good pictures, sir?" I asked him cheerfully.

"No, I didn't," Mr. Miller said—and it was a sort of snarl. "But I'll tell you one thing. Any blame fool who says owls can't count is a liar!"

On the way home Mr. Miller finally told us what had happened.

About an hour after we went walking, the owl came back. She lit on her nest and then she turned around and took a good long look at the little tent, which was on a level with her, and only about six feet away.

Mr. Miller was busy inside the tent focusing his camera and getting ready to take the owl's picture, when she asked: "Who-WHO-OO-who-WHO-OO?"—and took one leap.

The next thing Mr. Miller knew the front was ripped right out of the tent and the owl was looking him in the eye from about a foot away.

Mr. Miller accidentally dropped his camera; and then of course he had to hurry down to see if it was all right. And that was when we got back to the bluff.

I guess it wasn't a very good day for Mr. Miller, but it wasn't too bad for us. Mr. Miller said he had seen three young owls in the nest and he thought they were about halfway grown, which meant they were about the right age to take home for pets.

All we had to do now was to figure some way to get hold of them.

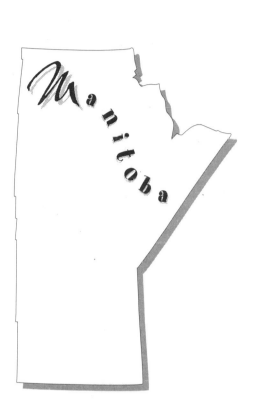

from

Who Is Frances Rain?

by

MARGARET BUFFIE

Fifteen-year-old Lizzie is spending the summer at her Gran's cabin on Rain Lake in the northern Manitoba wilderness. The tensions in her family are so great that Lizzie escapes to Rain Island for some peace. It is there that she puts on an old pair of spectacles and sees someone else on the island. Could it be the ghost of Frances Rain, who once lived there?

I took my sketchbook and pencils and sat back down in the veranda. I tried to sketch what I'd seen on Rain Island. Sometimes, when I've transferred something onto paper, I understand a lot more about it. Not this time, though. I held up my pencil drawing of the small cabin. I still couldn't understand where it came from.

If that had been Frances Rain's hand I saw, then why me? Why did I see it? Looking closely at the soft, blurry cabin, I suddenly felt a strange ache deep inside. It's hard to explain, but it was as if the cabin was changing me, as if I was growing outside of me—growing into someone else—someone different and lonely and sad. I slammed the book shut. The feeling disappeared.

I stood up and paced the veranda. Was I going stark raving nuts?

Who was this Frances Rain and how could my own drawing give me the willies? *Who was Frances Rain?*

I sat down. She was a teacher and prospector, Gran said. I'd read enough to know that prospecting was no sissy occupation. There were hard climbs through rocky hills, tough slogging through wet muskeg and hordes of blackflies and mosquitoes. There would be long hours spent hammering away at rocks in the high bush country. Then back to her little castle and moat.

Had she chosen to live her life the way she'd wanted, or had she been running away? I thought about Dad. Which one had he been doing?

Here I go again, I thought. Questions and no answers. I can't even answer why my own father left two years ago. How could I possibly find out why Frances Rain came here all those years ago?

All I knew was that I'd live my life the way I wanted, too. And I wouldn't leave anyone behind. Because I wouldn't get married. I'd become a writer or artist. Definitely *not* an archaeologist. Feeling good about my mature decision, I watched the sun go down. Pink and orange edged clouds drifted above the cabin and lit the veranda with a warm glow. The low putt-putt of a small boat moved across my line of vision. Alex angled the boat towards shore. Tim lumbered onto the dock and held the boat while Erica scrambled out, batting mosquitoes with her hat. The three of them swatted bugs, talking and laughing. They stampeded up the path and crowded onto the steps trying to escape the vampire horde.

"Hey, Lizzie," said Erica, "guess how many I caught? Six! Big ones." She held her arms wide apart.

They argued for a while about who caught the biggest.

"We'll fight this out in the morning, little one," said Tim. "Right now, your eyes are at half mast. Bed!"

Erica was too tired to fight it. She mumbled something about a zillion pound pickerel and wandered sleepily out of the room. Tim sank into one of the big chairs. I expected Alex to make up some excuse to go home, but he sat down beside me. I was glad that it was dark enough to hide the stupid grin on my face. We settled back and looked out over the dusky lake. Bugs tapped and hummed against the screens.

"Do either of you believe in ghosts?" Tim asked, casually.

"Ghosts?" we repeated in unison. Only in my case, it kind of croaked out.

"Not ghosts necessarily," said Tim, "but something paraphysical or otherworldly, if you like."

Alex stared at him. "Why are you asking us? Planning on a good ghost story?"

"No. It's just that... well... the funniest thing happened when we were out on the lake," said Tim. "I've always been a bit—what the Scots call 'fey.' My grandmother was a Scot and she knew when something was going to happen. I can't do that, but I've been into a few houses where I felt... something. A kind of pressure. Anxiety. And a few times, I've been told that the house was thought to be haunted."

"A pressure?" I gasped. "Like when someone pushes on you?"

"A bit like that. But as soon as I leave, the feeling just goes, and I usually convince myself that I ate too many onions for dinner or drank too many beers. Speaking of beers." He got up.

"Wait a minute," I demanded. "You can't just leave. What happened on the lake?"

"Yeah." Alex leaned forward. "That's dirty. Tell us."

Tim fell back on his chair and laughed. "Tell you so you can jeer at me and make fun, huh?"

"No," I said. "Honest. Come on. Give."

"You'll be disappointed, kiddo."

"If you don't tell me, I'll tell Mother that you're dying to go back to the city tomorrow."

He guffawed. "Anything but that! Jeez! You'd make a good interrogator. Get 'im where it hurts. OK, what happened was this. We were just on our way back and we were passing that big island... the one over there... you can almost see it from here."

I felt my scalp prickle.

"We putted around it, trying for that one last bite, eh, Alex? Well, that's when I felt that pressure I was telling you about. And when I looked over at the island, I thought I saw someone standing on the rock jutting out from it on the far side. But then Erica got her line tangled in mine, and when I looked back, I didn't see anything."

"That's when you asked me if there was a cabin on the island," said Alex. "I wondered why you asked that."

Tim nodded. "But even while you were telling me that no one lived on the place, I saw a light flicker in amongst the trees."

Alex laughed. "You told me you needed a leak, and would I drop you off for a second."

"I couldn't very well tell you that I wanted to check out ghosts, could I?"

I heard my own voice in the distance. "Did you land?"

He nodded. "I just walked a little way up this slope, but I could see there wasn't a cabin anywhere. And there definitely wasn't any light. The mosquitoes drove me back to the boat. Anyway, we circled the entire island afterwards and there wasn't even a canoe pulled up anywhere. But I'll tell you this. The whole time I was on that island, I felt an unearthly sadness all around me." He sat back. "Now call me a fool."

"This person you thought you saw," I asked, trying to sound casual. "Could you make him out? Was it a man or a woman?"

He thought for a minute. "You know, now that I think of it, I would have said it was a woman . . . no . . . I couldn't be sure. All I really saw was a sort of flicker." He smeared his hand all over his face and pulled his beard. "I don't know. Probably imagined the whole thing." He grinned sheepishly.

"Weird," said Alex. "Definitely weird."

"I told you you'd start calling me names," chuckled Tim.

"Oh, I didn't mean . . ."

"It's OK, Alex," said Tim, flashing his sugar cubes in the air. "Now, may I get that beer? See you later, kids."

"You didn't tell me your mother had married a madman," said Alex, when he'd gone. I knew he was only kidding, but I guess I was pretty edgy by this time.

"How do you know what he saw or didn't see? You really think he would have told us if he hadn't seen something? You're just like Evan. Think you know everything."

"I was only—"

"It took a lot of guts to tell us that story. If it happened to me, I wouldn't tell anyone. And lots of people—important, intelligent people—have seen ghosts!"

He jumped to his feet. "Hey! Cool down. I was only kidding. If Tim says he saw a ghost, he saw a ghost. Don't get crazy." He shook his head.

"Oh, so now *I'm* crazy . . ."

"Will you get serious? How come you're so worked up all of a sudden? You'd think you'd seen a ghost, not Tim."

"And if I had, you'd be making fun of me! Loonie Lizzie, maybe?"

I was acting stupid, but I couldn't seem to stop myself. Acting stupid is like a virus—comes on you without warning.

He held up both hands. "I believe him, OK?" He began to walk backwards to the door. "Look, I'm not looking for a hit in the nose. Besides, May will be wondering where I am."

I came to my senses too late. "Listen, Alex... I'm sorry. I don't know why I'm jumping down your throat. Everyone around here is tense right now, OK?"

"No kidding. But, no big deal, eh?" He was still backing away. "I gotta go or May'll have my head. I'll see you around, eh?" He took the steps two at a time.

"How about fishing again?" I called.

"Right. Sure. See you around," he said, stiff back and all.

Feeling like a number one hysterical schmuck, I watched the little red and green lights on his boat move across the water. Between Evan and me, we'd done a good job of getting rid of Alex Bird. He'd never talk to me again. He probably thought I was really nuts. I should have told him. But how could I? "By the way, Alex, I not only saw the ghost Tim saw, but the house she lived in." Great. Loonie Lizzie.

Somehow, I had to resolve the mystery of Frances Rain. For a long time, I stood on the veranda and stared over the flat silver bay. In the distance, the island was etched darkly against the navy sky, and I knew that under those distant trees, the golden spectacles were waiting for me.

*   *   *

I was up and out at dawn. After leaving a scribbled note for Gran, I tiptoed down the stairs into a heavy wet mist. The bushes and trees loomed out of the fog, not a breath of air stirring their branches. I'd gone fishing lots of times in thick mist, and the lake on mornings like this was as flat as an antiqued mirror.

I lowered the Beetle into the water and wiped off the cold dew on the seats. Through a spot of thinning mist, a small section of hazelnut bush quivered suddenly and I heard the chink of tiny coins in a warbler's pocket. Someone was up besides me.

I pushed off from shore, my clothes stinking from the mosquito repellent I'd sprayed all over them. This time I'd brought my sketchbook along with my lunch, my bathing suit and a small tape recorder.

The silent mist smothered the Beetle and me with its damp breath. I heard Bram's thin yelp from the veranda, but I couldn't bring him in case he messed up my experiment. Because that's what I was going to do. View the whole thing as a scientific experiment: taking notes on my tape recorder and making sketches. If I'd had a camera I would have brought it. Evan, the rat, refused to lend me his and Tim had an expensive Pentax, which looked like it needed a consulting engineer to travel with it.

Shafts of sunlight, rising above the trees, cut through the fog and soon I was travelling under a layer of disappearing mist. I docked easily and pulled the canoe up onto a grassy ledge.

Clear daylight came to the island like a window shade steadily opening. It hit my shoulders where I sat leaning against an old pine, warming me through my heavy sweater. Time for action.

Working up my nerve, I crept towards the campsite. The spectacles were right where they'd fallen two days ago. I grabbed them, ran back to the old pine near the shore and carefully cleaned them with a soft cloth I'd brought along. From where I was sitting I could just make out the green hump of the cabin's remains.

"I've decided to record everything I see," I said into the little holes of the tape machine. I felt a little silly but who was here to see me? "I am now going to place the glasses on my face... well, on my nose... that is... put them on." I cleared my throat. "I am going to put them on... now."

The visions came quickly. The path appeared just to my right, the cabin straight ahead. I looked towards the shore, and my heart did a flip flop.

A small dock, its stringers lying well up on the rocky shore, appeared before my eyes, but I could still see the Beetle behind a thickish film. There were two canoes tied to the dock—one a big freighter, the other a small Peterborough, like the Beetle. I tried to describe what I saw without babbling.

The cabin stood low and silvery in the early morning sun. Long-ago leaves danced their shadows across the green roof. When I listened to the tape later, I was surprised at how matter-of-fact I sounded—that is, until all hell broke loose. Figuratively speaking, of course.

"The cabin door seems to be slightly open," I heard myself say, sounding a little like a CBC news correspondent. "As I look around me, it's a clear spring day. Some of the trees are just budding. I wish... uh... uh, wait. There seems to be... there seems... what? The door is opening... in front of me!"

I can laugh now, but at the time, it was like being kicked in the chest. Every muscle went into rigor mortis. The door was opening all right. I waited, my mouth hanging open. Then it shut. The door, that is.

"I don't see anyone," I said in a strangled whisper. "Whoever closed it must still be in the cabin... wait... I see... I see, I see something moving... uh... it's a person. I think. I can barely see them... him... I can see suspenders, clear as a bell... now trousers—grey I think, and black, thick hair. It's a woman! She's looking towards the lake. Towards me?"

She grew clearer and clearer, almost like a Polaroid picture developing. I felt as if I was talking through a throat that someone's hands were squeezing shut.

"She's turning... going back into the cabin. Wait. Now she's back with a pair of binoculars. It must be Frances Rain. It has to be. Omigod! What am I seeing? I'm seeing a ghost. I don't believe it!" I ran out of breath.

The woman looked through the binoculars at the lake, and I saw her lips move. Then she shook her head and lowered the glasses. She seemed pretty tall. She had wide shoulders, but was slim in the legs and hips. Her skin was darkly tanned and her clothes were rough looking, the shirt rolled up at the sleeves, the high laced hunting boots scuffed right up to the knees.

Gulping, I continued, my voice rasping out the words. "She's turning . . . she's looking this way . . ." Silence for at least a minute while I debated what I was going to do if she came my way, then, "Now she's walking . . . looking . . . coming . . . TOWARDS ME!"

All you can hear on the tape after that is a couple of seconds of a rustling sound followed by a few loud clunks when the recorder hit against some rocks. Brave reporter. Miss nothing. That's me. I'd thrown myself on the ground behind some bushes.

From down amongst the twigs and dirt, I saw her legs and booted feet silently pass close by me along the path. One of her laces had a couple of knots in it, I noticed, and one trouser leg was patched at the knee with a lighter fabric.

Stranger yet was that, at the same time, I could actually see the dim outline of the background trees. My trees or hers, I wondered? It gave me a jolt. I could see her so clearly, yet see through her at the same time.

I lay there until I caught my breath, finally crawling to my

knees and peering over a low bush. I saw a boat, with two pad-
dlers and two seated passengers, out on the lake. It was a
freighter canoe. The crackled grey hull cut deeply through the
smooth spring waters, moving rapidly towards the woman waiting on shore.

*   *   *

I pushed my hair out of my eyes and walked around to the path,
keeping a sharp eye on the woman just in case she spotted me.
I followed the path until I was about ten feet from the shore. Just
to be on the safe side, I hid behind the trunk of a wide jack pine.
Would she be able to hear my voice, I wondered, turning the tape
recorder on again.

"Ahem!" I said loudly. "Ahem, ahem."

No response. So I described the people in the canoe.

"The two men paddling have dark skin and braided hair and
are wearing identical blue and white plaid shirts," I whispered
loudly.

As they moved closer, I realized they were, in fact, twins. They
sat unsmiling at either end of the canoe. The man at the back
slid his paddle tight against the side of the canoe while the other
one rested his across the gunwale. The steerer brought the canoe
neatly up to the dock. It slid to a stop, seeming to pass through
my own little Beetle at the same time.

Now I was able to see the two passengers on the floor of the
canoe—a man and a girl. He was big and wide, dressed in a
black coat and wide-brimmed hat. He tried to stand up, making the canoe wobble. The guide at the rear pointed at the floor
and said something. The girl clutched at each gunwale and
closed her eyes.

The man sat down again, but I knew from the angry movements of his jaw and his jabbing finger that he was not happy with the orders. The guide looked straight ahead, ignoring the lethal finger. I had the feeling that he'd heard it all before.

The girl kept her eyes closed until the canoe stopped rocking. She opened them again when Frances stepped onto the dock. The girl gazed up at her shyly, eyes squinting against the sun. The man in black looked up, too, and I saw his face clearly for the first time. It had a flabby chin that hung from ear to ear. His close-set eyes looked like two pushed-in eyes on a flat potato. His nose was a small smudged thing, but his mouth was like a frog's—a wide moist slit.

I shuddered when I saw it. The look he gave Frances should have knocked her over, but it didn't. She even offered him a hand up.

He ignored her hand and sat where he was, staring at her. She shrugged and walked by, stopping to speak to the guides. The paddler in front hopped out and held the canoe steady.

The Toad Man stepped heavily onto the dock. He was big all right, even taller than he looked sitting down, and really wide, with rounded shoulders under the dark overcoat and the huge fur collar. He took off his hat. The scalp underneath was flat and freckled and edged with a thin fringe of white hair.

I dived behind a tree as his nasty gaze swept the island. When I worked up my nerve to look again, the girl was out of the canoe. She was very thin and wore a long maroon coat and matching bonnet, trimmed with silver buttons. The skinny ankles underneath ended in a pair of thick-soled shoes.

Frances led the way onto shore. Only the two guides stayed back, the steerer sitting in the canoe, his brother crouching on the dock, his arms resting on his knees.

The girl looked around the island with interest. She was about thirteen or fourteen, her face pale and narrow with a big pointed nose reddened with cold. Not pretty. I almost felt sorry for her, but there was something in that face that made me think underneath the pale skin and shyness there was a pretty determined person. I think it was the steady gaze of those dark blue eyes. I liked the look of her.

I was busy describing everything, when she did something that shocked me right down to my sneakered soles. She put her hand in her coat pocket, brought out a pair of gold-rimmed spectacles and put them on. My spectacles!

I was so stunned that it took me a second or two to realize that she was watching Frances and the big man arguing, their arms flying in all directions. Standing there, threatening each other with fierce faces, they suddenly looked a lot alike.

The man kept pushing three fingers in front of Frances's face and she kept leaning back, pushing them angrily away, shaking her head. I watched his mouth form the words, "Three months and no more." Was this how long the girl was going to stay? Was he staying, too? What was going on?

The girl looked for support from the two solemn-faced Indians, but they'd suddenly found their moccasined feet fascinating. When she pushed herself between the two angry people, they both edged her aside.

As suddenly as it began, the argument stopped. Just like that. Frances nodded at the old man and he turned away. The guides looked at each other and shrugged. The girl slumped down on a rock by the shore, staring dismally over the water, her back to the others.

The big man, his face as black as thunder, plodded heavily up to the girl. To my surprise, the hard flat face softened for just one second when he looked down at her bent head, the frog's mouth working as if he were about to speak. When her chin tilted up, the hard look washed back over his ugly face. He spoke with short sharp gestures, holding up his three fingers again, then stomped back to the dock and got into the canoe.

The girl took two or three steps in his direction, one hand outstretched. He took no notice of her. Finally, she dropped her shoulders and waited silently for him to leave.

The twins removed two small boxes and a suitcase tied with a big leather strap from the canoe and placed them carefully on the dock, nodding shyly to Frances. The one on the dock stepped down into the canoe. We watched it move slowly and steadily away. The Toad Man didn't look back once.

Abruptly, Frances turned and with long strides began to walk back up the path to the cabin. She was almost level with me when she hesitated and said something over her shoulder to the girl, who was still standing by the shore, shifting from one large foot to the other. Frances spoke again and the girl turned and picked up her luggage.

I continued to mumble into the recorder, wanting to describe everything I saw, but I felt uneasy with Frances so close. I had this weird sensation of watching a huge, dim television set. Maybe these people weren't even ghosts. Maybe I was peering through a warp in time, looking through a clouded window into the past.

"The sun is glinting off Frances's hair. I can see strands of silver in it. She's that close! She's slim, but she looks as strong as a man. The girl's coming closer. They both look nervous. It's like they've just met. The girl looks anorexic. I wonder if she's been sick. Maybe that's why she's here. A rest cure or something. Funny, the girl's hard to make out; she keeps fading. Frances is as clear as a bell."

Frances's hand lifted, hesitated and touched the girl's shoulder lightly. It was then that I saw the signet ring.

"Hey! That ring. It *was* you I bumped into!" I called out in a loud voice.

She'd heard me.

I could feel a tingle rush down my arms and legs and through my body. She twisted her head sharply to look in my direction. I stood like an idiot gaping at her. Did she see me, too? She blinked rapidly, tilting her head to one side. A brown hand came up to shade her eyes—eyes of piercing blue that seemed to hold me to the spot. Too terrified to move, I looked at the girl, but she was gazing around searching for whatever had caught Frances's attention.

I stepped back, looking down to make sure that I didn't trip over anything. It wouldn't have mattered because my feet weren't there. Or my arms—or my legs. I wasn't anywhere to be seen.

Frantically I searched for myself. I felt around but couldn't see my hands feeling my body, although I felt a faint pricking of pins and needles at each spot I touched. Horrified, I looked up and saw the same amazement in Frances's eyes. I felt for the glasses and in one hard pull they were off. As I lay in a heap, waiting for the roller coaster to grind to a halt, one thing kept pounding in my head. She saw me. Frances Rain saw me.

Gloria

by

TIM WYNNE-JONES

The author's usual quirky humour, economy of language and cele-bration of being young are evident in this story set in the southern Ontario countryside.

It was one of those March Sundays when you had to have somewhere distant to get to. A destination. Rugs, Greg, Mac-Duffy, Marsha and I—we decided on the old barn at the back end of the property. There were enough boots for everybody—Marsha borrowed my sister's—and we set out.

Mom called us back. You'll need jackets, she said. It will be much cooler in the woods.

But she was wrong, and we wore the jackets around our waists, liking the goose bumps on our bare arms, pushing each other over into the granular snow.

We heard a red-tailed hawk overhead squealing asthmatically at something. MacDuffy said it was us. We were invading the hawk's territory. So we pushed him into a really big drift. Mac-Duffy, not the hawk.

We followed the hardened cross-country ski tracks, but our feet broke through again and again, winter giving way under us with every step. In the meadow the sun was high and MacDuffy took off his shirt. On any other day this could have ruined things; I mean, with Marsha there. Did he do it to impress her? Should I take off my shirt, too? If I did, would Marsha notice how pale my skin was next to his? On any other day. But it was one of those Sundays when nothing stupid mattered.

We reached the cedar woods that skirted the edge of the big swamp.

"Bet you a Ski-Doo's gone through," I said.

And Marsha said, "Didn't know you were a poet."

Nobody would take my bet. That's because we all knew there would be one. And, sure enough, there was a gaping hole in the ice halfway out, the snowmobile still sitting in it, prow high, water lapping up over the seat. It looked like some woebegone creature—a black pygmy hippo with yellow racing stripes. We stood watching it for a while, waiting for a dead body to float to the surface beside the machine. Nothing. You'd have to try pretty hard to drown in our swamp.

Last summer we came down here and MacDuffy led us, thigh-deep, through the muddy waters looking for snapping turtles. We filed behind him. We weren't afraid; he was an Indian. We didn't know that for sure—nobody had actually asked him—but he had black hair and dark skin and he knew stuff we didn't about things like the territories of red-tailed hawks. If he said he could catch us a snapper, then he could. He never bragged.

Suddenly he stopped and held up his hand. We didn't see anything but we held our silence (and our crotches).

What was it? Had he heard something? Had Snapper talked to him? No—bubbles. He followed them. Then with both hands he reached down, lightning quick so that the murky waters slopped against his chest, and came up with the biggest turtle I had ever seen. Its horny shell was as big as a serving platter. It reared its dinosaur head trying to take a piece out of MacDuffy's arm, while its legs tried to swim in the air out of his grasp.

We waded ashore and watched it chomp sticks in half with its powerful jaws and beak. Then we let it go.

That turtle was somewhere out there now, sleeping under the mud, dreaming egg-shaped dreams.

As for the Ski-Doo—someone would come for it in a four-by-four with ropes and a come-along and a case of beer and probably a dog or two to bark a lot and get in the way. It was a tradition in these parts.

Marsha wanted to walk out to the Ski-Doo. The ice looked OK, and it probably was. But the snow around the edge wasn't. She went up to her knees in it. Freezing-cold muddy water poured into her boots. She grabbed on to me and I pulled her out. Rugs got her boots. They came out with a sucking noise—*thuck!* He emptied out the water. By mistake he emptied out one of her socks, too. No one could find it.

"That's OK," said Greg. "I've got another one." He pulled a sock out of his pocket. He had an extra sock in his pocket. He didn't know why. We all laughed ourselves crazy. Then Marsha leaned against me while Greg wiped off her foot and put on the almost clean white sock.

"If this fits, you get to marry the prince," he said.

I stared hard at the Ski-Doo with Marsha leaning against me for support, trying not to lose my balance and sink like her missing sock into the gumbo. Did she look at me when Greg said that?

We reached the barn at last and found an old ladder in the long grass. We tried climbing it without leaning it against anything. MacDuffy said he was afraid of heights, but he smiled when he said it, so I couldn't tell if he was fooling. I got up two rungs; so did Marsha. Greg got up three. Rugs got to the fifth rung, but it broke and he fell fantastically with a loud splat into the melting snow. He laughed so hard that he couldn't get up. We all laughed and threw ourselves on our backs in the muck.

Then Greg thought of using the ladder as a stretcher. He and I jumped to our feet and piled Rugs on board. MacDuffy held Rugs down with a hand on his stomach and Marsha said she was the nurse and kept applying handfuls of snow to his forehead whenever he tried to sit up. We tore off around the barn with Rugs hanging on for dear life.

That's when we came upon the fox.

It was dead by the barn door, its snout full of porcupine quills.

"Probably rabid," said MacDuffy. "A fox isn't dumb enough to attack a porkster unless it's gone loco."

We let Rugs get up. We lay the ladder on the ground. How dazzling the fox was under the hot sun.

"Don't touch it," said MacDuffy. We knew that. Especially not its spit. There was spit all over its face. MacDuffy said we would have to phone the Ministry of Natural Resources. They would send someone up from the city and he would cut the fox's head off and take it back to town for testing.

"Why just the head?"

"That's where the disease is."

"Couldn't we just bury it?"

"No. Leave it."

Then Greg said, "I don't think so." And we looked up where he was pointing into the tall blue sky. There was a turkey vulture sailing on a thermal in a circle high above the barn. The first one of the season.

Using sticks, we loaded the fox onto the ladder/stretcher and carried it into the barn. Marsha cleared a flat spot and laid down a floor of old planks. The rest of us went looking for rocks. Careful not to touch the dead animal, we built a cairn of large stones over it. We filled in the cracks with smaller stones. Nothing could get at it now.

The barn sat on a knoll just up from an abandoned train bed. Rather than go back through the woods the way we had come, we walked along the train bed out to the concession road.

We were quieter now. Wetter—that was part of it. But also there was the dead fox on our minds like a hot ember burning behind our eyes. In the quiet I could hear Marsha's boots squelching with every step. There were red strands in her brown hair and gold ones. I'd never noticed that before. Shimmering.

I thought of as many words as I could to describe the way it looked:

Glittering.

Glimmering.

Gleaming.

Flickering.

Glinting.

I was so busy thinking about her hair that I didn't notice what the others did. Animal tracks. MacDuffy saw them first.

The animal tracks crossed the dirt concession road that led back to our place, walked along the shoulder a ways and then headed down into the woods on the east side of the road. They were bigger than any deer prints we had ever seen. An elk? A moose? We looked to MacDuffy for the answer.

Probably a moose.

This was thrilling. We squatted around a perfect footprint. A moose for sure. And if moose, then timber wolves next. And then the whole northern wilderness moving slowly southward.

"Makes sense," said Rugs. "All the factories in town are moving south to the States, Mexico."

His dad had lost his job the month before.

I imagined a flock of factories migrating overhead to warmer climes. And then I imagined lynxes and caribou and snowy owls coming to take their place.

Marsha picked up a fist-sized rock from the side of the road.

"We'll all become hunters and gatherers," she said.

"You'd better get quieter boots," I said.

It was the last leg of our trip and already growing colder as the sun sank below the trees. With the sun behind it we saw the ragged old truck sailing slowly our way as if not powered by an engine at all. It was the Considines. I didn't know them, but I knew their truck. It was probably the oldest active vehicle in the whole of the county. Considine couldn't get parts for it any more, so when something was broken, he made it from scratch. My father said he had pretty well rebuilt that truck part by part.

We watched the truck approaching as silently as a ghost, a silhouette against the setting sun. They lost a kid, the Considines. We all knew that. But none of us knew exactly what that meant. Did it die at birth? Had it gone through the ice? Did it die at all, or did it just move to the city and forget to write? Or had they left it outside the grocery store in its baby carriage, and it had ended up in Neverland like Peter Pan?

The truck rolled closer and we realized that Considine had turned the engine off, letting the long slow hill carry them on down at its own speed. We waited at the bottom.

Mrs. Considine rolled down the window. I had never talked to them before. They weren't our kind of people.

There was a dog on the front seat with them. It had its head in a large bag of potato chips.

"You seen a cow?"

They had lost their cow. First their kid and now their cow.

A cow. Rugs was the first to get it. He hooted and slapped his leg. Then, at about the same moment, the rest of us got it.

We pushed MacDuffy up to the window. He looked sheepish. We kept shoving him in the back until he told the Considines about the moose tracks on the road.

The dog smelled MacDuffy's hand, licked it. Maybe he smelled fox. MacDuffy patted it. We all did. There was potato chip dust all over the dog's muzzle. Mrs. Considine offered us some chips. Greg reached out to take some. Rugs grabbed his arm away.

"It's full of dog cooties."

Greg turned away as though he were going to be sick.

"No, thanks," said Marsha. Politely, for all of us. The rest of us were trying not to laugh. Greg was making barfing noises.

Mr. Considine started his engine. They thanked us for the information.

"With any luck those tracks'll lead us to Gloria," said Mrs. Considine.

The cow's name was Gloria.

We wandered the last bit of the way up the long slow hill, quietly swinging sticks, kicking at stones, looking for Gloria's tracks.

"I wish we could find that cow," said Marsha. She was walking beside me. "We could sell it for magic beans."

"Maybe the Considines would rather have a cow," I said. I

knew I would rather have magic beans, but I wasn't sure about the Considines.

"Maybe they could plant a magic bean," said Marsha after she'd thought about it for a minute, "and climb the beanstalk and find their kid."

Sunday ended. That happens, though it wasn't easy to let it. But then some days taste so good they are like promises. I was supposed to study for a science test. I fell asleep after dinner with my textbook on my face.

I dreamed I was climbing a giant beanstalk. Marsha was just ahead of me.

The next thing I knew there was a dull morning light and my sister was bringing me a cup of tea. We take turns; it was her week. She was smiling from ear to ear. She pointed to the window. It was snowing. I was about to curse when I realized it was *really* snowing! Sitting up, I could see that the snow was up past the bumper of the car and blowing around crazily. There would be no bus, no school. It was winter's last gift.

Then, beyond the car in the woods, standing motionless in the trees as white and black as a snowy day, I saw the Considines' cow. Gloria. My sister raced for the phone. She came back a minute later. The Considines were on their way.

Then she sat wordlessly at the foot of my bed and we drank our mugs of tea. It was sweet—she always made it too sweet— but better than any other cup of tea I'd ever tasted. Every sweet hot mouthful was like a taste of heaven.

from

To Dance at
the Palais Royale

by

JANET MCNAUGHTON

*On her seventeenth birthday in 1928, Aggie leaves Scotland to take
a job as a domestic in Toronto, where her sister Emma already works.
Her employers' son, Rodney, and his friend Rose persuade Aggie to
go secretly with them to dance at the Palais Royale on Lake Ontario.
Aggie's escort, Rose's brother Bobby—who doesn't know she is a servant—asks her to go to Centre Island with him the next day.*

Sunday afternoon was bright and sunny. Aggie had no trouble
pretending she was going to the domestics' church service.
She didn't even have to worry about Emma, because Emma had
a boyfriend now and almost always spent Sunday afternoons with
him. Aggie was glad of that for another reason: she couldn't imagine what Emma would say if she knew Aggie was going to dances
and teas with her employers' son.

After lunch, Aggie slipped upstairs. The blue kid evening shoes
Rose had picked for her yesterday would not do for afternoon.
She quietly crept to Mrs. Stockwood's closet and traded them,
being careful to take an older-looking pair this time. Just yesterday, "borrowing" shoes from Mrs. Stockwood's closet was unthink-
able. She slipped the shoes to Rodney. He would hide them in
the car so Aggie would be able to change out of her old shoes on

the way to the ferry docks. Aggie dressed quickly. In the navy silk dress Mrs. MacDougall had given her, she could almost believe she *was* an heiress from Scotland. Rodney waited in the car by the little park around the corner, just as he had the night before.

Aggie had visited Toronto Island with Emma, who liked Hanlan's Point with its amusement park and bandstand. Centre Island had summer hotels and picnic grounds. It was more sedate—not to Emma's liking, so Aggie had only been there once.

"We'll go to Centre Island," Bobby said as they met at the foot of York Street. "Hanlan's is so crass." The island shimmered out on the lake as they boarded the *Trillium*.

Aggie liked the tubby ferries with their black wooden hulls and flower names: the *Primrose*, the *Bluebell*, the *Mayflower* and the *Trillium*. Out on the water, the sturdy *John Hanlan* came towards them, heading from the island to the city. The *Hanlan* was a smaller boat, sharp-prowed and graceless. Black smoke poured from her funnel. She made the bigger ferries seem like fat, contented swans.

"Oh, the *Hanlan*," Rodney said. "They're taking it out of service soon."

Bobby looked at him with curiosity.

"How on earth do you know that?"

"I read it in the paper."

"Rodney remembers everything," Rose said.

"What will happen to that boat?" Aggie asked. She couldn't say so now, of course, but the *Hanlan* was the first ferry she'd taken to the island. She was fond of the homely old boat.

No one had any idea. As the *Hanlan* passed, Aggie thought: everyone in Canada is in such a hurry to leave the past behind. No one wants the old things. And she silently wished the *Hanlan* goodbye.

When Aggie and Emma came to the island, they always brought their own lunch, usually a bunch of bananas purchased at a city fruit stand for a nickel, eaten on a park bench. Now, as the *Trillium* slipped back towards the city, Bobby led the way to Manitou Road on the far side of the island.

"I think we'll go to Gin's Casino," he said.

Aggie stopped dead in confusion. Gin's Casino sounded like a speakeasy, a place where people would gamble and drink hard liquor.

"I dinna think..." she began, her voice trailing off.

Rose looked at her with concern for an instant and then laughed.

"Oh, Agnes, Gin's is just a restaurant with a dance floor. They don't have a liquor licence or anything."

"They do have the best ice cream on the island, though," Bobby said. As Rose and Rodney went ahead he added, "I'm sorry, Agnes. I wouldn't have alarmed you for anything in the world."

Manitou Road, the main street of Centre Island, was so busy it seemed like the heart of a small town. The restaurant overlooked the dance floor—empty of course. There was no dancing on Sundays.

Rose wore a pale blue linen suit, her rope of pearls, blue lace gloves, and a broad-brimmed straw hat that almost covered her face completely. Aggie had no summer gloves. The hat she wore to church was so shabby she'd left it in the car with her old shoes. Looking at Rose, she realized that her one good dress, even the borrowed shoes and stockings were not enough. Pretending to be something I'm not is hard, she realized, almost impossible. How could I keep up with Rose? I'm glad, Aggie thought, that this will be the last day of pretending—well, almost glad. It was hard to feel happy about the black uniform and mountains of laundry that were waiting for her tomorrow.

After tea, they walked back to view the city skyline. Bobby took Aggie's elbow as they walked across the grass, just as Davy used to in Scotland. The harbour shimmered blue and cool between the island and the hot city. Bobby pointed to the tallest building on the skyline, still no more than a tower of raw steel girders, half clad in stone.

"That new skyscraper is going to be the Royal York Hotel," Bobby said. He sounded as if he owned it himself. Aggie remembered how the skeleton of the Royal York had greeted her when she stepped out of Union Station with Emma.

"You seem very proud of it," she said.

Bobby nodded.

"I'm proud of the whole country. Every bit of it. The Great War is behind us. We have nothing but peace and prosperity to look forward to. With hard work and ambition, any man can make his fortune in Canada." He smiled at her. "Will you pass through Toronto again on your way home?"

Rodney, who was standing nearby, overheard and spoke up quickly.

"I'm afraid Agnes will take the train straight through to Montreal on the return trip. Won't you, Agnes?"

Aggie realized that Rodney had decided the game had gone far enough.

"Oh, aye, we've some friends in Montreal who'd like to see us before we sail," she improvised.

"But surely you could stop over in Toronto just for a day or two," Bobby said. His distress was obvious.

"The tickets are purchased," Rodney said, "and we must avoid hurting anyone's feelings." He looked pointedly at Aggie.

"That's true," Aggie agreed. "If I were to change my plans now, feelings would certainly be hurt."

Bobby didn't try to hide his disappointment. Aggie realized that Rose was not simply imagining things. Bobby did care for her, or at least for the wealthy young visitor from Scotland that she seemed to be. As they went towards the ferry dock to go home, Bobby slipped a small card to Aggie.

"My address," he said. "Perhaps you'll write to me."

Aggie stared at the card, not knowing what to say. She was as fond of Bobby Chandler as she'd ever been of any young man. But how could she agree to write from a place she wouldn't be? She looked up at Bobby. He blushed.

"Yes, well," he said, "I understand how busy your life must be." He turned away quickly. Aggie realized that Rodney might be too late in his bid to prevent hurt feelings.

Later, as they were stepping off the ferry in the city, Aggie caught the heel of Mrs. Stockwood's shoe in a space between the boat and the ramp. She pitched forward, almost falling, and the heel broke off.

"Oh no," cried Aggie, horrified. She could lose her job for this. Bobby looked puzzled.

"It's only a shoe," he said, then added, "Oh, I see, you're worried about leaving tomorrow. Well, there's a shoemaker in Union Station. I'm sure he'd be able to take care of it for you before you board your train."

Rodney picked up the heel and pocketed it.

"Don't worry Agnes, I'll see that it's fixed before it's needed again." And he helped Aggie limp to the car.

Aggie looked back over her shoulder at Bobby and Rose. In her panic, she hadn't said a proper goodbye. Bobby met her eyes briefly with his direct, open gaze. Then he looked away without attempting a polite smile. He took Rose by the arm and they turned towards their car. Just before they did, Rose winked at Aggie, but suddenly none of it seemed like a joke any more. The afternoon sun was oppressively hot. The shoe that had not broken had given Aggie a blister and worn a hole in one of the lovely silk stockings.

The shoes were still missing on Monday afternoon when Mrs. Stockwood burst in through the front door.

"Home again. Oh, isn't it lovely to be back?" she cried. Aggie came into the hall, willing herself to think of anything but shoes. Rodney followed his mother with the suitcases. His father had taken a taxi directly to his office.

"Really, Mother, anyone would think you'd been gone for weeks," Rodney joked.

"Well, it felt like weeks. Please take the bags upstairs, Rodney. I'm so hot and tired. What I need is a nice bath. Agnes, please unpack for me."

Aggie followed Rodney and his mother up the lovely staircase. She was wearing her drab black uniform again. To Aggie as well it seemed impossible that only three days had passed since the Stockwoods left. The shimmering evening dress was packed in Rose's canvas bag again, waiting for the moment when Aggie could slip it back to her. The enchanted weekend was over. Once again, Aggie was working hard to make other people's lives easier.

As Aggie unpacked Mrs. Stockwood's clothes, she tried to avoid looking at the closet floor, where dozens of shoes were lined up neatly. She felt a bit like a murderer at the scene of the crime. Rodney had taken the shoe to be repaired early that morning, as soon as he could. He was certain he would be able to slip the pair into the closet before his mother noticed. Aggie was not so sure. Every time she thought about it, her heart pounded. This will be my punishment, she thought, for leading Bobby Chandler on.

Downstairs, the front doorbell rang. Before she could leave the bedroom, she heard Rodney say, "I'll get it." When Aggie reached the top of the stairs, she saw Rodney holding a large paper cone that looked like flowers. He quickly reached inside, found a small card, glanced at it and tucked it into his pocket.

"Was someone at the door?" Mrs. Stockwood came out of the bathroom in her pink silk robe and padded over beside Aggie.

"Yes, Mother. Florist," Rodney said. Aggie noticed he had turned bright pink.

"Oh, how lovely!" Mrs. Stockwood hurried down the stairs. "Who could they be from? Find the card. There must be a card."

Rodney helped his mother tear the paper away from the flowers—pink lilies and salmon-coloured gladioli. Of course there was no card.

"Isn't that odd," Mrs. Stockwood said when they'd finished searching. "Perhaps I should call the florist."

"I'm sure they're for your wedding anniversary," Rodney said quickly.

"Oh, of course, they must. But who sent them? And why isn't there a card?"

"Perhaps the card was lost in transit. Linda must have had them sent, don't you think?"

Aggie knew Mrs. Stockwood could not imagine Rodney would ever mislead her.

"Yes," she said, "you must be right. Now look at me, in my dressing gown in the middle of the day. I'd better get dressed." And she padded back upstairs. "Just put those on the dining-room table, would you, Rodney?"

"I've finished unpacking, Mrs. Stockwood," Aggie said when Mrs. Stockwood reached the top of the stairs.

"Oh fine, dear. That will be all for now."

As soon as his mother was out of sight, Rodney jerked his head towards the dining room, then disappeared with the flowers. Aggie followed.

"These," he whispered, pointing towards the flowers now on the dining-room table, "are actually for you." He extracted a small card from his pocket. "Miss Agnes Maxwell" was inscribed on the envelope. Aggie opened it.

"'Bon voyage,'" she read, "'from your new Canadian friend, Bobby.' Oh dear."

"Oh dear, indeed. We let this go too far. If Mother or Mrs. B. had opened that door, we'd both be in hot water and you might be out of a job."

Aggie looked at the flowers. No one had ever sent her flowers, and these were the most beautiful ones she'd ever seen.

"I feel terrible," she said. "It was so thoughtful of Bobby."

"You ought to be thinking of yourself, Agnes, not Bobby. We still have to get those shoes back into Mother's closet. Bobby will survive. We had no way of knowing this would happen. We were just going to a dance. The main thing is to make sure he never finds out. I'm sure Mother won't suspect a thing if you just act normal."

Aggie tried to follow Rodney's advice, but she kept the card in her uniform pocket and went into the dining room whenever she could. Flowers for me, she chanted silently to herself as she worked, flowers for me.

Rodney told Rose, who had to see the flowers. Rodney and Aggie managed a moment when Mrs. Stockwood, still tired from the trip, was napping, and Mrs. Bradley was busy with the gardener outside.

"Oh, it's so romantic!" Rose said, touching the petals of a lily. "I didn't know Bobby had a romantic bone in his body. Roddy, why don't we tell him?"

"What!" Rodney was so loud that Aggie was afraid his mother might hear.

"No, really. He's obviously in love with Agnes. He'd come in here and sweep her off her feet. They'd get married and live happily ever after."

Rodney looked more serious than Aggie had ever seen him. He ran a hand through his thinning blond hair.

"Rose," he said, "this is not a romance novel. This is Toronto. This is 1928. Bobby thought Agnes was a young woman of good family, of money. Young lawyers do not marry domestic servants. I'm sorry, it just isn't done."

Rose looked disappointed, but she didn't argue. And although Aggie felt her cheeks burn, she knew Rodney was right.

In her room that night, Aggie held the two cards in her hands, the one Bobby had given her on the island, and the one that came with the flowers. The flowers themselves would be gone soon. Rodney was right, of course. Bobby Chandler would not fall in love with a domestic. But what if he had already fallen in love and then found out ... She shook her head. I'll soon be as daft as Rose, she thought.

The next morning, Rodney was off early for tennis, before the courts became unbearably hot. It was almost lunchtime when Mrs. Stockwood called Aggie to her bedroom.

"Agnes," she said, "when you were unpacking did you see my navy shoes? The ones with the two thin straps and the little gold buckles?"

Aggie's heart began to pound. "Not while I was unpacking, Mrs. Stockwood," she said, truthfully. "Did you take them to Quebec?"

"No, I don't believe I did. They ought to be here somewhere. Perhaps you could help me look."

Aggie did, feeling more guilty by the moment. She hadn't seen Rodney before he left that morning to remind him to pick up the missing shoe. What if he forgot?

Aggie was beginning to wonder if it wouldn't be better to confess when Rodney passed the bedroom door a few minutes later, still dressed in his tennis whites.

"Anything wrong?" he asked.

Mrs. Stockwood told him. Aggie held her breath.

"Oh," Rodney said, "I believe I saw shoes like that in the hall closet this morning when I took my racquet out. Could they be there?"

"Well, I suppose. Agnes, please check for me. I'd like to wear those shoes this afternoon."

Aggie found the shoes just where Rodney had left them. It was impossible to tell the heel had been repaired. A wave of relief swept over her. I dinna deserve to get off like this, she thought. But she had.

The blast furnace heat of July gave way to the cooler clarity of August. Summer was almost over, and Aggie began to realize how much she would miss Rodney when he returned to Queen's. Rose's visits would stop then too. And what would she do without Rose? Now, as Aggie went about her work, she listened for the sound of their laughter, not with envy as she had at the beginning of the summer, but with a sense of longing and loss. She tried never to think about Bobby. But sometimes, in her dreams, she found herself walking by Lake Ontario, looking out over the moonlit water, or back at the shimmering city. The attentive young man at her side was always Bobby. She never saw his face, and they never spoke. He was simply a solid presence at her side, someone to depend on. These dreams stayed with her, creating a kind of fog that comforted her and kept her from thinking too much about what might have happened—and what would not.

She caught herself staring off into space when she should have been working, and more than once she came into a room, knowing there was a reason for being there, but unable to remember it. Mrs. Bradley was right about knowing your place, Aggie told herself. Perhaps it would be better to spend more time with Emma. But Aggie didn't want to deal with Emma, or the new boyfriend Aggie had never met. With Emma, she could only be Aggie Maxwell, a domestic servant. Aggie would rather cling to the magic of that weekend when she had been someone else.

Before Rodney returned to Queen's, the house erupted in a small frenzy of activity. Just the perfect argyle socks must be found to match Rodney's new navy blazer, and dozens of white linen handkerchiefs monographed with "RS" were necessary, apparently, for success at university. Then of course there were the truly important matters: winter coats (two) with matching gloves, hats and scarves. And boots so strong and finely made that toes could pass the winter in them without ever feeling cold. Rodney stood at the centre of all the fuss like the calm eye of a storm, tolerating it for the sake of his mother and Mrs. Bradley. It was not unlike the bustle before his arrival in the spring, but now Aggie understood why. How could anyone not like Rodney? When she compared her faded image of the stuffy, spoiled young man she had expected with the Rodney she had come to know, she was amazed that anyone could be so wrong. And she knew she would miss him.

Rose participated in the selection of winter clothes, but Aggie could see her heart wasn't in it. One afternoon, when Rodney had been called away to express his opinion on neckties, Rose lay across an easy chair in the sitting room with a shoe dangling from one foot, while she flipped listlessly through a winter catalogue. Aggie was supposed to be ironing. Instead, she stayed. She hadn't had a chance to talk to Rose alone since the flowers came.

"I dread this fall," Rose said to Aggie. Then she brightened a bit. "Bobby promised to take me out more often, though, now that I'm almost eighteen. I hope he means it."

"How is Bobby?" Aggie asked, trying to keep her voice even. Rose sat up.

"He still looks at the mail, first thing every night when he comes home. He still looks disappointed, every single night. And sometimes he asks, ever so casually, if Rodney ever hears from that charming cousin of his in Scotland."

Aggie knew she was blushing. She didn't care.

"What do you say?"

"I tell him that Agnes is known to be terrible about letters, that Rodney says she almost never writes anyone. Oh, Agnes, I really wish you could see him. If you were together again, I'm sure it would work out. He's really got it bad."

Rodney entered at that moment.

"Someone sick?" he asked.

"Housekeeper's son has the chicken pox," Rose said smoothly. She held up the catalogue. "How do you feel about these cufflinks, Roddy?"

Aggie remembered the ironing.

Later that afternoon, Aggie sat in the kitchen with a cup of tea while Mrs. Bradley worked on the grocery order.

"Olives, picked onions . . . lots of extras this week," she said. "The missus has her heart set on giving Rodney a big send-off Saturday night. I'll teach you how to make those pinwheel sandwiches if you like. We'll be up to our ears in fancy tidbits for the next few days."

Aggie smiled.

"I'd like that."

Mrs. Bradley sighed.

"This place sure will be quiet with Rodney gone again. Seems the summer went by so quickly. Oh well, he'll be home at Christmas. Perhaps that won't seem too long."

The party made so much work that it was easy for Aggie to forget everything else for a few days. When she wasn't helping Mrs. Bradley, she was busy with cleaning that hadn't been done since spring. By Saturday, everything was perfect—except the weather. It was hot again, as hot as July. Mrs. Stockwood decided to have the party outside. In the afternoon, Aggie helped Rodney and Rose take down the badminton net and string Japanese lanterns across the garden. They seemed almost impossible to untangle, but at last the garden was crisscrossed with delicate paper globes.

Rose ran her arm over her forehead as she climbed down from the ladder.

"Whew, it's hot. Is that the last of them, Roddy?"

"I'm not sure," Rodney said, "I'll check the loft in the garage."

As soon as he disappeared, Rose whispered to Aggie, "I've got a surprise tonight. Wait and see."

She must have a going-away present for Rodney, Aggie thought. Then Rodney emerged from the garage with another tangled mass of lanterns.

"Oh no," Rose groaned, and they set to work again.

By evening, sheet lightning flashed behind low clouds.

"I do hope it doesn't rain," Mrs. Stockwood said.

"Now dear," Rodney's father said, "you know sheet lightning

doesn't always mean rain. Let's get those lanterns lit. If it starts to rain, we'll just move everything inside."

Aggie changed into a fresh uniform before the party started. Her little attic room was stifling, but through her tiny window the garden was transformed. Pink and green and blue and orange paper lanterns glowed softly, perfectly still in the hot night air. Gradually, the garden began to fill with guests.

"Real champagne!" Rose said as she slipped into the kitchen. "This is swell."

Aggie was filling a tray of flute glasses with champagne.

"This is perfect," Rose said. "It couldn't be better. Will you bring that tray into the garden when it's full?" Aggie nodded. "Terrific. See you out there."

And she was gone with a swish of her electric blue evening gown.

The sheet lightning flashed again as Aggie carefully swung the screen door open and, balancing the silver tray, stepped out into the night. The air hit her like something damp and solid. So many people were in the garden now she couldn't tell who was there. The Japanese lanterns cast a gentle glow over everything. Rodney approached, looking surprisingly serious. "Agnes," he said, "could I have a word with you?"

"As soon as I finish with this tray…" Aggie started to say, but Rodney's friends came for him before she could finish. He glanced back anxiously as he was spirited away. Aggie could barely see Rose in one of the few chairs, facing some young men who stood with their backs to the house. Rose, Aggie knew, would want champagne, and tonight she would have a glass. Aggie made her way through the crowd, stopping whenever she was close enough to anyone to offer them a drink. Finally, she reached Rose.

"Champagne, miss?" she said, bending down.

"Yes, thank you," Rose replied. She winked at Aggie.

Aggie straightened and turned to face the young men who were talking to Rose. Directly in front of her, frozen in mid-laugh, stood Bobby Chandler. Somehow Aggie managed to keep her grip on the tray, but everything around them faded into the distance.

There was no doubt in Aggie's mind that Bobby knew exactly who she was. The laughter on his face shaded to surprise, then just before the anger, there was a flash of hurt and disbelief.

"Excuse me," he said, not to Aggie, but to the young men around him. He turned on his heel and walked away. Rose, who had seen Bobby's face from where she sat, stood up. Together, the girls watched Bobby leave the party. Neither of them moved as his tires squealed out in the quiet street.

Lightning flashed and thunder cracked almost overhead. The clouds burst and torrents of rain came down on the party. Young women shrieked, throwing flimsy summer shawls over their heads as they ran for the house. The dry earth gave off a dusty scent as the rain soaked in, like a sigh. Aggie and Rose stood, unmoving. Rain fell into the champagne flutes and bounced off the silver tray Aggie still held in her hands.

One by one, the beautiful Japanese lanterns went out with a hiss, and were ruined by the rain.

from

Angel Square

by

B R I A N   D O Y L E

It is December 1945 in Ottawa, and Tommy, who thinks of himself as The Shadow, is trying to find out who beat up his best friend Sammy's father in the streetcar barns. He has heard that a boy called Lester Lister was there that night with a girl. Tommy and his friend Gerald decide to interview Lester.

We walked over the St. Patrick Street Bridge and up Springfield Road on to Acacia Drive and into Rockcliffe Village where everybody was rich.

All the streets in Rockcliffe are called Avenue and Way and Terrace and View and Place and Drive and Vista and names like that.

In Lowertown all the streets are called Street. Cobourg Street. Friel Street. Augusta Street. York Street. If a street was really in bad shape (houses all falling over and broken sheds and fences full of holes and broken windows and raggedy kids and older brothers back from the war always drunk) it wouldn't even be called a street. Like Papineau, for instance. Not Papineau Street, just Papineau. You ask Chalmers Lonnigan, "Where do you live, Chalmers?"

"I live on Papineau."

"Is that a street or an avenue?"

"I dunno."

Gerald and I had been together in Rockcliffe before.

We specially liked to go over right after supper when it was dark. We'd have our supper about five-thirty or six but the people in Rockcliffe had their supper about half past seven or eight. Rich people eat later for some reason.

Maybe it was because they weren't very hungry.

Lester Lister told me it wasn't called supper anyway. It was called dinner.

In Lowertown we ate our dinner at noon.

In Rockcliffe they'd have their dinner at supper time and their lunch at dinner time.

Pretty confusing.

We'd gone over a couple of times when there wasn't much to do and looked in people's windows. We weren't looking in windows in Rockcliffe to see people taking their clothes off or anything like that. We'd look to see what they were having for supper (dinner) and try to guess what they were saying to each other by reading their lips.

It was hard to figure out what they were saying. Whatever it was, it didn't look very interesting. They weren't talking about germs, that's for sure, or turkeys.

Sometimes they wouldn't say anything for a long time. They'd just look at their fireplaces or their plates and not move their lips at all.

They were probably thinking about important matters concerning the world or Germans or something.

Or maybe they were all just thinking about money.

We arrived at Lester's fancy house and went up on the big veranda and rang the bell.

Gerald spit over the railing just as Mrs. Lister opened the door.

"Could I speak to Lester for a moment, please?" I said.

Mrs. Lister looked at Gerald and me like we were some kind of Martians or something.

"I'm afraid he's having dinner at the moment," she said. (It was about nine o'clock at night so of course they were having dinner.)

"It's about school," I said. "It's really very important."

"Just a moment then," she said, and left us standing out there in the cold.

Pretty soon Lester came out, slipping on a fur hat so he wouldn't get his brain exposed to the winter. As soon as he closed the door and stepped out on the veranda, Gerald crowded him up against the wall.

"Tonight you were in the car barns doing naughty things with Miss Fleurette Featherstone Fitchell and looking for your wallet which you lost the night somebody beat up Sammy Rosenberg's father. You and Miss Fitchell saw something that night that she won't tell us about but that you *will* tell us about because if you don't, we're going to spoil your dinner by telling Mummy and Daddy that you are studying hamburger buns and cigars with Miss Fitchell some nights instead of being where you're supposed to be, wherever that is."

It was so easy. For Gerald.

Yes, they were there, Lester said, in a whiny voice, they were there, but he's never going there again, honest, and that night they heard the yelling and they saw the man in the hood and they saw him hit Mr. Rosenberg and they saw him run away after Mr. Rosenberg fell down and they saw something fall out of the man's pocket and they were so scared but Fleurette picked it up and they ran out and when they reached the entrance a man stopped them and said that they'd better not say anything to anyone about this or they'd be awful sorry and then they ran home.

"What did she pick up, Lester? What was it?" I said.

"It was just a comic," said Lester. "Just a stupid comic book. It fell out of the man's pocket." Lester was fiddling with his fur hat.

"OK, Lester," Gerald said, "go in and finish your dinner." Lester went in and shut the door quietly.

We stood on the St. Patrick Street Bridge for a while watching the ice and talking and then we went home.

A comic book.

Just a comic book.

But it was something.

It was a clue.

*　　*　　*

By Friday there was so much snow that every plow was out and the teams of men and the big sleighs were out all day and all night.

Each box sleigh is pulled by a team of horses and each sleigh has one driver and ten shovellers. The horses stand in a cloud of their own steam and their whiskers are frozen white and their manes hang down with gobs of ice. The ten shovellers shovel the snowbank into the sleigh and shout and swear and laugh and sing and play jokes on each other.

And that day the bells on all the harnesses were tinkling and jingling in Lowertown on the last day of school before Christmas, the first Christmas after the war.

Angel Square was raging; everybody was trying to get a good day of fighting in before the holiday.

All over the square the Jews and the Dogans and the Pea Soups were running head first into each other like mountain goats.

At school Blue Cheeks was in a very Christmassy mood and only gave out lines to Killer Bodnoff and Fleurette Featherstone Fitchell for passing pictures of hamburger buns and cigars back and forth.

I wrote a note to Fleurette and passed it to her when Blue Cheeks wasn't looking.

> FFF.
>
> Lester said you have the comic book the man dropped in the car barns that night.
>
> I want it.
>
> If you don't give it to me I'll tell Mrs. Lister about you and Lester and you'll never see him again.
>
> Signed
Tommy

I watched her face as she read it. She was moving her lips. When she was finished she looked over at me and nodded. Her note to me said this:

> Meet me after school gets out.
>
> Signed
Fitchy

We were getting out at noon and so our last class was with Mr. Maynard. We sat around chatting and making cards. I made a card for him with a picture of a moon eclipse on it and some little noiseless bells.

I wrote this on it:

Merry Christmas, Mr. Maynard. I loved what you said about the leaf on the moon.

Tommy

Then the bell rang and everybody ran out on Angel Square and tried to get home. The school was suddenly quiet.

I slipped into Blue Cheeks's room and wrote a Christmas message on his empty blackboard. It was a sentence he could have a lot of Christmas fun correcting over the holidays.

It said this:

The boy wrote Merry Christmas to his teacher and then quietly left the room on the blackboard.

Signed
The Shadow

It was his favourite kind of sentence. A wrong one.

I met "Fitchy" in the schoolyard and walked with her to her house on Friel Street.

"I don't like Lester Lister any more, anyway," she said. "He ran away and left me. He's a coward."

I waited outside her back door while she went in to get the comic. There were a whole lot of cats under her back shed looking out at me standing there in the falling snow.

She came back out with the comic but she didn't give it to me right away.

"Do you want to come in the back shed with me?"

"I can't," I lied. "I've got to go to work."

"He was going to give me a watch for Christmas," she said.

"It's better this way," I said and I touched the hand that was holding the comic.

"I guess so," she said. "Lester Lister is a coward." She let go of the comic.

"You're not a coward, though," she said.

"Thank you," I said.

"It's OK if you call me Fitchy."

"Thank you, Fitchy."

On the way home I studied the comic book. It was a war comic with different pictures of Japs and Germans being stabbed and blown up.

Up on the corner somebody had written an initial.

The letter L.

The man who hit Sammy's father had written that letter there maybe.

L.

At home, while my sister Pamela was crushing me at the door, I could smell cake and fruit. Usually I didn't smell anything at our house. Funny how other people's houses smell like something but your own never does. Maybe it's because you're so used to your own house.

Gerald Hickey's house always smelled like onions and starch.

Sammy's house always smelled like incense and pickles and fish.

CoCo Laframboise's house smelled like beans and pie.

Lester Lister's house smelled like shellac.

Dad was home early too and he and Aunt Dottie were talking about turkeys and chickens again and this time Dad was saying he was having trouble getting *chickens* even and how Devine's and the other stores in the market were all out of them.

They were saying that it looked like we were going to have to have Mock Duck again.

Mock Duck is a big slab of meat piled up with dressing and then rolled up like a jelly roll and tied up with lots of thick string.

One Christmas my Uncle Paddy ate a piece of string from the Mock Duck about as long as his arm and Dad and I went out in the kitchen with him to help him pull it all out. It reminded me of a movie I once saw where Laurel and Hardy ate some wool socks and had to pull the long threads out of their mouths at a fancy dinner.

Aunt Dottie said Uncle Paddy ruined our whole dinner. I guess she was right. It wasn't very Christmassy watching a guy eat string for about fifteen minutes.

But I like my Uncle Paddy. He's a nice man. He's pretty cuddly. And big. Even bigger than Dad. He's in the Air Force Police. He is a very loud sneezer. Once he sneezed so loud that the cat ran head first into a wall.

Uncle Paddy has huge arms and wrists. One of his wrists is thicker than Gerald Hickey's neck. So is the other one.

Dad was putting on his coat and his scarf and was saying he had to go up to the Union Station to meet the soldiers coming in. One of his friends would be there. He was a Cameron Highlander.

His name was Frank. Back from the war.

I said I'd go with him because I had to go uptown to some stores to hunt for some Christmas presents.

We got off the streetcar and walked across Rideau Street into the Union Station. The *U* in the word *Union* was shaped like a *V*.

We went over to talk to a Red Cap in a red cap, a cousin of Dad's from up the Gatineau who stuttered. They talked and laughed for a few minutes and we talked about money then the Red Cap reached in his pouch where all his tips were and filled my hand with nickels.

"Merry Chri-Chri-Chri-Chri . . ." he said. "Come back to-to-to-tomorrow and I'll give you some more."

There were mobs of people all bundled up and stamping snow and we started down the long wide stairs to where all the thousands of soldiers were with their knapsacks and gear. Everybody was kissing and hugging and running and squealing and crying. Over the loudspeakers, Bing Crosby was singing "I'm Dreaming of a White Christmas." There was a huge Christmas tree twinkling in the middle of the floor and decorations and streamers crawled up the walls.

You had to lean way back to see the ceiling.

Steam floated in through the iron gates where the trains were.

We waited and watched for about a half an hour but there was no sign of Dad's friend Frank. Dad met one soldier he knew who said yes, Frank was on the train but he didn't know where he was now.

Dad said he'd go down to the market and look for him around there, so I said goodbye and went hunting for presents.

I went to Charles Ogilvy's, Murphy Gamble's, Bryson Graham's, Reitman's, Caplan's, Lindsay's, Orme's, Shaffer's, Stein's, Larocque's and Freiman's.

It was in Freiman's I saw it.

It was on the glass counter with a sign beside it. The sign said "For that girl of girls." Then there was a picture of Rita Hayworth.

Richard Hudnut's Three Flower Gift Set

Picture her rapture on finding this set
beneath the tree Christmas morn.
Soft green embossed gift box contains
Hudnut's lovely

FACE POWDER, ROUGE, LIPSTICK,
TOILET WATER, PERFUME, TALCUM,
VANISHING CREAM, BRILLIANTINE,
COLOGNE and CLEANSING CREAM

$7.50

I put two dollars down and asked the lady if she could hold the Richard Hudnut Three Flower Gift Set until Monday, the day before Christmas. Then I would bring in the rest of the money.

She said that I could.

She had a face like she was a sort of Virgin Mary. A little bit of a little smile, eyes looking up and to the right, head a bit on one side, and a halo sitting just over her head with nothing holding it up.

But it wasn't really a halo, it was some silver spray on a mirror right behind her.

In Freiman's I also found a duck for my sister Pamela. I always got her a little yellow duck made of rubber. You squeezed the duck and it went quack for you.

She really enjoyed the duck even though she got the same thing the year before. It was always like a new present because she didn't have very much of a memory. Every day she'd have to find out about squeezing the duck and making it do a quack. And she'd always laugh just like it never happened before. Every day she had a chance to be happy. Then the duck would be worn out by summer and Aunt Dottie would throw it away and she'd forget all about it.

Then the next Christmas, the duck, all over again, and happy, all over again.

She was lucky in a way, not knowing anything. She didn't have to know about Sammy's dad or a man named L or anything about the war or the fights on Angel Square or the Ritchie's Feed and Seed bags or Delbert Dilabio or Arnie Sultzburger.

Maybe she was lucky.

Or maybe not.

She also didn't know about Gerald or Sammy or CoCo or the lovely Margot Lane or Lamont Cranston or The Shadow or Mr. Maynard.

Maybe she wasn't lucky.

I don't know.

Then, in Freiman's, I saw Dad's present.

It was a Flat Fifty.

A Flat Fifty is a tin box (flat) with fifty cigarettes inside. You buy them for special occasions or if you have fancy tables in your house you can put one of these fancy flat tins out so that your guests can help themselves, don't mind if I do.

I buy Dad a Flat Fifty every Christmas. I always mean to change and get him something different but for some reason, just at the last minute, I wind up getting him another Flat Fifty. It's almost like being hypnotized. I'd be determined not to get him a Flat Fifty again but then I'd be in a store, Christmas shopping, and I'd see all the Flat Fifties stacked up with Christmas bows on them and I'd go over, pulled over there by some big magnet, and my mouth would open and I'd hear it say, "Flat Fifty, please."

I couldn't seem to help it.

And Christmas morning Dad would pick up his present from me and he'd weigh it in his hands and he'd feel the shape of it and he'd say, "I hope it's a Flat Fifty!" and then he'd rip the paper off.

"It is! It is a Flat Fifty! Just what I wanted. Thank you very much!" he would always say. And then when Aunt Dottie was opening hers from me (I always got her chocolates, I couldn't help it) Dad would say, "I wonder if it's chocolates." And then when Aunt Dottie would finally get it open (it took her about an hour to unwrap because she wouldn't tear the paper) Dad would yell, "It is! It is chocolates! Let's have a couple!"

"No, you're not having any, I'm saving these for *myself* for a change this year," Aunt Dottie would say and put them on the floor beside her.

(Uncle Paddy was there one Christmas Day and stepped in Aunt Dottie's chocolates by mistake—squashed every one of them.)

Then, after we helped Pamela open her duck and got her to squeeze it and make it quack a few times, Aunt Dottie would send me down the cellar to the cold storage to bring up some shortbread with the half cherry on each one and the Christmas cake wrapped in wax paper and we'd have a little snack.

So I went over to the counter with the Flat Fifties all stacked up with the Christmas bows on them and my mouth opened and I heard it say, "Flat Fifty, please!"

That was enough shopping.

I walked home through the gently falling snow. The lights from the people's windows along York Street were yellow and warm. Some cats picked their way into the laneways.

I passed the school and crossed Angel Square all alone. It was a beautiful square in the late winter afternoon.

All alone on Angel Square.

I came up Papineau and turned the corner onto Cobourg Street.

Dad and some soldiers were out in front of our house taking pictures of each other. One soldier, who seemed to be quite clumsy and off balance all the time, was trying to take a picture of Dad and the other two soldiers. Dad was in the middle. He had one arm around each soldier.

The soldier taking the picture was looking down into the camera, shading it with one hand and backing up, trying to get everybody in the picture. He had the camera down about at his waist and he had one eye closed while he backed up the side of the snowbank.

Quite a few people saw him when he fell backwards over the bank and did a complete backroll and got his head stuck in the deep snow. The camera flew out onto the streetcar tracks.

A streetcar with a driver and two inspectors was going slowly by, heading for the car barn; a lot of kids, making their snow forts, stopped and watched; three people pushing a car onto Desjardins Street saw; Chalmers Lonnigan peeking around Papineau saw; some Dogans looking out over their half-built snow fort up from St. Patrick Street saw; Aunt Dottie upstairs in her poem room, probably looking out, saw; Pamela, for sure, looking out her window through her frost frame saw.

It was Dad's friend Frank home from the war.

The streetcar quietly crushed the camera.

I took the comic over to Gerald's house and we studied it. We took it over to CoCo's house and we studied it.

L.

That night I went to my choir practice at St. Albany's Anglican Church.

I went up the hill on King Edward to the corner of Daly and followed in the deep footprints around the side of the church where some of the others in the choir had stepped. I went through the little green door and down the wooden stairs to the practice room.

It's a room like the room at Talmud Torah where I do the floors. There are even pictures on the walls of other choirs and soloists. But they don't wear little caps; they have on black cassocks and white surplices.

Lester Lister was standing beside me, singing. In the middle of the hymn we had a conversation. It was easy. You sang what you wanted to say instead of the words in the Hymn Book.

Instead of:

> *Holy, Holy, Holy,*
> *Merciful and Mighty*
> *God in three persons*
> *Blessed Trinity*

I sang:

> *Got the comic from her*
> *Says she doesn't like you*
> *Says you are a coward*
> *'cause you ran away.*

When the hymn got to the second finish, instead of the real words, Lester sang:

> *I don't like her either*
> *She's just a dirty slut*
> *Now I can forget about*
> *The watch I said I'd buy.*

Lester Lister. What a slimy person.

I knew Gerald would meet me after practice because he always did on Fridays.

I walked slowly up Rideau Street waiting for him to surprise me like he always did. It was a game we played. If he got me, I would buy the drinks; if I saw him first, he would buy.

He was nowhere in sight.

Then I felt the gun in my back. I was about halfway home coming up Rideau Street on the north side right near Imbro's Restaurant.

Usually I would turn into Imbro's (and Gerald and I would have a cream soda), his gun still on me the whole time.

"Turn in here, copper," Gerald would say, "and don't look around or I'll drill ya!"

Inside the restaurant I'd have my hands up, not high but halfway up and wrists a little loose. Gerald would push me over into a booth for two near the door.

"Two cream sodas, doll, and be quick about it!" Gerald would say to the waitress. She would smile and be right back with the two bottles. I would pay the fourteen cents.

"OK, sucker," Gerald would say, "drink up and let's scram, pigeon!"

Then, if the waitress came by again, Gerald might say: "You know, honey, you're much prettier when you're angry!"

The girl would just laugh because she was used to this. She'd heard it all before. It was the same every Friday night. Every time I got paid at choir.

"Stop that eternal pacing up and down!" Gerald might say to Louis, the owner, if he was around.

"A man like you could have an accident on the street, for instance. Hit and run driver maybe. You never know." They were things that people said in movies. Gerald would have his hat pulled down over his eyes and a fake cigarette hanging out of the corner of his mouth.

Louis would just laugh. He'd heard it all before. On Friday nights. My pay night at choir.

Outside, the Friday night was dressed up for Christmas on Rideau Street. The hydro poles were wrapped in boughs and the streetcars had a wreath in each front window. The shops had Coca Cola Santas hung up in the windows and some had small Christmas trees with flashing lights. Imbro's had some bells on the door and if you went out into the middle of Rideau Street and looked downtown, you could see a big tree on top of Freiman's and maybe a lot of other blue and red colours down there.

Gerald and I did part of our game with the waitress and Louis and then we discussed the comic.

Gerald said he thought that the L could stand for Lonnigan. Chalmers Lonnigan's father. He hated Jews. It might be him. It was worth a try. Gerald said he thought he worked at the museum.

I said goodbye to Gerald and went home.

Dad and I listened to part of the Friday night fights on the radio.

It was Tony Janero and Humberto Zavala. We didn't find out who won because the tubes got weak in the middle of round seven.

Finally all we could hear was the cat purring and now and then a streetcar going home to the barns, the rumbling muffled by the snow, shaking the house a little bit.

Aunt Dottie had hung some balsam boughs on the wall going upstairs. They smelled deep and fresh.

I went to sleep with Christmas in my nose and Margot Lane in my head.

Tomorrow Gerald and CoCo and I would have a talk with Chalmers Lonnigan and see if we could find out anything.

from

Shadow in
Hawthorn Bay

by

J A N E T   L U N N

When Mary was almost twelve, her beloved cousin Duncan left the Highlands of Scotland with his family for Upper Canada. Now it is 1816, four years later, and Mary, who is gifted with second sight, hears Duncan imploring her to come to Canada. She decides that she must answer his call.

Quarters in the hold of the *Andrew MacBride* were a nightmare. Mary's berth was the top one of three, set in a row only two feet from other rows, in a space no crofter would stall three dozen cows and sheep in. It was to house two hundred people. What air there was was soon dark and fetid with the odours of the two hundred unwashed bodies, their breath, their excrement, and their cooking. It was dark and it was cold—cold for being so airless, as the Highland wind and rain had never been cold.

Out on deck the sea terrified her. It rose to the heights of the highest hills, it fell to the depths of the deepest glens, in a constant motion that seemed to threaten, with each new swell, to engulf the ship that rode it so precariously.

Although she was violently sick to her stomach from the pitching and rolling, Mary was so glad the voyage had actually begun that, almost, she did not mind. In the bunks below hers were Kirsty and Iain Mackay, their new baby, and Kirsty's mother, Elizabeth Finlay. When she first met her Mary saw the grey mist of death around Kirsty's pale hair but she could not bear to say so. The family were so good to her, so genuinely eager to share their provisions, that soon she was cooking her porridge and potatoes with them, helping to care for the baby and commiserating with them over their sorrows.

They had come from a glen to the north and west of Mary's, they told her one evening after supper. "And had our houses burned out behind us so we could not go home"—there were tears in Kirsty's blue eyes, there was bewilderment in her soft voice as well as bitterness—"so our chiefs could have our land for the sheep. Our own chiefs whose fathers were our fathers, whose mothers were our mothers."

Iain said nothing, but the set of his red head bent over the rattle he was whittling for the baby bespoke not only bitterness but resignation.

"It is a new land we go to." Elizabeth's bonnet strings bobbed with her firm nod. "A good land, we will be well there." Elizabeth's husband was already in Upper Canada awaiting them.

"A good land." They were the words Uncle Davie had written. It was what he had said when he had first talked of leaving the glen. Thoughts of leaving the Highlands had been in the air for three generations, to be sniffed out of corners and tasted on the wind. They had begun after the Scottish followers of Prince Charles Edward Stuart, the Bonnie Prince, had lost to the English at the bloody battle of Culloden Moor, sixty-nine years earlier, in 1746. Many of the Highland men who had survived the battle had been exiled. Later, others had chosen to leave with their families. The settlers in America and the Canadas had written home to say that it was fine to have no landlords. Shipping companies had posted bills in all the market towns saying that land across the sea could be had for only a few shillings. Preachers, influenced by wealthy landowners or honestly feeling it would be better for the people, preached that it was a gift from God. Mr. Graeme at St. Kilda's told his congregation, "He has given you a chance to repent you of your sins and begin life anew." And Uncle Davie Cameron had sat afterwards by the Urquhart hearth and called emigration wisdom.

"Wisdom is it, Davie Cameron?" James Urquhart had raised one red eyebrow scornfully. "We have been in this glen from time immemorial, Urquharts and Camerons alike." But Uncle Davie had sold up and gone with Aunt Jean and Duncan and Callum and wee Iain. The family had settled in the backwoods of Lake Ontario country, among refugees from the revolution in America.

Uncle Davie had written again and again to beg James and Margaret to join him in Upper Canada. War had broken out anew in 1812 between the British colonies in Canada and the thirteen old colonies, now called the United States, but "we are not much troubled here on our island at our end of the loch," he had said and had drawn them a map to show how to find him. Mary had pored over it, learning it by heart, trying in her mind to fill it with hills and streams and crofts, trying to see Duncan's dark forests, aching to see him in his new world. But the second sight did not come to her at will, it came and went unbidden. Duncan and his dark forest had remained stubbornly beyond her view.

"And here am I, now," she thought, looking around her at the sorry gathering of exiles, "with these poor souls who have no homes left to go back to."

The exiles did their best to be cheerful. Hector Macmillan, the piper, played dance tunes and melodies they all knew how to sing, and there were story-tellers. But the sailors sometimes played cruel jokes on the passengers in the hold and stole their provisions—the Mackay family lost their dried berries, their bit of salt fish, and a bag of oats. After four weeks the drinking water was stale and scarce and a lot of the food had spoiled. Many people had sickened of dysentery and malnutrition. Peggy Gordon grew hysterical from homesickness, Jamie Mathieson swore he would jump overboard before he would pick one more rat from his oats. Kirsty Mackay weakened day by day from the poor food and, one stormy night, she died in her sleep. Her thin body was rolled in her plaid and Colin Macleod, who had been the dominie back in Kirsty's glen, read psalms from the Bible, and her body was cast into the sea.

For one horrible instant, as Mary watched the plaid sink, she felt an almost overpowering urge to jump after it. It was as though she were the one sinking and had to leap in to save herself. Forcing back the sensation of black, suffocating water, she clung to the ship's rail until her knuckles went white and her breath came in sharp gasps. Afterwards she wept until there were no more tears in her. She crouched on the deck and wearily rested her head against the railing, her hair whipping about her in wet swirls. The frenzy that had been driving her for so long had abated, the headache was gone. In their place she was filled with a sadness that drained her of all other feeling.

She did not want to sleep again in the hold. She ate her oats raw, on deck; she wrapped herself in her plaid and tried to sleep with her head on her sack, braving the waves that passed over her, the winds that threatened to hurl her overboard. But the waves were too powerful and in the end the wind caused her to flee in terror to her berth below. Hugging herself, saying charms over and over, she kept the fears at bay.

The day after Kirsty Mackay died, when the emigrants had come together on deck around the piper, Mary took the baby from its grieving father and stood at the edge of the gathering. After the piper had played "The Flowers of the Forest" she sang a lullaby for the baby and for Kirsty. All the days afterwards she took the baby to walk with her around and around the deck.

Three weeks later the ship sailed into the gulf of the St. Lawrence and began its journey up the great river towards Montreal. At first the fog was too thick for anyone to be able to see anything. When it finally lifted Mary could not believe they were on a river, it was so wide. As the days passed it gradually narrowed and the shores became visible, faintly at first, then more and more clearly—low and rolling to the south, high and rising towards the Laurentian Mountains away to the north.

Along both shores were farms and villages with neat little white houses and tall shiny church spires. The distant mountains brought a joy to Mary's heart. "The forests are so far from where the people must be," she thought. "Why do you mind them so, Duncan? Are the hills so different from our own?"

Slowly they made their way up the river, past settled islands, the mouths of smaller rivers, and more and more villages—everywhere the signs of settled countryside. High on its promontory, the city of Quebec guarded the river. Mary thought that, but for there being no castle, it must be as fine, even, as Edinburgh itself—the fort, the stone houses both down along the shore and up above the cliff.

They finally docked in Montreal on a morning in mid-July. The day was already hot and damp and the air was full of bugs. The quay gave off an odour of dead fish, of cargoes and people emerging from ships from all over the world. Mary felt overwhelmed by the noise of hundreds of people all shrieking and shouting at each other in different languages. It was not what she had expected of a city in Duncan's "dark forest."

She determined not to stay in this hot, stinking, crowded place a single moment. She would have struck out for the spot on Uncle Davie's map called Collivers' Corners in Upper Canada with no delay but Elizabeth Finlay invited her to travel with her party. Elizabeth Finlay and Iain Mackay, and a few others who were headed west, were travelling on that day by coach. "And there's room for you," Elizabeth told Mary, "room going begging." Carefully not looking at Mary's bare feet, her now faded and threadbare blue skirt and worn blouse, she insisted, "Mairi, in these long, sad weeks, you have become very dear to us—to Iain and to me and to the wee bairnie. Why do you not come with us all the way?"

Mary, looking from Elizabeth's kind, worn face to Iain's weary one, read in their eyes—without the need of second sight—the hope that she would marry Iain and be mother to the baby.

"I will come with you, and many thanks, as far as Cornwall on the river, but I must go on to Loch Ontario."

They did not have to stay the night in Montreal since the stage-coach in which Iain had booked passage left immediately for Upper Canada. It wasn't long before the road grew narrow and the forests grew thick. There was little light. Mary began to understand why Duncan had written "dark with forest." In some places the trees were the familiar birch and aspen. In other places all she could see was cedar and tamarack swamp. But along most of the route were giant pines rising a hundred feet and more into the air, their trunks over six feet across, their branches starting only thirty or forty feet from the ground and meeting high above the rough road. Before the coach had driven very far into the forest

Mary had to restrain herself from pushing open the door, jumping out, and running back to the river, back to the city, to where those gigantic trees would not close in on her so relentlessly. Firmly she said to herself a charm against danger.

I will close my fist
Tight I will close my fist
Against the danger
That I have come within.

With each passing mile from Montreal, the smaller, rougher, and farther apart were the settlements—squares and notches cut out of the wilderness. Many of them were only one or two rude shacks, with blankets for doors, surrounded by a few feet of raw tree stumps with the cut-down trees in high piles at the edge of the clearing. "Bush country," a fellow traveller called the woods they rode through. His voice was loud and nasal and his English flat and harsh to Mary's ears used to the soft sibilant sounds of Gaelic.

The coach lurched and bumped along the deeply rutted road, now and again all but capsizing on a protruding root, a stump, or a large boulder. Occasionally there was relief from the endless trees when the road ran alongside the St. Lawrence River, past rapids or through more settled villages where there were a few stone or frame houses with flowers and vegetables growing around them. The journey took two days with two overnight stops at dirty little inns that stood at crossroads along the way.

At last they reached Cornwall, a sizeable town on the river with several inns, mills, and blacksmith shops. There Mary parted from her friends, they to travel north, she to follow the map she had memorized so carefully.

"I know it is many miles yet to Loch Ontario and farther still to the island where Uncle Davie lives but I will be well." She drew the map for them on the back of the paper packet that still held Mrs. Grant's letter and they asked the innkeeper about the distance. "Yep," he said, "looks to be up past Kingston way—be about a hundred miles."

"Mairi, you will get lost in this strange place. You are unprotected. Come with us for now and we will get word to your uncle. He will surely come for you."

"I cannot." Mary smiled. She took Elizabeth's hand. "I will not be lost. I have my map. The sound of the river will be always beside me. And—and I have money. I will be well." Mary hugged them all. "Fare you well." She kissed the baby once more. "Remember me."

But she did not have money and, alone, she did not feel as brave or cheerful as she let on. She, who had never been afraid of much of anything in either the seen or the unseen world, was afraid of this strange land, of strange people—Indians, about whom she had heard so many frightening stories, and others who spoke English so loudly in such flat accents; and even more, so much more, she was afraid of the forest that seemed to come at her from a depth of darkness too black to fathom, too powerful to escape.

Humming "The Battle Song of Harlaw" to keep up her courage, she set out with a will and walked steadily until nightfall. The road was very rough even on feet toughened by fifteen years of treading on rocks and sharp, cropped Highland grass. Her two shawls began to seem a real burden. There was no wind, the heat lay heavy and damp and thick, and the bugs were an unbelievable torment. In the Highlands the black clouds of whining, itching mosquitoes were unknown. Overhead where the trees almost met there were crows and jays and waxwings, birds she knew, and enormous pigeons of a kind she did not. They seemed to her friendly and, with their coo-roo-coo-roo, a bit of comfort in this strange place.

She passed half a dozen homesteads and several travellers on horseback, in carts, and once in a coach. She stopped at a log shack to ask for a cup of milk. A small, grey-looking man was sitting on a stump in the dooryard. "This ain't no inn and we don't feed beggars," he growled.

Before Mary could respond, a woman appeared from the interior of the cabin, equally grey-looking.

"Git along!" she spat. "Git along outta here."

Mary stared at her in horror.

"Scat," hissed the woman.

Mary left, dazed. She could never have imagined a human being talking to a stranger, a traveller, like that, "as though I were a dangerous beast," she muttered to herself.

Maybe because she was so shaken by the experience, maybe because she was bone-weary, Mary made a mistake. She had been running, walking, and running again along the ever-narrowing road for some time when she stopped. She was hungry and she was bitten from head to foot by mosquitoes, and while she had been running the tree-dim world had turned to night. She listened.

"I cannot hear the river." She was frozen with fright. She realized that it had been some time since she had seen either a dwelling or another traveller. She looked down and saw, by the bit of daylight that remained, that the road was no longer much more than a foot path. She began to hear the sounds of the woods at night as though she had just wakened from a sleep—wolves howling nearby, owls hooting, frogs croaking, other unfamiliar cries and calls, and all around her rustlings and gruntings in the underbrush.

"Duncan!" she whispered. "Duncan, I am lost." She hugged her two plaids as though they were her only comfort in the world.

Through the dark and the trees she saw a flicker of light. She ran towards it—off the path and into swamp water up to her hips. She screamed. She grabbed at a low branch of a cedar tree. She pulled herself up—and came face to face with a dark man looking down at her. She gasped, let the branch go, and would have fallen back into the swamp if the man hadn't grasped her by the arm and shoulder and pulled her back onto firm ground.

"Please," she pleaded in Gaelic, "please, let me go." She could not understand his reply. It was not English. She could see now that he was naked from the waist up. An Indian! A savage! She wrenched her arm free and ran. She fell, picked herself up, stumbled and ran again, gasping and sobbing, until she fell over a root.

She lay there, gulping in air, trying to calm herself, listening for the sound of feet coming after her. She could hear no feet. She heard the animals, she heard the owls—and then she heard the river.

"The river!" She sat up and looked around. She could make out nothing but the shape of evergreen trees.

"I do hear it," she whispered. "I will not leave this place until morning comes. Och, Duncan, what a terrible country this is. How will I find my way out of this wilderness? Is there no one to rescue me? My poor white bones will be found, years from this day, all picked over. My luck has surely left me." In a panic she felt into the pocket under her petticoat for the spindle whorl and for Mrs. Grant's letter. Safe. In spite of herself, she leaned against the trunk of a tree and dozed fitfully, like a cat, starting to wakefulness at every new sound.

At first light she saw that the wider road was only a few feet from where she sat. "What a foolish lass I am," she reproved herself. If she hadn't been so tired and so wet and dirty, she might have laughed. As it was, grimly she straightened her blouse and her skirt now stained with brown swamp water and pulled her fingers through her tangled hair. She picked up her shawls—Mrs. Grant's wrapped carefully inside her own—held her shoulders back, and started west along the road. She was too afraid of getting lost again to go down to the river to wash or drink.

Rescue did come and in an unexpected form. Mary hadn't been walking for more than half an hour when a coach rattled by. It stopped just up the road.

A woman's head in a fashionable bonnet poked out of the window. "Dear, dear," she fluttered, "what can you be doing on this desolate stretch of road at such an hour, child? It's only just gone seven."

Mary wanted to say, "What is it you think I am doing? I am making a fine meal of meat and drink on this white linen cloth you see spread out before your eyes." What she did say was, "I am on my way to Collivers' Corners, ma'am—on Loch Ontario."

"Why, that's a blessing. We're on our way to Amherst. That's on Lake Ontario."

"Mama, Josie's wet herself." A tousle-headed boy put his head out of the window beside his mother's.

"Just a minute, Charles, just a minute. Oh dear, oh dear! We've lost our nanny. It's so sad. Maggie died on board ship and I don't know what we shall do. I . . . you . . . we . . . you wouldn't be able to help with the children, would you? You do seem small." The woman looked doubtfully at Mary's ragged, grubby state. "They're very sweet," she added.

By this time the three children had crowded their mother out of the window and Mary could see, at once, that they were not sweet.

"I can see that they are," she agreed, "and I will be happy to help you care for them." Before the woman could change her mind, Mary hopped up onto the step and was in the coach.

The mother, an English woman named Sophie Babbington, had no rein on her children, and they, delighted to have a fresh victim, climbed all over Mary, shrieked in her ear, pummelled her viciously, pulled her hair, and fought with each other across and on top of her. Mary didn't care. Mrs. Babbington had a wicker hamper full of cold chicken and white bread, and cold tea and fruit, food Mary had never eaten in her life, and the coach was steadily moving westward towards the dot on Uncle Davie's map that was labelled Collivers' Corners.

At Prescott, where the rapids ended, Mrs. Babbington, without a word, bought Mary a ticket on the ship that would take them up the river to Kingston on Lake Ontario and, from there, to Soames for Mary, and on to Amherst for herself and her children. She took a room in an inn at Prescott, saw to it that Mary had a bath, and gave her a skirt, a petticoat, a blouse, and a pair of shoes that had been the nanny's. Maggie had been only a little larger than Mary and the clothes did very well. They were clean but every bit as heavy as Mary's own in the heat. With a sigh, Mary bundled up her own rags to salvage as best she could another day. After a night's sleep in a real bed, even though none too clean and shared with all three children, she felt considerably brighter and well able to tackle the rest of her journey.

By the time their ship neared the island the children were Mary's devoted slaves. She had told them stories from Cornwall to Prescott, from Prescott to Kingston, from Kingston to Soames, each story more terrifying than the last. She had told them she was a witch and taught them nonsense rhymes in Gaelic that she said were evil spells. When the time came for her to leave them at Soames they all cried and Mrs. Babbington begged her to stay with them.

"I declare, the children have never behaved themselves so well. I don't know how you manage them!" Mrs. Babbington had slept in the coach from the moment she had picked Mary up, and as soon as they boarded the ship she had left the children completely to her.

Mary was as grateful to Mrs. Babbington and her children as they to her. They had kept her so busy she had had no chance to think of anything else. "*Beannachd Dhé leat*, may the blessing of God attend you," she said as she left them on the wharf at Soames. "I will not forget your kindness."

Soames was a prosperous village with five docks, short streets running from them to a main street where there were three inns, a couple of blacksmith shops, a livery stable and two mills. At one of the blacksmith shops Mary was told, "It ain't more'n eight miles to Collivers' Corners. Like as not you can get a lift if you wait."

She did not wait. Eight miles was nothing to walk. But the trees, once she had left the village, seemed taller and if possible even more formidable than the ones near Cornwall. And there was a steady wind here that moved the enormous treetops so that they seemed to be singing a constant, low, keening song. The road was much like the one out of Montreal and Cornwall. "Government road," the blacksmith had told her proudly, "wider than most. Goes all the way to the town of York, more than one hundred miles west of here."

As she tramped along in the half-light, Mary concentrated on the familiar sounds of pigeons and doves cooing. She started at the sight of strange animals and she tried not to acknowledge the terror that rose in her throat when she glanced into the dark trees hemming her in. She did not hear the horse and cart approach. She jumped and whirled around at the sound of a drawn-out "Whoa!"

"Didn't mean to scare you." The tall boy driving the cart looked concerned. "It ain't exactly that these here wagons is quiet or sneaky. Hop aboard if you like."

He was a tall, brown-haired boy perhaps three or four years older than she, with a broad, open face. Without a word she climbed up beside him.

"I'm Luke Anderson." He eyed her curiously. Mary told him her name and where she was headed. As she sat beside Luke, Mary's head reached only to his shoulder, and her feet did not quite touch the floor. She wished, for once, that she were not so small. With her feet dangling down like that she felt foolish. Once or twice Luke offered conversation but, when Mary did not respond, fell silent. He remarked about a bird in sudden flight and a deer that bounded across the road. Once they had to stop when a strange, ungainly, dark-furred animal lumbered across the road. "Raccoon," Luke replied to Mary's astonished question. Otherwise they rode for almost two hours in silence. The only sounds were the dull thud-thud of the horse's hoofs on the dirt road and the chatter and whistle of the birds at the edge of the forest.

They came in sight of the village at last—a blacksmith shop, a general store, a scattering of log cabins and frame houses and, across a small stream, a dark red house beside a tall stone mill.

"That's the Corners," said the boy. Only then did Mary tell him, "I am wanting to find Davie Cameron and his family."

"Oh, that's too bad. That's really too bad. They took off from here not two weeks ago."

"Took off?" Mary stared blankly at Luke.

"They gave up. Took off. Went home to where they come from. After—"

"Went home?" echoed Mary.

"It was after—" Luke began again.

Mary put out her hand as if to stop the words she knew were coming next, words she had known she would have to hear from the day Kirsty Mackay had died, the day her headache had stopped. Then, because she could not bear to hear this stranger speak them, she said them herself.

"It was after Duncan died," she said.

from

Looking at the Moon

by

K I T   P E A R S O N

This is the beginning of the second volume of a trilogy about Norah and Gavin, who were sent to Toronto from England in 1940 to live as the "war guests" of wealthy Aunt Florence and her daughter Mary. It is set at the family's summer cottage on Lake Joseph in Muskoka, Ontario.

I look so ugly!

Norah peered over her brother's head at the photograph, while Aunt Mary held open the Toronto newspaper and read aloud from the "Personal Notes" for August 2, 1943:

> Mrs. Wm. Ogilvie, her daughter Miss Mary Ogilvie, and their young war guests, Norah and Gavin Stoakes, have just returned from a trip to Vancouver. They will be spending the month of August at "Gairloch," their summer home in Muskoka.

In the picture above the caption Aunt Florence sat stiffly on the chesterfield, looking as majestic as usual. Gavin was perched on its right arm and Aunt Mary smiled timidly on the far left.

Between the two women scowled Norah, her face all nose, and her arms and legs as skinny as toothpicks.

"What does 'Wim' mean?" asked Gavin.

Aunt Florence laughed. "William, pet. It's an abbreviation." She took the paper from her daughter to examine it more closely. "Must you always frown, Norah? At least your new dress looks presentable. We'll buy two copies so we can send one to your parents. Won't that be nice?"

Norah shrugged. She ran out of Ford's Bay Store, where they had picked up the newspaper while they waited for the launch. Standing on the dock, she hooded her eyes with both hands and gazed hungrily out at the lake.

At last they'd arrived! The hot, hundred-mile drive from Toronto had seemed endless. Norah had smouldered with frustration while they wasted a whole hour in Orillia, having lunch with friends of the family. During the meal she'd made so many hints about the time that Aunt Florence had marched her out to the car and made her wait there without dessert.

After Orillia Gavin had slept, but Norah had squirmed in the back seat, while Aunt Florence nattered to her daughter about their friends' connections. "Let's see now . . . Alma Bartlett married Harry Stone... wasn't he the brother of William Stone?" For all of July, during their trip to British Columbia, Norah had been subjected to the same boring gossip. *Who cares?* she wanted to scream.

But now she watched the dancing waves and sniffed in the balsamy smell that was always her first sensation of being back in Muskoka. A breeze lifted her sticky hair. She knelt on the dock and dipped her hands in the clear water. She splashed it into her face, then took a drink. All summer she had been waiting to feel and taste the lake again.

And in a very short while she would be at Gairloch itself! She hadn't been there since last October; now that there was gas rationing, and you couldn't buy new tires, they no longer came up in May. Norah still hadn't forgiven Aunt Florence for cheating her out of a whole month on the island. And a month spent almost entirely in Aunt Florence's company had been too much to bear.

Norah was used to her guardian after living with her for almost three years. After a rough beginning they had reached a sort of truce. But lately Aunt Florence's fussiness had driven her wild. Kind Aunt Mary understood that Norah was growing up, but Aunt Florence still treated her like a child.

"I'm thirteen!" she had protested, when Aunt Florence had brought home the "presentable" dress before their journey— impossibly babyish, with puffed sleeves and a sash. "I'm a teen-ager now—why can't I pick my *own* clothes?"

"A teen-ager!" Aunt Florence had sniffed. "I don't hold with these newfangled notions. There's no such thing as a teen-ager. In our family you are a child until you leave home and then you're an adult. I don't want to hear that word again."

And all Norah could respond was, "Yes, Aunt Florence," as sulkily as she dared. Whenever she tried to explain *her* side of things, Aunt Florence just said "Sauce!" and closed the conversation. Norah remembered having loud, satisfying arguments with her mother. But her mother was in England and Norah hadn't seen her since she and Gavin had been sent to Canada to be safe from the war. With Aunt Florence she was supposed to behave like a polite guest and keep her mouth shut.

At last the launch curved around the headland, and Norah saw her "cousins" Janet and Flo in it, waving. She shouted and waved back and jumped away her car stiffness. Now she had five whole weeks of freedom ahead of her, when she could have as little as possible to do with bossy adults. She glanced down at the comfortable shorts she was only allowed to wear up north. Maybe she didn't *really* want to be a teen-ager, not yet...

"Norah, Norah!" Janet was leaning over the bow screaming her name. The spray flew into her mouth, making her choke. Flo pulled her back and waved.

All summer Aunt Florence had nagged at Norah to smile more often. Now she grinned so hugely her cheeks felt as if they were cracking. There had been "cousins" in Vancouver, but they were all boys and not very friendly. Flo and Janet were like real cousins. Sometimes Flo seemed distant—she was seventeen—but Janet was only a year older than Norah.

As soon as the launch putted up beside the dock, Janet leaped out and grabbed Norah, whirling her around. "Oh, *Norah,* you've finally come! It's been so boring without you!"

"Hi, kiddo," smiled Flo, tying up the boat efficiently. "Thank goodness you're here—now I can get this pesky sister out of my way."

"Your hair's longer!" cried Janet. "I like it. Do you like mine? I put it in pincurls now." Janet's hair was a blonde fuzz that emphasized her fat cheeks. She hugged Norah again, then controlled her excitement as the aunts and Gavin, loaded down with bags of groceries, came out of the store.

"Hello Janet, hello Florence." The cousins were kissed and exclaimed over. Gavin beamed up at everyone, his eyes the same bright blue as the water.

"You might have helped us carry these, Norah," said Aunt Florence. Norah ignored her as they all found places in the long boat. She ran her hands over its mahogany sides and leather seats. The launch was called *Florence*—not after Aunt Florence but after her mother. But Norah thought it suited her guardian to have the same name as the luxurious boat, whose luminous wood, thick glass windscreen and shiny brass all glittered with importance.

She watched carefully as Flo turned the key to start the ignition. Only the older teen-agers were allowed to drive the *Florence*, but you could run the smaller launch by yourself when you turned thirteen. She hoped the grown-ups would remember that before she had to remind them.

"Isn't it great to be back?" whispered Gavin. He leaned against Norah and the two of them threw their faces back to drink in the spray, keeping watch for their first glimpse of the island.

All of the Drummond clan were on the dock to greet them. Aunt Florence stepped out regally and accepted the homage of her sisters, brother, in-laws, nieces and nephews as if she were their ruling monarch—which, being the eldest, she was. Norah barely noticed which of the grown-ups was kissing her. She was too busy taking in the white dock, the grey boathouse with its fancy railing and, best of all, the circular cottage waiting above.

"*Bosley!* Look, Norah, he remembers me! Wave, Boz!" Uncle Reg's black-and-white springer spaniel had bounded onto the dock and leapt at Gavin. Then he lifted one of his paws in greeting while everyone laughed.

Norah kicked off her shoes, wriggled through the excited group and ran up to the cottage. The stone steps were cool and rough under her tender feet. She dashed into the kitchen.

"Hanny! We're back!"

Hanny, Aunt Florence's cook in the city, turned around from the stove and opened her arms. Norah ran into them and their noses collided. They both laughed.

"Norah, what a treat to see you again! Did you have a grand trip? I got all your postcards, and Gavin's too—where is he?"

"Down at the dock, still being kissed," grinned Norah. She circled the spacious kitchen, grabbed a cookie off a plate and plopped herself on top of the old pine table, munching noisily.

"Not before dinner and no sitting on my clean table," said Hanny automatically, but her lined face still smiled. "Oh *my*, I've missed you all this month—even Mrs. O! The family seems rudderless without her here."

"How is Mr. Hancock?" asked Norah politely. Hanny's husband was retired, but he always came up with her in the summers to help out.

"Having a nice, lazy time as usual. He gads about fetching mail or taking your uncles fishing, while I slave away in a hot kitchen. Though I must say your aunts are very helpful." Hanny pushed her untidy hair under its net and turned back to the stove. "Now, Norah, it's lovely to see you but we'll have to talk later. You're all eating together this evening—all twenty of you!—and I'm not nearly ready. You'd better skedaddle—unless you'd like to peel some carrots."

Norah left quickly in case Hanny meant it. Before the family came in she made a swift inspection of the rest of the cottage: up the stairs and down the slippery hall, peeking into each of the huge bedrooms, then through the sunny dining room into the living room.

Nothing had changed; nothing ever did. Old photographs dotted the panelled walls. Cups from regattas, faded rugs and comfortable wicker furniture filled the dim space. A faint smell of wood smoke came from the massive stone fireplace. In an alcove beside it was the same wooden puzzle that had been there for years, its pieces scattered on a small table. Above it was Aunt

Florence's mother's collection of china cats, and the knot board where all the children, including Norah, had learned to tie knots.

Norah ended her tour on the veranda, her favourite part of the cottage. She ran all around its wide circumference, then leaned against one of its thick cedar posts and watched the clan parade up the steps—as if she, not Aunt Florence, were the ruler of Gairloch.

Surely, the black cloud of angry misery that had hung over her almost constantly since she had turned thirteen would now dissolve.

* * *

The long evening meal was over, the younger children had gone to bed, and the two generations of aunts and uncles, whom Flo had long ago christened "the Elders," were relaxing in the living room.

Norah sat on the rug opposite Janet, her calm mood already vanished. She was trying to concentrate on a game of slapjack, but inside she seethed at what Aunt Mar, her least favourite Elder, had just said to her in the kitchen.

"Look how you've grown, Norah! You'd better ask Aunt Florence to buy you a brassiere before school starts."

How dare she make personal remarks like that! At least the two of them had been alone, bringing out the dessert plates.

Norah tugged angrily at the skirt Aunt Florence had made her change into. The Elders changed for dinner every night, but the children only had to when they had what the younger cousins called a Big Dinner together.

It wasn't dark yet and Norah hadn't even had time to explore. She kept glancing out at the beckoning evening. Finally she couldn't bear to be inside a moment longer.

"I'm going for a walk," she whispered to Janet. She slipped out of the room and ran down to the boathouse to change. Comfortable again in slacks, an old shirt and bare feet, Norah strode along the shoreline path that circled the island. A chipmunk skittered out of her way and soft pine needles crunched under her feet.

Soon she reached the tiny log cabin that was the children's playhouse. No one seemed to have used it since she and Janet, with Bob and Alec—cousins on the Ogilvie side—had called themselves the Hornets and pretended the playhouse was a gangsters' hideaway. But this summer Bob and Alec hadn't come.

Four yellow-and-black striped masks hung on nails inside the door. Norah closed it quickly. It seemed much longer than a year ago that they had played that silly game.

Beyond the playhouse was the babies' beach. Norah rolled up her pant legs and paddled, her feet stirring up silt. The bay was so shallow that it looked brown, every ripple of sand showing through its crystal surface.

Her next stop was the gazebo perched on a rocky point at the far end of the island. An empty cup and saucer had been abandoned on the bench inside. Norah knew she should take them back to the kitchen, but that would slow her down.

She passed the windmill which pumped up water for the tank behind the cottage. Then she cut through the woods in the middle of the island, weaving through tree trunks and ferns until she reached a clearing. Here stood two extra cabins for overflowing family and guests. Behind them was Norah's favourite place on the island, the high rocky promontory that overlooked it all. Her feet reached for the familiar footholds as she scrabbled up the rock to the level platform on top. There she collapsed, panting and sweaty.

She ran her hands over the streaky pink rock and gazed down at the massed green foliage beneath her. Beyond it stretched the lake. Clumps of land—other islands and long fingers of mainland—broke up its flat expanse.

Vast as it was, this lake was the smallest of three huge ones that were joined together by narrow ribbons of water. But their lake was the deepest, Norah thought with satisfaction, and the most beautiful. She never tired of watching its colour change from silver to blue to green. Now its surface reflected the pink-tinged sky. The slanting light picked out each rock, tree and wave.

Norah let out a relieved breath—finally she was alone.

Her first encounter with the Drummond clan each summer was always overwhelming. Ten adults and eight children were here this month and they were all related. Norah had heard the expression "blood is thicker than water"; Ogilvie and Drummond blood seemed thicker than most. Over the summers she had grown used to the family's established rituals, jokes and conflicts. She knew as well as all the cousins that Aunt Bea was shrill and giddy because she resented Aunt Florence being the eldest, and that Uncle Reg played practical jokes on his two sisters whenever he had the chance.

But although the family was always warm towards their two war guests, Norah often felt as though they belonged to an exclusive club she and Gavin could never join. Every once in a while the family shared something that excluded them. This evening, for example, they had all started talking about Andrew, an unknown cousin who was supposed to arrive tomorrow. Andrew's funny expressions when he was four, the time he ran away and hid under the canoe when he was eight, the plays he made up... all through dinner they had discussed him.

But Aunt Mar's rude comment had been much worse than the

chatter about Andrew. Norah knew she needed a brassiere; she just couldn't bring herself to ask Aunt Florence for one. And anyway, shouldn't Aunt Florence notice for herself and suggest it?

It was difficult to believe that the two mounds on her chest, that had appeared almost overnight, really belonged to *her*. This last year she was sure her nose had grown as well. It seemed to fill up her whole face like a beak.

Dad had a nose like that—but it didn't matter on a man. Thinking of Mum and Dad produced the usual small ache, like prodding a sore spot. When she and Gavin finally went back to England, would her parents recognize this new person with a beaky nose and breasts like a woman's?

One day in the spring, as she was waiting nervously to attend her first mixed party, Norah had asked Aunt Florence if she was pretty. She knew Aunt Florence would tell her the truth; she didn't believe in false flattery.

"You are when you smile," was the brisk reply.

That meant she *wasn't* pretty, for if she always had to smile to enhance her looks, she couldn't be. It was also an infuriating way for Aunt Florence to get in some advice, instead of just answering the question.

Now she scraped away lichen from the rock. Why wasn't the magic of Gairloch making her troubles disappear, the way it usually did?

Tired of her own thoughts, Norah slithered back down the rock. She would go and check on Gavin. All of the boys except the two youngest ones slept in half of the old servants' quarters behind the cottage. The Hancocks slept in the other half. Norah poked her head into the large room that the family called the "Boys' Dorm." With Bob and Alec away, only three small boys, Peter, Ross and Gavin, occupied cots. All three were fast asleep.

Norah went in and bent over Gavin. As usual he clutched "Creature," his toy elephant, in his fist. She covered him up more closely. Even though the gentle little boy was everyone's favourite, the family accepted that Norah was the one who was really responsible for him. She had never forgotten how she had neglected that responsibility when she'd first come to Canada. Now her love for Gavin was the most constant element in her life here.

She heard laughter coming from the water's edge; the others must have already gone to bed. Norah wished she could go straight down to the boathouse, where all the girls slept, but one of the family rituals was saying good-night.

Aunt Anne and Uncle Gerald, who stayed in one of the cabins with their two youngest children, had already retired. The rest of the Elders were playing bridge.

"I'm going to bed now," Norah announced.

"I was just going to call you," said Aunt Florence. "What were you doing out there all by yourself? Janet was upset you left so abruptly."

Norah shrugged. On the first night back at Gairloch you were expected to kiss everyone. Dutifully she made her rounds. "Goodnight Aunt Florence... Aunt Mary... Aunt Catherine... Aunt Bea... Aunt Dorothy... Uncle Barclay... Uncle Reg... Aunt Mar." Whew! Eight kisses, some on papery cheeks or rough skin that needed a shave.

She fled to the toilet, then down to the dock. The boathouse was built directly over the lake. On this side of the island the water was so deep that the boats could be driven right into their slips, like putting a car in the garage. Before she went up the stairs, Norah paused to admire the family's fleet. Inside, the *Florence* bobbed beside the smaller launch—the *Putt-Putt*—and the heavy old rowboat. The sailboat was moored outside and the canoe was overturned against a wall.

She looked for her mug and toothbrush on the shelf built under the window. It was in the same place it had been last Thanksgiving. Norah brushed her teeth vigorously and cleaned the brush in the lake. Ignoring the bar of soap beside the mug, she splashed her face and dried herself with the fresh towel waiting for her on her hook.

She stood for a moment, listening to the haunting wail of a loon. A few stars had already appeared and the fat moon made a silver trail on the water. Norah drank in a gulp of cool night air, then climbed up the stairs to the "Girls' Dorm."

The familiar space seemed to welcome her. Everything was the same: the messy clutter of clothes and bathing suits, the dark wooden walls, the nails to hang their things on and the faded gingham curtains they always left open.

"Where have *you* been?" Clare asked her. "Moon-gazing? Maybe our Norah has been having romantic thoughts."

Norah pulled off her clothes and got into her pyjamas without answering. Clare was so impossible, no one took her seriously. She was sitting on the edge of her bed, plucking at her ukelele and yowling "You Are My Sunshine" out of tune.

"*Please* stop, Clare," begged Sally. "I'm trying to go to sleep."

Clare's pretty, pouty face looked up. "Then go back to the cabin with your parents and little brothers," she said rudely. "If you want to be out here with the *big* girls, you have to put up with us." She began again, even louder.

Abashed, Sally sank down into her pillow. She was only seven and in awe of her older cousins. But Flo reached over and snatched away Clare's ukelele.

"You're too noisy," she said calmly. Ignoring Clare's protests, she blew out the lamp. "Get into bed, everyone, and keep quiet so Sally can go to sleep."

The five girls lay in bed for a few silent moments. The loon warbled again and something, a frog or a fish, splashed briefly. Waves lapped soothingly against the sides of the boathouse. Norah snuggled farther into her narrow but cosy bed, feeling as usual as if she were *on* a boat. She began to think of the treats that waited for her tomorrow... the first of a long string of days when there was nothing she *had* to do.

Then, as usual, they all began talking again, as revived and wide-awake as if they had had hours of sleep. Only Sally dozed. The others sat up in bed, their faces white ovals in the moonlight.

First Flo, Janet and Claire finished telling Norah everything she had missed in July: the Port Clarkson Regatta, the *Ahmic* steamship accident, and how Uncle Gerald had seen a bear swimming from one island to another.

"Aunt Bea tried to organize us like Aunt Florence," giggled Janet.

"We had to recite *poetry* every night," complained Clare. "It was terrible."

"I hate to admit it, but it's a relief to have Aunt Florence back," said Flo. "Now it's your turn, Norah. Tell us all about your trip!"

Norah began with the only good part—the train. They had slept in narrow bunks with straps to hold them in; the train rocked them to sleep every night like a noisy cradle. "The meals were *wonderful*, and really fancy, just like in a restaurant. There were white tablecloths and finger bowls and we had roast beef and trout and things like that."

She couldn't find words to describe her astonishment at how huge Canada was; the train seemed to go on forever, unfolding mile after mile of empty country. She remembered her first awestruck glimpse of the Rockies, their sharp peaks outlined against a hard blue sky.

Nor could she explain how being on a train had made her realize that, in a way that hadn't been true when she had first come to this country, the war seemed to have finally touched Canada. Every day she and Gavin walked the length of the whole train, through crowded cars full of soldiers and solitary, worried-looking women who soothed crying children.

She went on to describe Vancouver with its rounded mountains rising straight up from the sea; and the Ogilvie cousins whom the Drummonds had never met.

"Vancouver was sort of like England," said Norah. "But there was nothing to do there except visit a lot of boring relatives. Do you know they even had black-outs? After Pearl Harbor, because they're so close to Japan."

Clare interrupted her. "Did *you* know that I have a boyfriend, Norah? Now that I'm fifteen, I'm finally allowed to date. His name's John and he's planning to join the RCAF. He's—"

"Spare us the details," Flo broke in. "We're already so tired of hearing about him."

"But *Norah* hasn't heard," persisted Clare. She continued to go on about how dreamy her new boyfriend was until Flo interrupted her again.

"You don't even know what loving someone is," she said quietly. "Wait until he *does* join up. Like Ned..."

"Who's Ned?" Norah asked, because she knew Flo wanted her to.

"He's *my* boyfriend, and he's in the army and stationed overseas. I write to him three times a week."

"She also writes to two other boys," said Janet. "She uses so much paper that Mother makes her buy her own."

"Well, it's important," said Flo. "They need to be cheered up."

Norah turned over impatiently. Flo seemed much more grown-up this summer, as if she had already entered the strange adult world that was still closed to the rest of them. And she wished all of them would stop going on about *boys*. They were just like her friend Dulcie. This past year Dulcie had "discovered" boys. She was always moaning about being too young to go to dances, and she didn't understand when Norah said she wasn't interested. At least Janet wasn't like that yet.

But then Janet disappointed her too.

"What do you think of Frankie, Norah?" she asked. "I think he's the greatest thing since canned peas."

Flo roared with laughter. "Sorry, Janet," she choked, seeing her sister's hurt face. "But when you try to use expressions like that you sound so—"

"I don't want to hear how I sound," interrupted Janet huffily. "I was asking Norah a question. What do you think of Frankie?"

Norah knew she meant Frank Sinatra. "He's OK, I guess," she sighed. She didn't mind the mellow voice which seemed to be on the radio every time it was turned on. But she was tired of him. Her other city friend, Paige, had every one of his records and played them until Norah wanted to scream. At least they didn't have a phonograph in the boathouse.

The conversation turned to a comparison of their school years in Montreal and Toronto. They had a lot to catch up on since last summer.

"Stop *talking*," moaned Sally, turning over and going back to sleep. Norah herself was drifting through whole patches of conversation. Then Janet asked her a question. "Have you ever met Andrew, Norah? I can't remember if you were here the last time he came."

"No, I haven't. Who *is* this Andrew, anyway?" she added irritably.

"He's the only son of Uncle Ralph and Aunt Constance," explained Flo. "Uncle Ralph was my mother's and Clare's father's brother—he died about five years ago. They used to come to Gairloch every summer but then Aunt Constance married again and Andrew had to move to Winnipeg. He's been back a few times for a visit. And tomorrow he'll be here again! He's transferring to the University of Toronto this fall."

"He's *dreamy*," said Clare. "He visited us in Montreal last year and all my friends were envious. If he wasn't my cousin I'd have a huge crush on him."

"He's the best person in the family," said Flo. "We were really close when we were kids."

"The last time he came he taught me how to dive," said Janet. "Wait till you see how handsome he is, Norah!"

Norah pretended she was already asleep. What a bore this Andrew sounded! And what a bore the cousins were going to be, if all they wanted to talk about were boys and singers.

And yet, since she was now a teen-ager too, shouldn't she be more interested in those things? She didn't want to be as childish as Sally or as grown-up as Flo. But it wasn't much fun to flounder in between.

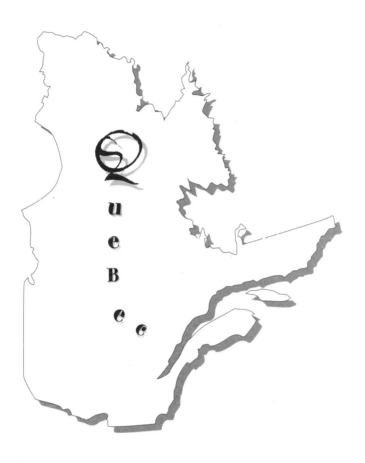

Moon Prayer

by

R O C H   C A R R I E R

In the late thirties and early forties in a small Quebec village a small boy talks to God about the tribulations, confusions and joys of his young life.

Today, God, I'm going to pray in my bed instead of going to the church. Thank You for the beautiful day You gave the Earth. I caught three big trouts in the Famine River, but I threw back a big carp. God, Your carp are really poor quality. They can't take the summer heat. Their flesh decomposes as if they were dead. But anyway, the bees and the butterflies seemed to be happy about everything. The day passed as quickly as the night does when you're asleep. I picked some strawberries, too. I brought home my trouts and a pailful of strawberries, already hulled. I'm not the kind of lazybones that picks strawberries and then doesn't hull them. But I think You could have made straw-berries that don't have hulls. They'd be easier to pick.

Our mother sent me out to cord some wood. It's the begin-ning of July, and the sun's so hot you melt in your pants. But our father's getting ready for the winter. He's bought his wood, enough to heat every igloo at the North Pole and the polar ice cap, too. And we're the ones that have to cord it. Summer holidays would be the best time in my whole life if it wasn't for cording that wood. Sometimes when I look at the mountain of wood waiting for me, I wonder if I wouldn't be better off in school, learning lists of grammatical exceptions and how to make fishes plural.

It was really beautiful today. You should have seen Your sun, and the colour of the barley and the spruce trees. You should have heard Your birds singing and Your insects buzzing. You should have seen Your snakes baking their skins on piles of stones: You'd have been proud of Yourself. Days like that mean that the eternal goodness of Your Heaven overflowed onto Earth. I want to thank You, God, for the beautiful day. Even if tears are pouring out of my eyes, I'm really quite happy. It's dark in my room but You can see me. The tears are on account of our Uncle Marcel.

You're the only one that knows I'm bawling like a baby. When I cry I don't make any sound, I don't sniff or squawk. I suffer my sorrow in silence, as they say on the radio. If my brothers hear me crying they'll make fun of me and call me a baby. One sob and they'll be in my bed, landing on me with their feet and slapping me with their pillows. I'd rather keep my suffering inside for a while. My pillow's all wet. I really shouldn't be suffering like this after such a beautiful day.

Our Uncle Marcel is young and he's taller than me. He must be at least thirteen or twelve, our uncle. He's the one that holds the censer in the church procession. If you ask me, I think he'd rather be holding some girl's hand. Uncle Marcel smokes on the sly. That's a secret, but I can tell You because You've seen him. His mother, our grandmother, doesn't know. I think I'll tell her tomorrow. Uncle Marcel upset me a lot tonight. I know he smokes because he offered me his cigarette and he said:

"If you don't tell my mother, your grandmother, I'll let you take a puff."

I didn't take one puff, I took a dozen. All at once I felt like a man: I was dizzy and I wanted to throw up. My guts were squirming, my head was spinning. I still didn't say anything to Uncle Marcel's mother, our grandmother. Tomorrow, if You let me live long enough to open my eyes, I'm going to tell our grandmother on him because he upset me so much. I can't stand it when people laugh at me because I'm not as big as the others and because I'm younger.

Our Uncle Marcel is proud. He's always got a little mirror in one hand, and with the other hand he's always combing his hair. He wants the girls to think he's handsome. I'm going to tell our grandmother that he made me smoke. Then Uncle Marcel will be sentenced to stay in his room for quite a few nights. He'll have to go quite a few days without combing his hair because he'll have to go quite a few days without any girls seeing him. My pillow's all wet with tears, God, and I don't like going to sleep feeling sad.

Tonight our father said:

"The Moon's as full as a woman."

I didn't understand what he meant. I looked at the Moon. She was like a great big orange on a tablecloth, as blue as the sky, that had little holes like moth-holes in it, for the stars. The Moon also looked like the big round head of a man, without any hair or a toupee or a body, but with eyes and a nose and a mouth. If the Moon was full, she was full of light. And I was looking up at her.

I wished I could reach up and touch Your Moon. I wished I could climb onto the Moon and scoop up a handful, like a handful of earth or a handful of snow. I wished I could see what it was made of. Is the Moon a ball of fire? Is the Moon just an explosion? Is the Moon solid like Earth? Is it a big diamond? Is it like a huge scoop of ice cream you can lick? Is it hot like fire? Is it cold like ice? Anyway, it's beautiful to look at. It's so far away from Earth that looking at it for a long time makes you dizzy, like when Uncle Marcel made me smoke a string cigarette. Our Uncle Marcel hasn't got any tobacco. He won't steal any from his father, our grandfather, because he says he's not a thief, so I bring him string from our father's store.

God, You hung the Moon so high up in the sky, it would take four hundred years to get there by train. That's what the nun at school told us. She didn't say how long it would take to build the railway. You'd have to know how long it took to build the railway that goes from one end of Canada to the other. And then calculate the distance between Earth and the Moon. Then divide that distance by the length of Canada. And then multiply the quotient obtained by the time needed to build the Canadian railway. The Moon's far, far away, farther than the end of our lives.

Nobody on the gallery outside our house dared to talk. We were all looking at the Moon. We were as quiet as if we were scared. It was a nice kind of fear, though. A gentle fear. The sleepy kind of fear when you don't understand something beautiful that you wish you could understand. It was as if the gallery had moved like a boat in the water. The men were smoking. The women were quiet, too. You could hear yourself breathe. That was the only sound our lives were making. The Moon was beautiful, round and yellow and shiny. There were a few stars, but you just knew that on this night, the sky was made for the Moon. It was really hard to believe that some of the stars were hundreds of times bigger than the Moon: they seemed to be hundreds of times smaller. The Moon was the queen of the stars, I tell You.

Maybe the Moon isn't a star because it doesn't have points like a real star, but anyway, she was really shiny and far away up in the sky where the stars are, and where You are too, God. The sky You created on the first day of Creation is very beautiful; I wonder if it's become more beautiful since. You created it perfect, but if it's more beautiful now, it's Your fault. Thank You for beauty, God.

There were quite a lot of us out on the gallery. The men didn't dare to smoke. The children were quiet. We felt as if we weren't exactly on the Earth: as if we'd floated a little on our gallery, between Earth and the Moon. And it felt as if Earth was flying in the sky.

There was practically a crowd of us out on the gallery: Monsieur Philippe from the elections and Roméo the ice-cream man and Juste and Madame Juste and Roland and Réal and Gaston who make heels for ladies' shoes; there was Dorval who sells horses and all my brothers and sisters and the seminary student who's learning to read from a breviary and the thirteen Chabotte children. And then there were my friends Roger and Lapin. I'm pretty sure I've left out some but You saw them all, God, all sitting on the gallery and not talking.

Everybody was looking at the sky that had never been so bright. The sky was as blue as in the middle of the day. The sky above the village seemed as light as a curtain when the wind blows in. Behind the curtain, it was as if we could see You. It felt as if You were there. As we listened, it was as if we could hear You smoking Your pipe up in Heaven. But there wasn't any smoke: the sky was clean, without a cloud. In the cities, apparently, people never see the sky on account of the black clouds the factories make. I imagine people get out of the habit of looking at the sky, so they forget. Since people forget the things they don't see very often, they must forget You, too, God.

Our Uncle Marcel was sitting out on the gallery too. He was quiet because if he'd said anything, our grandmother who was out there too, rocking, would have told him to go and make his noise somewhere else. He'd been quiet for a long time. Even though there weren't any girls to admire him, our Uncle Marcel's hair was combed better than anybody's; he looked really sharp. Uncle Marcel's the best player in any game; he's the fastest runner; he's got the worst temper. If there's girls around, it's Uncle Marcel they like best, and that makes me proud.

Our Uncle Marcel isn't one of those people who walks by you with his nose in the air so he can't smell you, as if you were a cat turd. He's practically twice as old as I am, but sometimes he plays with me as if he wasn't an uncle and he was the same age as me. Sometimes we even have fights. We roll in the grass like real enemies, but we laugh, and then we roll some more and we bang into each other and give each other wrist burns and we kick and rip each other's shirts and hit our heads on the grass and put our hands around each other's necks and choke, but we choke from laughing, too. Sometimes I cry because I'm smaller and because Uncle Marcel is better. But I'm proud of our uncle, even though I never win a fight with him. I don't know anybody else that's got an uncle who plays with him and rolls in the grass all the way from the road down to the vegetable garden. Everybody else with uncles has old uncles who are bald and scared they'll fall down and break their bones and kick a bucket. I'm really proud of our Uncle Marcel. Sometimes I try to comb my hair like him. When I'm grown up like him I'll be the best, like him, and I'll have the worst temper like him and I'll hit the ball as far as he does. The girls will know I'm the best.

Our Uncle Marcel was looking at the Moon, too, and he was quiet. But then all of a sudden he talked. Beside the house You planted a willow tree, an old, old one that was there long before the house. It's way higher than the house and its trunk is as wide as my bed. Four or five other trunks are growing out of the first one. Sitting on one of its branches is like climbing on the back of our father's horse.

The Earth had turned, or maybe the Moon had moved, and Uncle Marcel said in my ear, so he wouldn't interrupt the other people's thinking:

"See that? The Moon's in the willow tree."

I looked with the eyes You gave me, God, and I saw the Moon in the willow tree, just like Uncle Marcel said.

"See? The Moon's up there on the biggest branch of the willow."

He said this in a whisper, and he was pointing at the Moon. Some of the people sitting on the gallery looked where his finger was pointing.

"Look, up there, leaning against the tip of the biggest branch: it's the Moon."

I stood up to get a better look. It was true. Uncle Marcel had noticed before any of the others that the Moon had stopped; she'd landed on the biggest branch. The Moon was hooked onto the end of the biggest branch, way up high above the roof of the house, higher than the chimney, almost as high as the church steeple, practically at the top of the willow.

"Yes, you're right," I said to our Uncle Marcel, "I can see the Moon perched at the very end of the biggest branch."

This time he spoke out loud:

"Want me to go up and get you a couple of handfuls of moon?"

"Yes," I told him, "I want three handfuls of moon, or four."

Everybody on the gallery heard our uncle, and they heard me answer. Everybody watched our uncle get out of his chair, walk down off the gallery, got to the willow, jump up, and then, with his neatly combed hair and his nice clean clothes, start to climb that tree, as limber as a cat, without mussing his hair. Everybody was watching our uncle, especially that Clémence Chabotte who'd just arrived, she's the sister of Juste Chabotte's boys. I was really proud of our Uncle Marcel. I didn't know anybody else with an uncle like mine, that could climb a willow tree to bring down a handful of moon for his nephew. I stood up so I could watch him better. He was already high up; I could see the leaves stirring and tossing higher and higher. And then, all of a sudden, very high up, almost at the very end of the big branch, I saw our uncle right beside the Moon. I saw him touch the Moon. And then I saw him pull off a handful, two handfuls, three handfuls of moon; I saw him scoop up some moon the way you scoop up water in your hand. I was so happy! I was going to have some pieces of the Moon! I didn't know anybody else that had pieces of moon. I'd take them to show at school. No other uncle would dare to go up as high as our Uncle Marcel. I was proud, God, prouder than I'd ever been in my whole life.

Our uncle climbed back down as easily as he'd gone up. He came back to the gallery, slowly and carefully because he was carrying moon dust. It was fragile, I told myself. It could die and turn grey like ashes. It could scatter in the wind. Our Uncle Marcel was being careful. He was protecting his harvest. He was taking tiny little steps. He was hardly lifting his feet as he came towards us, with both hands closed around his catch that seemed to want to fly away like a bird. When he got really close to me, our Uncle Marcel said very loud:

"Still want a piece of moon?"

"Yes!"

I was so happy, I almost shouted.

Everybody came over quietly, like in church, to get a look at the piece of moon our Uncle Marcel had gone to get me in the sky, at the tip of the willow tree. He told me:

"Count to three. At three I'll open my hands..."

I was a little bit scared. I'd never touched moon before. Was it cold like ice? Was it hot like bread? I got my own hands ready to move fast.

He counted: "One, two... three..."

Our Uncle Marcel's hands were partly open and I caught the piece of moon. It was cool and wet. Everybody was looking at me. I was looking at the piece of moon. It wasn't shiny. It was wet. Crumpled. I looked more closely. It wasn't shiny. It wasn't ashes. It wasn't moon. It was a handful of leaves. So then I yelled:

"That isn't moon, it's willow leaves."

They all burst out laughing as if I'd made some funny joke. Everybody. Even our Uncle Marcel, who never laughs for fear of mussing his hair. Even Your seminary student. Even that Clémence Chabotte, who must think her Marcel's the best. I burst into tears like a bomb. Honest, God, I've never cried so hard in my whole life.

When I'm very old I'll still remember that Moon. It's so sad when grown-ups play tricks on you. I'm going to stop praying to You now, God, and I'm going to cry into my pillow because I still haven't cried out all my sorrow.

The Witch Canoe

by

MARY ALICE DOWNIE

The author retells one of Quebec's most well-known folk tales, about the strange vessel known as "la chasse-galerie."

This, said my grandmother, is a tale that your grandfather experienced himself. I tell it in his very own words. Always he would begin:

> Cric, crac, girls and boys!
> *Parlons, parlee, parlow!*
> The whole thing if you want to know,
> (Pass the spittoon to Fiddler Joe!)
> *Sac-à-tabi, sac-à-tabac,*
> All who are deaf will please draw back.

I warn you now, I intend to begin my story by making a big sign of the cross. That will be a setback to the Devil, who always tries to snatch a poor shantyman's soul at this time of year by promising him all kinds of nonsense. I have seen enough in the shanties to understand all his tricks.

It was New Year's Eve many years ago in the depths of the forest in the Ross timber camp at the head of the Gatineau River. Winter had set in and the snow was already piled up to the roof of the shanty. The boss of the camp, as was the custom, had sent us a small barrel of Jamaica rum. Our Near Year's dinner was cooking on the stove; a *ragoût* of pig's feet it was. A big kettle half-full of molasses simmered on the fire. Later there was to be a candy-pull.

My comrades and I were gathered around the fireplace that night making merry, and if it is true that small rivulets make large rivers, it's just as true that small drinks empty large barrels. The rum was powerful enough, I can assure you. At about eleven o'clock I began to feel dizzy and I lay down on my buffalo robe to take a nap before the midnight jump we always took over the head of a pork-barrel from the old year into the new.

I had slept for quite a while when I was shaken awake by the second boss, Robert Vessot.

"Hormisdas," he said. "It's after midnight. You're late for the barrel-jump. Our comrades have gone to the other camps. But I'm going to Lavaltrie to see my sweetheart. Will you come with me?"

"To Lavaltrie!" I said. "Are you mad? It's 300 miles away. You can't travel that distance through the forest in two months when there aren't any roads beaten in the snow. And what about our work the day after tomorrow?"

"Imbecile! Don't you understand? We'll travel in our bark canoe. We'll be back in time for breakfast."

I understood. Robert wanted me to join him in running *la chasse-galerie*. I was to risk the salvation of my soul for the fun of going to Lavaltrie to give the girls a New Year's kiss. Now it was true that I wasn't much good. I didn't practise my religion and I took a drink too much now and then, but there was a big difference between that and selling my soul to the Devil.

"Not on your life!" I said. *"Pas un tonnerre!"*

"You're an old woman," Robert sneered. "There's no danger. We can go to Lavaltrie and be back in six hours. Don't you know that with *la chasse-galerie* we can travel 150 miles an hour? We must not pronounce the name of the good Lord during the voyage and we must be careful not to touch the crosses on the steeples when we travel. That should be easy enough. All a man has to do is look where he goes, think about what he says and not touch a drop of liquor on the way. I've made the trip five times and the Devil hasn't got me yet. Come, *mon vieux*, be brave and in two hours we'll be in Lavaltrie. There are already seven of us, but we have to be two, four, six or eight to make up the crew."

"That's all very well, but we must make a pact with the Devil and he's not the kind of merchant I want to bargain with."

"A mere formality, if we're careful where we go and don't drink. Come! Our comrades are waiting and the canoe is already in the clearing. Come, come!"

I went outside the shanty with Vessot and saw the six men waiting for us, paddle in hand. The large canoe lay on a snowbank. Before I had time to think twice I was seated in the bow waiting for the signal to leave. I felt confused, but Vessot gave me no time for reflection. He was a tough customer. It was whispered in the camp that he hadn't been to confession for seven years.

He stood in the stern.

"Are you ready?" he shouted.

"Ready!"

"Repeat after me:

"Satan! King of the infernal regions, we promise to sell our souls if within the next six hours we pronounce the name of the good Lord, your master and ours, or if we touch a cross on the voyage. On that condition you will transport us through the air wherever we may want to go and bring us back safe and sound to the shanty. *Acabris, Acabras, Acabram! Fais-nous voyager par-dessus les montagnes!*"

Scarcely had we said the last words when we felt the canoe rising in the air. Up, up, up it went to five or six hundred feet. I felt as light as a feather.

At Robert's command we began paddling like the sorcerers we were. With the first paddlestrokes, the canoe shot off like an arrow and up we went under the protective wing of the Devil himself. I could hear the bow of the canoe whizzing through the crisp night air.

We went faster than the wind. During the first fifteen minutes we sailed over the forest, seeing nothing but the dark heads of the great pines. It was a beautiful night. A full moon lit the sky like the midday sun, but it was very cold and our moustaches were frozen while our bodies were soaked with sweat. We paddled like demons at work in the place below.

Soon we saw a glistening belt of ice that shone like a mirror. It was the Gatineau River. Then we could make out the lights in the farmhouses. The tin-covered steeples passed under us as quickly as telegraph poles flash by a train; the spires shone in the air like the bayonets of soldiers drilling on the Champ de Mars in Quebec.

On we went, like a pack of devils. We flew over forests, rivers, towns and villages, leaving a trail of sparks behind us. Vessot, the madman, steered us because he knew the route; and soon we came to the Ottawa River. We followed it down to the Lac des Deux Montagnes.

"Look out!" Robert said. "We'll just skim over Montreal and frighten some of the fellows who are out later than they should be. Hormisdas, clear your whistle and sing us your best canoe song."

After the excitement of the trip, I was ready for anything. We could see the lights of Montreal already. With a skilful twist of his paddle Robert brought us down level with the towers of Notre-Dame. I cleared my throat and began. I meant to sing *"Canot d'écorce,"* but to my horror I heard myself singing another song, while my comrades joined in the chorus:

> "Satan our master fair,
> Heave us up in the air ...
> Wing, wang, wong!
> Wong, wang, wing!
> Drive us along
> On night's dark wing!"

Although it was nearly two o'clock in the morning, four men stopped in the middle of the street to watch us go by. We flew so fast that we passed Montreal in a twinkling. We began to count the steeples as we neared the end of our voyage: Longue-Pointe, Pointe-aux-Trembles, Repentigny, St.-Sulpice, until at last we saw the twin spires of Lavaltrie gleaming beyond the dark pines.

"Over there," Robert shouted. "We'll land on the edge of the wood in Jean-Jean-Gabriel's field. We'll go on foot from there and surprise them at the dance."

Five minutes later our canoe lay in a snowbank beside the wood and we trudged toward the village Indian-file. This was difficult, because the snow came up to our waists and there was no trace of a road.

We could see a light in Jean-Jean-Gabriel's house. Robert, who was the most daring of us, knocked on the door, but there was no one there except a servant. He told us the old folks had gone for a snack at Robillard's and the young people of the village were across the St. Lawrence at Wilfrid Auger's.

"Let's cross the river," said Robert. "We'll find our sweethearts there."

We went back to our canoe, reminding each other not to pronounce those words, to touch anything shaped like a cross or to take a drop of liquor. There were only four hours left. If we wanted to escape old Nick's clutches, we had to be back at the shanty before six o'clock. He wasn't the sort to let us off if we were late.

"Acabris, Acabras, Acabram! Fais-nous voyager par-dessus les montagnes," Robert shouted and off we went again, paddling through the air, renegades every one of us. We crossed the river in less time than it takes to tell it and landed in a snowbank close by Wilfrid Auger's house. We could hear the dancers laughing and see their shadows through the brightly lit windows.

We dragged our canoe to the river's edge and hid it among the hummocks made by the ice-shove.

"Now," Robert said. "No nonsense, do you hear? Dance as much as you like, but don't take a single glass of rum or whisky. At the first sign, follow me out. We can't be too careful."

He knocked loudly at the door. Old Wilfrid answered it himself and the guests welcomed us with open arms.

"Where do you come from?"

"I thought you were in the shanties up in the Gatineau."

"What makes you come so late?"

"Have a drink."

Robert came to our rescue. "Give us a chance to take our coats off and dance. That's what we came for. If you still feel curious in the morning, I'll answer all your questions then."

I had already spied a pretty girl, so I asked for the next dance, which was a four-handed reel. She accepted with a charming smile that made me forget I had risked the salvation of my soul for the pleasure of cutting pigeonwings as her partner. The dancing went on for two hours and if I say so myself, we shanty fellows cut a figure that made the hayseeds tired before morning. I was so busy with my partner that at first I didn't notice that Robert was visiting the sideboard rather often. It never occurred to me that he would get tipsy after all the lectures he had given *us*.

Four o'clock struck. My comrades began to edge out of the house, but I had to drag Robert away from the sideboard. We had just two hours to reach the camp and 300 miles to ride in our canoe, under Beelzebub's protection.

We left the dance like wild Indians without saying goodbye to anyone. We found our canoe safe in the hummocks, but we were all furious when we discovered that Vessot had been drinking. He was to steer the boat and that was no job for a drunken man.

The moon wasn't quite as bright as it had been when we left the camp. I was determined to keep a sharp lookout ahead for accidents.

"Steer straight for the mountain the minute you see Montreal," I said to Robert.

"I know my business," he growled. "You mind yours!"

What could I do? Before I had time to decide, he shouted:

"*Acabris, Acabras, Acabram! Fais-nous voyager par-dessus les montagnes!*"

Up we went again, like a bolt of lightning. We were steering southwest, if the wild way Robert managed our boat could be called steering.

We nearly shaved the steeple off the church of Contrecoeur, and instead of going west Robert took us toward the Richelieu River. Minutes later we were skimming over Beloeil Mountain. We came within ten feet of hitting the big cross that the bishop of Quebec had planted there.

"To the right, Robert! Go to the right, or you'll send us all to the Devil!"

Instinctively he turned and we headed straight for the mountain of Montreal. We could see it in the distance by the dim lights of the city.

I was frightened. If Robert kept on steering this way we'd never reach the Gatineau alive. The Devil was probably smacking his lips at the prospect of making a New Year's meal of us.

The disaster was not long in coming. While we were passing over the city Robert gave a loud yell. He flourished his paddle over his head and gave it a twist that sent us plunging into a snowdrift in a clearing on the mountain-side. Luckily for us, the snow was soft and we weren't hurt. The canoe wasn't injured either, but Robert got out and said he was going downtown to have a glass. We tried to reason with him but in vain. He would go down if the Devil himself were to grab him on the way.

I whispered to my companions and before Robert knew what we were doing, we had him down in the snow. We bound him hand and foot and put him in the bottom of the canoe. We gagged him too, to stop him from saying any words that might damn us.

"Acabris, Acabras, Acabram! Fais-nous voyager par-dessus les montagnes!"

Up we went again, this time steering straight for the Gatineau. I took Robert's place at the stern.

We had only an hour to reach camp and we all paddled for dear life and eternal salvation. We followed the Ottawa River as far as Pointe-Gatineau and then steered due north by the polar star. We were flying through the air until that rascal of a Robert managed to slip his bonds off and pull off his gag. Before we knew it, he was standing up in the canoe, paddle in hand, and swearing like a pagan. If he said a certain sacred word, our end had come. It was out of the question to calm his frenzy. We were floating over a pine forest only a few miles from camp. Our position was desperate. Robert was waving his paddle like a shillelagh, flourishing it so wildly that he threatened every moment to crush someone's head.

I was so excited that I made a false stroke with my paddle and let the canoe drop level with the pines. It struck the top of a big tree and tipped over. We all fell out and began dropping down from branch to branch like partridges. I don't know how long I took to come down because I fainted before we reached the ground. My last recollection was of dropping down a well without ever reaching bottom.

Next morning I awoke in my bunk! Some of our comrades had brought us back to the shanty. They had found us up to our necks in a snowbank at the foot of a monster pine tree.

No one was seriously hurt, but we were all bruised and scratched and there were several black eyes. Our companions said they found us sleeping off the effects of the night's frolic in the snow, and not one of us contradicted them.

It's not as amusing as some people might think to travel in

mid-air in the dead of winter under the guidance of Beelzebub, especially if you have a drunkard to steer your bark canoe. Take my advice and don't listen to anyone who tries to rope you in for such a trip. Wait until summer to visit your sweethearts, for it's better to run all the rapids of the Ottawa and the St. Lawrence on a raft than to travel in partnership with the Devil himself!

The Bear That Thought
He Was a Dog

by

C H A R L E S

G . D .   R O B E R T S

*This is one of the hundreds of stories by the poet and author who
made animal tales a hallmark of Canadian fiction.*

I

The gaunt, black mother lifted her head from nuzzling happily at the velvet fur of her little one. The cub was but twenty-four hours old, and engrossed every emotion of her savage heart; but her ear had caught the sound of heavy footsteps coming up the mountain. They were confident, fearless footsteps, taking no care whatever to disguise themselves, so she knew at once that they were the steps of the only creature that presumed to go so noisily through the great silences. Her heart pounded with anxious suspicion. She gave the cub a reassuring lick, deftly set it aside with her great paws, and thrust her head forth cautiously from the door of the den.

She saw a man—a woodsman in brownish-grey homespuns and heavy leg-boots, and with a gun over his shoulder—slouching up along the faintly marked trail which led close past her doorway. Her own great tracks on the trail had been obliterated that morning by a soft and thawing fall of belated spring snow—"the robin snow," as it is called in New Brunswick—and the man, absorbed in picking his way by this unfamiliar route over the mountain, had no suspicion that he was in danger of trespassing. But the bear, with that tiny black form at the bottom of the den filling her whole horizon, could not conceive that the man's approach had any other purpose than to rob her of her treasure. She ran back to the little one, nosed it gently into a corner, and anxiously pawed some dry leaves half over it. Then, her eyes aflame with rage and fear, she betook herself once more to the entrance, and crouched there motionless to await the coming of the enemy.

The man swung up the hill noisily, grunting now and again as his foothold slipped on the slushy, moss-covered stones. He fetched a huge breath of satisfaction as he gained a little strip of level ledge, perhaps a dozen feet in length, with a scrubby spruce bush growing at the other end of it. Behind the bush he made out what looked as if it might be the entrance to a little cave. Interested at once, he strode forward to examine it. At the first stride a towering black form, jaws agape and claws outstretched, crashed past the fir bush and hurled itself upon him.

A man brought up in the backwoods learns to think quickly, or, rather, to think and act in the same instant. Even as the great beast sprang, the man's gun leaped to its place and he fired. His charge was nothing more than heavy duck-shot, intended for some low-flying flock of migrant geese or brant. But at this close range, some seven or eight feet only, it tore through its target like a heavy mushroom bullet, and with a stopping force that halted the animal's charge in mid-air like the blow of a steam hammer. She fell in her tracks, a heap of huddled fur and grinning teeth:

"Gee," remarked the man, "that was a close call!" He ejected the empty shell and slipped in a fresh cartridge. Then he examined critically the warm heap of fur and teeth.

Perceiving that his victim was a mother, and also that her fur was rusty and ragged after the winter's sleep, sentiment and the sound utilitarianism of the backwoods stirred within him in a fine blend.

"Poor old beggar!" he muttered. "She must hev' a baby in yonder hole. That accounts for her kind of hasty ways. 'Most a pity I had to shoot her jest now, when she's out o' season an' her pelt not worth the job of strippin' it!"

Entering the half darkness of the cave, he quickly discovered the cub in its ineffectual hiding-place. Young as it was, when he picked it up, it whimpered with terror and struck out with its baby paws, recognizing the smell of an enemy. The man grinned indulgently at this display of spirit.

"Gee, but ye're chock-full o' ginger!" said he. And then, being of an understanding heart and an experimental turn of mind, he laid the cub down and returned to the body of the mother. With his knife he cut off several big handfuls of the shaggy fur and stuffed it into his pockets. Then he rubbed his hands, his sleeves, and the breast of his coat on the warm body.

"There, now," said he, returning to the cave and once more picking up the little one, "I've made ye an orphant, to be sure, but I'm goin' to soothe yer feelin's all I kin. Ye must make believe as how I'm yer mammy till I kin find ye a better one."

Pillowed in the crook of his captor's arm, and with his nose snuggled into a bunch of his mother's fur, the cub ceased to wonder at a problem too hard for him, and dozed off into an uneasy sleep. And the man, pleased with his new plaything, went gently that he might not disturb its slumber.

Now, it chanced that at Jabe Smith's farm, on the other side of the mountain, there had just been a humble tragedy. Jabe Smith's dog, a long-haired brown retriever, had been bereaved of her new-born puppies. Six of them she had borne, but five had been straightway taken from her and drowned; for Jabe, though compassionate of heart, had wisely decided that compassion would be too costly at the price of having his little clearing quite overrun with dogs. For two days, in her box in a corner of the dusky stable, the brown mother had wistfully poured out her tenderness upon the one remaining puppy; and then, when she had run into the house for a moment to snatch a bite of breakfast, one of Smith's big red oxen had strolled into the stable and blundered a great splay hoof into the box. That had happened in the morning; and all day the brown mother had moped, whimpering and whining, about the stable, casting long distraught glances at the box in the corner, which she was unwilling either to approach or to quite forsake.

When her master returned, and came and looked in hesitatingly at the stable door, the brown mother saw the small furry shape in the crook of his arm. Her heart yearned to it at once. She fawned upon the man coaxingly, lifted herself with her forepaws upon his coat, and reached up till she could lick the sleeping cub. Somewhat puzzled, Jabe Smith went and looked into the box. Then he understood.

"If you want the cub, Jinny, he's your'n all right. An' it saves me a heap o' bother."

II

Driven by his hunger, and reassured by the smell of the handful of fur which the woodsman left with him, the cub promptly accepted his adoption. She seemed very small, this new mother,

and she had a disquieting odour; but the supreme thing, in the
cub's eyes, was the fact she had something that assuaged his
appetite. The flavour, to be sure, was something new, and nov-
elty is a poor recommendation to babes of whatever kindred; but
all the cub really asked of milk was that it should be warm and
abundant. And soon, being assiduously licked and fondled, and
nursed till his little belly was round as a melon, he forgot the cave
on the mountainside and accepted Jabe Smith's barn as a quite
normal abode for small bears.

Jinny was natively a good mother. Had her own pups been left
to her, she would have lavished every care and tenderness upon
them during the allotted span of weeks, and then, with inex-
orable decision, she would have weaned and put them away for
their souls' good. But somewhere in her sturdy doggish make-up
there was a touch of temperament, of something almost approaching imagination, to which this strange foster-child of hers
appealed as no ordinary puppy could ever have done. She loved
the cub with a certain extravagance, and gave herself up to it
utterly. Even her beloved master fell into a secondary place, and
his household, of which she had hitherto held herself the
guardian, now seemed to her to exist merely for the benefit of
this black prodigy which she imagined herself to have produced.
The little one's astounding growth—for the cubs of the bear are
born very small, and so must lose no time in making up arrears
of stature—was an affair for which she took all credit to herself;
and she never thought of weaning him till he himself decided the
matter by preferring the solid dainties of the kitchen. When she
could no longer nurse him, however, she remained his devoted
comrade, playmate, satellite; and the cub, who was a roguish but
amiable soul, repaid her devotion by imitating her in all ways possible. The bear being by nature a very silent animal, her noisy

barking seemed always to stir his curiosity and admiration; but his attempts to imitate it resulted in nothing more than an occasional grunting *woof*. This throaty syllable, his only utterance besides the whimper which signalled the frequent demands of his appetite, came to be accepted as his name; and he speedily learned to respond to it.

Jabe Smith, as has been already pointed out, was a man of sympathetic discernment. In the course of no long time his discernment told him that Woof was growing up under the delusion that he was a dog. It was perhaps a convenience, in some ways, that he should not know he was a bear—he might be the more secure from troublesome ancestral suggestions. But as he appeared to claim all the privileges of his foster-mother, Jabe Smith's foreseeing eye considered the time, not far distant, when the sturdy and demonstrative little animal would grow to a giant of six or seven hundred pounds in weight, and still, no doubt, continue to think he was a dog. Jabe Smith began to discourage the demonstrativeness of Jinny, trusting her example would have the desired effect upon the cub. In particular, he set himself to remove from her mind any lingering notion that she would do for a lap-dog. He did not want any such notion as that to get itself established in Woof's young brain. Also, he broke poor Jinny at once of her affectionate habit of springing up and planting her forepaws upon his breast. That seemed to him a demonstration of ardour which, if practised by a seven-hundred-pound bear, might be a little overwhelming.

Jabe Smith had no children to complicate the situation. His family consisted merely of Mrs. Smith, a small but varying number of cats and kittens, Jinny, and Woof. Upon Mrs. Smith and the cats Woof's delusion came to have such effect that they, too, regarded him as a dog. The cats scratched him when he was little, and with equal confidence they scratched him when he was big.

Mrs. Smith, as long as she was in good humour, allowed him the freedom of the house, coddled him with kitchen titbits, and laughed when his affectionate but awkward bulk got in the way of her outbursts of mopping or her paroxysms of sweeping. But when storm was in the air, she regarded him no more than a black poodle. At the heels of the more nimble Jinny, he would be chased in ignominy from the kitchen door, with Mrs. Jabe's angry broom thwacking at the spot where Nature had forgotten to give him a tail. At such times Jabe Smith was usually to be seen smoking contemplatively on the woodpile, and regarding the abashed fugitives with sympathy.

This matter of a tail was one of the obstacles which Woof had to encounter in playing the part of a dog. He was indefatigable in his efforts to wag his tail. Finding no tail to wag, he did the best he could with his whole massive hind-quarters, to the discomfiture of all that got in the way. Yet, for all his clumsiness, his good will was so unchanging that none of the farmyard kindred had any dread of him, saving only the pig in his sty. The pig, being an incurable sceptic by nature, and, moreover, possessed of a keen and discriminating nose, persisted in believing him to be a bear and a lover of pork, and would squeal nervously at the sight of him. The rest of the farmyard folk accepted him at his own illusion, and appeared to regard him as a gigantic species of dog. And so, with nothing to mar his content but the occasional paroxysms of Mrs. Jabe's broom, Woof led the sheltered life and was glad to be a dog.

III

It was not until the autumn of his third year that Woof began to experience any discontent. Then, without knowing why, it seemed to him that there was something lacking in Jabe Smith's farmyard—even in Jabe Smith himself and in Jinny, his foster-mother. The smell of the deep woods beyond the pasture fields drew him strangely. He grew restless. Something called to him; something stirred in his blood and would not let him be still. And one morning, when Jabe Smith came out in the first pink and amber of daybreak to fodder the horses, he found that Woof had disappeared. He was sorry, but he was not surprised. He tried to explain to the dejected Jinny that they would probably have the truant back again before long. But he was no adept in the language of dogs, and Jinny, failing for once to understand, remained disconsolate.

Once clear of the outermost stump pastures and burnt lands, Woof pushed on feverishly. The urge that drove him forward directed him toward the half-barren, rounded shoulders of old Sugar Loaf, where the blueberries at this season were ripe and bursting with juice. Here in the gold-green, windy open, belly-deep in the low, blue-jewelled bushes, Woof feasted greedily; but he felt it was not berries that he had come for.

When, however, he came upon a glossy young she-bear, her fine black muzzle bedaubed with berry juice, his eyes were opened to the object of his quest. Perhaps he thought she, too, was a dog; but, if so, she was in his eyes a dog of incomparable charm, more dear to him, though a new acquaintance, than even little brown Jinny, his kind mother, had ever been. The stranger, though at first somewhat puzzled by Woof's violent efforts to wag a non-existent tail, apparently found her big wooer sympathetic. For the next few weeks, all through the golden, dreamy autumn of the New Brunswick woods, the two roamed together; and for the time Woof forgot the farm, his master, Jinny, and even Mrs. Jabe's impetuous broom.

But about the time of the first sharp frosts, when the ground was crisp with the new-fallen leaves, Woof and his mate began to lose interest in each other. She amiably forgot him and wandered off by herself, intent on nothing so much as satisfying her appetite, which had increased amazingly. It was necessary that she should load her ribs with fat to last her through her long winter's sleep in some cave or hollow tree. And as for Woof, once more he thought of Jabe Smith and Jinny, and the kind, familiar farmyard, and the delectable scraps from the kitchen, and the comforting smell of fried pancakes. What was the chill and lonely wilderness to him, a dog? He turned from grubbing up an ant stump and headed straight back for home.

When he got there, he found but a chimney standing naked and blackened over a tangle of charred ruins. A forest fire, some ten days back, had swept past that way, cutting a mile-wide swath through the woods and clean wiping out Jabe Smith's little homestead. It being too late in the year to begin rebuilding, the woodsman had betaken himself to the settlements for the winter, trusting to begin, in the spring, the slow repair of his fortunes.

Woof could not understand it at all. For a day he wandered disconsolately over and about the ruins, whining and sniffing, and filled with a sense of injury at being thus deserted. How glad he would have been to hear even the squeal of his enemy, the pig, or to feel the impetuous broom of Mrs. Jabe harassing his haunches! But even such poor consolation seemed to have passed beyond his ken. On the second day, being very hungry, he gave up all hope of bacon scraps, and set off to the woods to forage once more for himself.

As long as the actual winter held off, there was no great difficulty in this foraging. There were roots to be grubbed up, grubs, worms, and beetles, already sluggish with the cold, to be found under stones and logs, and ant-hills to be ravished. There were also the nests of bees and wasps, pungent but savoury. He was an expert in hunting the shy wood-mice, lying patiently in wait for them beside their holes and obliterating them, as they came out, with a lightning stroke of his great paw. But when the hard frosts came, sealing up the moist turf under a crust of steel, and the snows, burying the mouse-holes under three or four feet of white fluff, then he was hard put to it for a living. Every day or two, in his distress, he would revisit the clearing and wander sorrowfully among the snow-clad ruins, hoping against hope that his vanished friends would presently return.

It was in one of the earliest of these melancholy visits that Woof first encountered a male of his own species, and showed how far he was from any consciousness of kinship. A yearling heifer of Jabe Smith's, which had escaped from the fire and fled far into the wilderness, chanced to find her way back. For several weeks she had managed to keep alive on such dead grass as she could paw down to through the snow, and on such twigs of birch and poplar as she could manage to chew. Now, a mere ragged bag of bones, she stood in the snow behind the ruins, her eyes wild with hunger and despair.

Her piteous mooings caught the ear of a hungry old he-bear who was hunting in the woods near by. He came at once, hopefully. One stroke of his armed paw on the unhappy heifer's neck put a period to her pains, and the savage old prowler fell to his meal.

But, as it chanced, Woof also had heard, from a little further off, that lowing of the disconsolate heifer. To him it had come as a voice from the good old days of friendliness and plenty and impetuous brooms, and he had hastened toward the sound with new hope in his heart. He came just in time to see, from the edge of the clearing, the victim stricken down.

One lesson Woof had well learned from his foster-mother, and that was the obligation resting upon every honest dog to protect his master's property. The unfortunate heifer was undoubtedly the property of Jabe Smith. In fact, Woof knew her as a young beast who had often shaken her budding horns at him. Filled with righteous wrath, he rushed forward and hurled himself upon the slayer.

The latter was one of those morose old males, who, having forgotten or outgrown the comfortable custom of hibernation, are doomed to range the wilderness all winter. His temper, therefore, was raw enough in any case. At this flagrant interference with his own lawful kill, it flared to fury. His assailant was bigger than he, better nourished, and far stronger; but for some minutes he put up a fight which, for swift ferocity, almost daunted the hitherto unawakened spirit of Woof. A glancing blow of the stranger's, however, on the side of Woof's snout—only the remnant of a spent stroke, but enough to produce an effect on that most sensitive centre of a bear's dignity—and there was a sudden change in the conditions of the duel. Woof, for the first time in his life, saw red. It was a veritable berserk rage, this virgin outburst of his. His adversary simply went down like a rag baby before it, and was mauled to abject submission, in the smother of the snow, inside of half a minute. Feigning death, which, indeed, was no great feigning for him at that moment, he succeeded in deceiving the unsophisticated Woof, who drew back upon his haunches to consider his triumph. In that second the vanquished one writhed nimbly to his feet and slipped off apologetically through the snow. And Woof, placated by his victory, made no attempt to follow. The ignominies of Mrs. Jabe's broom were wiped out.

When Woof's elation had somewhat subsided, he laid himself down beside the carcass of the dead heifer. As the wind blew on that day, this corner of the ruins was a nook of shelter. Moreover, the body of the red heifer, dead and dilapidated though it was, formed in his mind a link with the happy past. It was Jabe Smith's property, and he got a certain comfort from lying beside it and guarding it for his master. As the day wore on, and his appetite grew more and more insistent, in an absent-minded way he began to gnaw at the good red meat beside him. At first, to be sure, this gave him a guilty conscience, and from time to time he would glance up nervously, as if apprehending the broom. But soon immunity brought confidence, his conscience ceased to trouble him, and the comfort derived from the nearness of the red heifer was increased exceedingly.

As long as the heifer lasted, Woof stuck faithfully to his post as guardian, and longer, indeed. For nearly two days after the remains had quite disappeared—save for horns and hoofs and such bones as his jaws could not crush—he lingered. Then at last, urged by a ruthless hunger, and sorrowfully convinced that there was nothing more he could do for Jabe or Jabe for him, he set off again on his wanderings.

About three weeks later, forlorn of heart and exigent of belly, Woof found himself in a part of the forest where he had never been before. But someone else had been there; before him was a broad trail, just such as Jabe Smith and his wood sled used to make. Here were the prints of horses' hooves. Woof's heart bounded hopefully. He hurried along down the trail. Then a faint, delectable savour, drawn across the sharp, still air, met his nostrils. Pork and beans—oh, assuredly! He paused for a second to sniff the fragrance again, and then lurched onwards at a rolling gallop. He rounded a turn of the trail, and there before him stood a logging camp.

To Woof a human habitation stood for friendliness and food and shelter. He approached, therefore, without hesitation.

There was no sign of life about the place, except for the smoke rising liberally from the stove-pipe chimney. The door was shut, but Woof knew that doors frequently opened if one scratched at them and whined persuasively. He tried it, then stopped to listen for an answer. The answer came—a heavy, comfortable snore from within the cabin. It was mid-morning, and the camp cook, having got his work done up, was sleeping in his bunk the while the dinner was boiling.

Woof scratched and whined again. Then, growing impatient, he reared himself on his haunches in order to scratch with both paws at once. His luck favoured him, for he happened to scratch on the latch. It lifted, the door swung open suddenly, and he half fell across the threshold. He had not intended so abrupt an entrance, and he paused, peering with diffidence and hope into the homely gloom.

The snoring had stopped suddenly. At the rear of the cabin Woof made out a large, round, startled face, fringed with scanty red whiskers and a mop of red hair, staring at him from over the edge of an upper bunk. Woof had hoped to find Jabe Smith there. But this was a stranger, so he suppressed his impulse to rush in and wallow delightedly before the bunk. Instead of that, he came only halfway over the threshold, and stood there making those violent contortions which he believed to be wagging his tail.

To a cool observer of even the most limited intelligence it would have been clear that these contortions were intended to be conciliatory. But the cook of Conroy's Camp was taken by surprise, and he was not a cool observer—in fact, he was frightened. A gun was leaning against the wall below the bunk. A large, hairy hand stole forth, reached down and clutched the gun.

Woof wagged his haunches more coaxingly than ever, and took another hopeful step forward. Up went the gun. There was a blue-white spurt, and the report clashed deafeningly within the narrow quarters.

The cook was a poor shot at any time, and at this moment he was at a special disadvantage. The bullet went close over the top of Woof's head and sang waspishly across the clearing. Woof turned and looked over his shoulder to see what the man had fired at. If anything was hit, he wanted to go and get it and fetch it for the man, as Jabe and Jinny had taught him to do. But he could see no result of the shot. He whined deprecatingly and ventured all the way into the cabin.

The cook felt desperately for another cartridge. There was none to be found. He remembered that they were all in the chest by the door. He crouched back in the bunk, making himself as small as possible, and hoping that a certain hunk of bacon on the bench by the stove might divert the terrible stranger's attention and give him a chance to make a bolt for the door.

But Woof had not forgotten either the good example of Jinny or the discipline of Mrs. Jabe's broom. Far be it from him to help himself without leave. But he was very hungry. Something must be done to win the favour of the strangely unresponsive round-faced man in the bunk. Looking about him anxiously, he espied a pair of greasy cowhide "larrigans" lying on the floor near the door. Picking one up in his mouth, after the manner of his retriever foster-mother, he carried it over and laid it down, as a humble offering, beside the bunk.

Now, the cook, though he had been undeniably frightened, was by no means a fool. This touching gift of one of his own larrigans opened his eyes and his heart. Such a bear, he was assured, could harbour no evil intentions. He sat up in his bunk.

"Hullo!" said he. "What ye doin' here, sonny? What d'ye want o' me, anyhow?"

The huge black beast wagged his hind-quarters frantically and wallowed on the floor in his fawning delight at the sound of a human voice.

"Seems to think he's a kind of a dawg," muttered the cook thoughtfully. And then the light of certain remembered rumours broke upon his memory.

"I'll be jiggered," said he, "ef 'tain't that there tame b'ar Jabe Smith, over to East Fork, used to have afore he was burnt out!"

Climbing confidently from the bunk, he proceeded to pour a generous portion of molasses over the contents of the scrap pail, because he knew that bears had a sweet tooth. When the choppers and drivers came trooping in for dinner, they were somewhat taken aback to find a huge bear sleeping beside the stove. As the dangerous-looking slumberer seemed to be in the way— none of the men caring to sit too close to him—to their amazement the cook smacked the mighty hind-quarters with the flat of his hand, and bundled him unceremoniously into a corner. "'Pears to think he's some kind of a dawg," explained the cook, "so I let him come along in for company. He'll fetch yer larrigans an' socks an' things fer ye. An' it makes the camp a sight homier, havin' somethin' like a cat or a dawg about."

"Right you are!" agreed the boss. "But what was that noise we heard, along about an hour back? Did you shoot anything?"

"Oh, that was jest a little misunderstandin', before him an' me got acquainted," explained the cook, with a trace of embarrassment. "We made it up all right."

Dreams

by

B U D G E   W I L S O N

A story that reflects the author's recurrent interest in the bittersweet period between childhood and adulthood.

I was sixteen years old when he took my dream away from me. It is not a small offence to be a stealer of dreams.

Our family lived in Mackerel Cove, a small fishing village on the South Shore of Nova Scotia. When I tell people that, when I point out the exact location, they look at me with a puzzled, almost incredulous expression. Sometimes that look is all I get. Other times, they give voice to their astonishment. "But how did you become what you are? How did you get from there to here?"

What do they think goes on in small fishing communities? Nothing? Do they assume that such places contain people with no brains, no ambition, no dreams? They look at me as though my skin had just turned green. As though I'd been cast in some inferior mould and had, by some miracle of agility or cussedness, found a way to jump out of it. By the time those questions started, I was a junior executive in an oil company, in the days before oil became a questionable commodity—in Toronto, where the mould is often even more fixed than elsewhere.

When I was a boy of eleven, the horizon was endless, physically and metaphorically. From our yellow frame house—which was perched on a hill, without the protection or impediment of trees— you could view the wide sea, stretching from the rocky point and behind Granite Island, disappearing beyond the edge of the sky, inviting dreams of any dimension. And in the foreground, four reefs threw their huge waves up into the air—wild, free.

I spent a lot of time sitting on the woodpile—when I was supposed to be cutting wood, piling wood, or carting wood— looking at that view. And thinking. Planning. Rumour had it that if you drew a straight line from our front door, right through the centre of that horizon, the line would eventually end up on the west coast of North Africa. How can Torontonians conclude that such an environment is limiting? They're lucky if they can see through the smog to the end of the block. I could go straight from the woodpile to Africa. Or I could turn left and wind up in Portugal.

And the wind. On that hill, where my great-grandfather had had the vision to build his house, the wind was always a factor. Even when it was not blowing. Then my mother would emerge into the sunshine or the fog, and take a deep breath. "Gone," she would announce. She hated the wind. She was from near Truro, where the slow, muddy Salmon River just limps along its banks, shining brown and slithery in the dead air. Dead air— that's what inlanders seem to want. Then they feel safe. Or peaceful. But those were two words that meant nothing to me at that time.

What is it about kids that makes them so blind and deaf for

so long? Some of them, anyway. How can they go charging into life with such a certainty that all is well? Without, in fact, a passing thought as to whether it is or is not? It's just there. Mackerel are for jigging, the sea is for swimming, a boat is for rowing around in. The gulls are for watching, particularly on those days when the wind is up, when they just hang high in the air, motionless, wings wide, riding the storm. I was like that when I was eleven, sailing along with no effort, unconscious of the currents and turbulence that surrounded me.

Twelve seems to be a favourite time for waking up. What is so special about twelve that makes it such a hazardous, such a brittle age? No doubt it's partly because of all those puberty things—those unseen forces that begin to churn up your body, making it vulnerable to dangers that didn't even seem to exist before that time. And with the body, so goes the head and the heart.

All of a sudden (it really did seem to start happening all within the space of a day), I began to hear things. Things like the edge in my mother's voice, the ragged sound of my father's anger. Where had I been before? Too busy on the woodpile, in the boats, at the beach—*outside.* Or when inside, shut off by comic books, TV, the all-absorbing enjoyment of food. And lots of arguing and horsing around with my brothers and sisters, of whom there were five. But, now, suddenly, the wind blew, and I heard it.

Once you have heard those sounds, your ears are permanently unplugged, and you cannot stop them up again. Same thing with the eyes. I began to see my mother's face as an objective thing. Not just *my mother*, a warm and blurry concept, but a face to watch and think about and read. It was pinched, dry-looking, with two vertical lines between the brows. Much of the time, I saw, she looked anxious or disenchanted. I didn't know the meaning of that word, back then, but I recognized the condition. She was thin and pale of skin—probably because she didn't like to be out in the wind—with a head of defeated-looking thin brown hair. I saw that for the first time, too.

Within twenty-four hours of my awakening, I felt that I had discovered and recognized everything. My mother, I knew, was worried about money—or about the extreme scarcity of it. That seemed a waste of time to me. There were fish in the sea, vegetables in the garden, loaves of bread in the oven, and second-hand clothes to be had at Frenchy's. But look again. Not just worry. Something else. And that, I knew, had to do with my father. I watched very carefully. He didn't ask for things. He demanded. "Gimme the sugar." "Let the dog out." "Eat your damn vegetables." He didn't praise. He criticized. "This soup is too cold." "There's a rip in them pants." And on pickling day, "Too blasted hot in this kitchen." As he made each one of these remarks, I would see a small contraction in those vertical lines on my mother's forehead. Not much, but to me it was an electric switch. I was aware of a connection.

With this new and unwelcome knowledge, I watched the other kids to assess their reactions. But they were younger than I was. So there was nothing much to watch. They continued to gabble on among themselves, giggling, pushing, yelling at one another. Even when my father would shout, "Shut up, damn you!" they'd all just disperse, regroup, and continue on as before. Well, not quite all. I focused on Amery, aged seven, eyes wide and bright, chewing on his nails. Awake, too, I thought, and felt a kinship with him.

My father didn't work as a fisherman in our little village. He was employed in the fish plant, gutting fish. Slash and gut, slash and gut, eight hours a day, five days a week, fifty weeks a year. Enough to limit the vision of any Bay Street Torontonian. I heard people in our village talk about what it was like to work with him. "A real jewel of a man," said one woman to my mother. "Patient, and right considerate. Always ready to help out." I looked at Ma while the woman was talking. I was thirteen by then, and very skilful at reading faces. She's struggling, I concluded, to keep the scorn out of her face. It was a fixed mask, telling nothing—except to me. A man friend of Pa's once said to me, "I sure hope you realize how lucky you are to have a father like him. He's some kind. A real soft-spoken man." I said nothing, and adjusted my own mask. When my father had left the house that morning, he'd yelled back at my mother, "Get your confounded books off the bed before I get home tonight! I'm sick of you with your smart-ass ways!" Then he'd slammed the door so hard that a cup fell off the shelf.

My dream was a simple one. Or so it may seem to you. I wanted to be the most talented fisherman in Mackerel Cove. Talented! I can see the incredulous looks on the faces of my Toronto colleagues. Do they really think that the profession of fishing is just a matter of throwing down a line or a net, and hauling up a fish? A good fisherman knows his gear, his boats, his machinery, the best roots to use when making lobster traps. He knows how to sniff the air and observe the sky for signs of unforecasted winds and fogs. He knows his bait, his times of day, his sea bottom, the choices of where to go and how soon. A talented fisherman knows all these things and much more. And—in spite of the wrenching cold, the disappointments, the flukey comings and goings of the fish population—he loves what he is doing with his life. I know this to be true. I spent half my boyhood tagging along with any local fishermen who'd put up with me—on their Cape Island boats, their Tancooks, or just in their dories.

No one on Bay Street can describe to you the feeling of setting out through a band of sunrise on the water, trailing five seine boats, a faint wind rising. Or the serenity that fills your chest as you strike out to sea, aimed at the dead centre of the horizon, focused on Africa. That's what I'd longed and hoped for from the time I was five years old. At sixteen, it was still my dream.

The exam results came in, just four days before my seventeenth birthday. I stood at the mailbox, holding my marks—the highest in grade twelve for the whole of the county. And more. The biggest university scholarship for that region, puffed out with some fat subsistence money donated by a local boy who'd made good on Wall Street. I took all of it and laid it on the kitchen table.

"I don't want it," is all I said.

My father and mother looked at the marks, read the letter, raised their eyes and looked at me. My mother had her mask on. Not my father.

"What in blazing hell do you mean—you don't *want* it?"

"I don't want to go to college. I want to stay here. I want to be a fisherman. The best one around. It's what I've always wanted, ever since I laid eyes on a boat."

My father stood up. He was skinny, but he looked big that day. With one abrupt gesture, he swept everything off the kitchen table onto the floor—four coffee mugs, *The Daily News*, cutlery, Ma's books, a pot with a geranium in it, a loaded ashtray.

"You want to be a fisherman!" he shouted. "Us with no gear, no wharf, no shed, no launch. Not even a decent size boat. No, young fella! You turn down that offer and you got but one route to take. Me, I'll teach you how to do it, because I'm the best gutter in the plant."

He paused for a breath. Then again—"*No*, dammit! You just

pitch out your fancy dreams and grab that scholarship, because I'm sure not gonna keep you here any longer come fall. Not if you can make money with that fool book-learning that your prissy ma seems to have passed along with her mother's milk." He smashed his fist down on the empty table, and kicked his way out the back door.

Ma died when I was twenty-four, just one week before I received my MBA from the University of Toronto. I'd picked up two other degrees on the way, and had sailed through university with accolades and scholarships. There I was, half an orphan, embarking on a life of prosperity and maladjustment, cut off by my past and my present from my original dream.

I skipped graduation and flew home for the funeral. I stayed three weeks. Pa was silent and shrunken-looking, although he was only fifty-five. He sat around a lot, guzzling beer, going through two packs of cigarettes a day. The only kid left at home was Amery, and he looked as though he'd like nothing better than to jump ship. Thin and fidgety, he'd startle if you so much as snapped your fingers. He was working in the plant, too. Gutting.

"Thinkin' o' closin' down the plant," said Pa, one day. "No fish worth a darn. Most o' the time, anyways. Foreign vessels scoopin' 'em all up before they has a chance to spawn."

He didn't say this angrily. He said it wearily, as though he had nothing but lukewarm water flowing through his veins. And no blood transfusion in sight.

The day I left, I waited until Amery and Pa had departed for work. Then I went out and sat on the woodpile. The offshore wind was blowing strong and dry, and the gulls were coasting around in the sky, wings spread, barely twitching. The sun was well up, casting a wide path over the ruffled water. While I watched, a Cape Islander crossed the path, low in the water with a big catch of mackerel. In the distance, the horizon stretched taut and firm, broken by the leaping waves of the four reefs.

I searched in vain for Africa. Apparently it wasn't there any more.

Prince
EDWARD
iSLand

from

Emily of New Moon

by

L. M. MONTGOMERY

Emily, orphaned after the death of her father, is taken to live at New Moon by her aunts and cousin. The "Emily" trilogy is vivid testimony to Montgomery's love for her island.

Emily found the drive through the blossomy June world pleasant. Nobody talked much; even Saucy Sal had subsided into the silence of despair; now and then Cousin Jimmy made a remark, more to himself, as it seemed, than to anybody else. Sometimes Aunt Elizabeth answered it, sometimes not. She always spoke crisply and used no unnecessary words.

They stopped in Charlottetown and had dinner. Emily, who had had no appetite since her father's death, could not eat the roast beef which the boarding-house waitress put before her. Whereupon Aunt Elizabeth whispered mysteriously to the waitress, who went away and presently returned with a plateful of delicate, cold chicken—fine white slices, beautifully trimmed with lettuce frills.

"Can you eat *that?*" said Aunt Elizabeth sternly, as to a culprit at the bar.

"I'll—try," whispered Emily.

She was too frightened just then to say more, but by the time she had forced down some of the chicken she had made up her small mind that a certain matter must be put right.

"Aunt Elizabeth," she said.

"Hey, what?" said Aunt Elizabeth, directing her steel-blue eyes straight at her niece's troubled ones.

"I would like you to understand," said Emily, speaking very primly and precisely so that she would be sure to get things right, "that it was not because I did not like the roast beef I did not eat it. I was not hungry at all; and I just et some of the chicken to oblige you, not because I liked it any better."

"Children should eat what is put before them and never turn up their noses at good, wholesome food," said Aunt Elizabeth severely. So Emily felt that Aunt Elizabeth had not understood after all and she was unhappy about it.

After dinner Aunt Elizabeth announced to Aunt Laura that they would do some shopping.

"We must get some things for the child," she said.

"Oh, please don't call me 'the child,'" exclaimed Emily. "It makes me feel as if I didn't belong anywhere. Don't you like my name, Aunt Elizabeth? Mother thought it so pretty. And I don't need any 'things.' I have two whole sets of underclothes—only one is patched—"

"S-s-sh!" said Cousin Jimmy, gently kicking Emily's shins under the table.

Cousin Jimmy only meant that she would better let Aunt Elizabeth buy "things" for her when she was in the humour for it; but Emily thought he was rebuking her for mentioning such matters as underclothes and subsided in scarlet conviction. Aunt Elizabeth went on talking to Laura as if she had not heard.

"She must not wear that cheap black dress in Blair Water. You could sift oatmeal through it. It is nonsense expecting a child of ten to wear black at all. I shall get her a nice white dress with black sash for good, and some black-and-white-check gingham for school. Jimmy, we'll leave the child with you. Look after her."

Cousin Jimmy's method of looking after her was to take her to a restaurant down street and fill her up with ice-cream. Emily had never had many chances at ice-cream and she needed no urging, even with lack of appetite, to eat two saucerfuls. Cousin Jimmy eyed her with satisfaction.

"No use my getting anything for you that Elizabeth could see," he said. "But she can't see what is inside of you. Make the most of your chance, for goodness alone knows when you'll get any more."

"Do you never have ice-cream at New Moon?"

Cousin Jimmy shook his head.

"Your Aunt Elizabeth doesn't like new-fangled things. In the house, we belong to fifty years ago, but on the farm she has to give way. In the house—candles; in the dairy, her grandmother's big pans to set the milk in. But, pussy, New Moon is a pretty good place after all. You'll like it some day."

"Are there any fairies there?" asked Emily, wistfully.

"The woods are full of em," said Cousin Jimmy. "And so are the columbines in the old orchard. We grow columbines there on purpose for the fairies."

Emily sighed. Since she was eight she had known there were no fairies anywhere nowadays; yet she hadn't quite given up the hope that one or two might linger in old-fashioned, out-of-the-way spots. And where so likely as at New Moon?

"Really-truly fairies?" she questioned.

"Why, you know, if a fairy was really-truly it wouldn't *be* a fairy," said Uncle Jimmy seriously. "Could it, now?"

Before Emily could think this out the aunts returned and soon they were all on the road again. It was sunset when they came to Blair Water—a rosy sunset that flooded the long, sandy sea-coast with colour and brought red road and fir-darkened hill out in fleeting clearness of outline. Emily looked about her on her new environment and found it good. She saw a big house peering whitely through a veil of tall old trees—no mushroom growth of yesterday's birches but trees that had loved and been loved by three generations—a glimpse of silver water glistening through the dark spruces—that was the Blair Water itself, she knew—and a tall, golden-white church spire shooting up above the maple woods in the valley below. But it was none of these that brought her the flash—*that* came with the sudden glimpse of the dear, friendly, little dormer window peeping through vines on the roof—and right over it, in the opalescent sky, a real new moon, golden and slender. Emily was tingling all over with it as Cousin Jimmy lifted her from the buggy and carried her into the kitchen.

She sat on a long wooden bench that was satin-smooth with age and scrubbing, and watched Aunt Elizabeth lighting candles here and there, in great, shining, brass candlesticks—on the shelf between the windows, on the high dresser where the row of blue and white plates began to wink her a friendly welcome, on the long table in the corner. And as she lighted them, elvish "rabbits' candles" flashed up amid the trees outside the windows.

Emily had never seen a kitchen like this before. It had dark wooden walls and low ceiling, with black rafters crossing it, from which hung hams and sides of bacon and bunches of herbs and new socks and mittens, and many other things, the names and uses of which Emily could not imagine. The sanded floor was spotlessly white, but the boards had been scrubbed away through

the years until the knots in them stuck up all over in funny little bosses, and in front of the stove they had sagged, making a
queer, shallow little hollow. In one corner of the ceiling was a
large square hole which looked black and spookish in the candlelight, and made her feel creepy. *Something* might pop down out
of a hole like that if one hadn't behaved just right, you know. And
candles cast such queer wavering shadows. Emily didn't know
whether she liked the New Moon kitchen or not. It was an interesting place—and she rather thought she would like to describe
it in the old account book, if it hadn't been burned—but Emily
suddenly found herself trembling on the verge of tears.

"Cold?" said Aunt Laura kindly. "These June evenings are
chilly yet. Come into the sitting-room—Jimmy has kindled a
fire in the stove there."

Emily, fighting desperately for self-control, went into the
sitting-room. It was much more cheerful than the kitchen. The
floor was covered with gay-striped homespun, the table had a
bright crimson cloth, the walls were hung with pretty, diamond-
patterned paper, the curtains were of wonderful pale-red damask
with a design of white ferns scattered all over them. They looked
very rich and imposing and Murray-like. Emily had never seen
such curtains before. But best of all were the friendly gleams
and flickers from the jolly hardwood fire in the open stove that
mellowed the ghostly candlelight with something warm and
rosy-golden. Emily toasted her toes before it and felt reviving
interest in her surroundings. What lovely little leaded glass
doors closed the china closets on either side of the high, black,
polished mantel! What a funny, delightful shadow the carved
ornament on the sideboard cast on the wall behind it—just like
a negro's side-face, Emily decided. What mysteries might lurk
behind the chintz-lined glass doors of the bookcase! Books were

Emily's friends wherever she found them. She flew over to the bookcase and opened the door. But before she could see more than the backs of rather ponderous volumes, Aunt Elizabeth came in with a mug of milk and a plate whereon lay two little oatmeal cakes.

"Emily," said Aunt Elizabeth sternly, "shut that door. Remember that after this you are not to meddle with things that don't belong to you."

"I thought books belonged to everybody," said Emily.

"Ours don't," said Aunt Elizabeth, contriving to convey the impression that New Moon books were in a class by themselves. "Here is your supper, Emily. We are all so tired that we are just having a lunch. Eat it and then we will go to bed."

Emily drank the milk and worried down the oat-cakes, still gazing about her. How pretty the wallpaper was, with the garland of roses inside the gilt diamond! Emily wondered if she could "see it in the air." She tried—yes, she could—there it hung, a yard from her eyes, a little fairy pattern, suspended in mid-air like a screen. Emily had discovered that she possessed this odd knack when she was six. By a certain movement of the muscles of her eyes, which she could never describe, she could produce a tiny replica of the wallpaper in the air before her—could hold it there and look at it as long as she liked—could shift it back and forth, to any distance she chose, making it larger or smaller as it went farther away or came nearer. It was one of her secret joys when she went into a new room anywhere to "see the paper in the air." And this New Moon paper made the prettiest fairy paper she had ever seen.

"What are staring at nothing in that queer way for?" demanded Aunt Elizabeth, suddenly returning.

Emily shrank into herself. She couldn't explain to Aunt Elizabeth—Aunt Elizabeth would be like Ellen Greene and say she was "crazy."

"I—I wasn't staring at nothing."

"Don't contradict. I say you were," retorted Aunt Elizabeth. "Don't do it again. It gives your face an unnatural expression. Come now—we will go upstairs. You are to sleep with me."

Emily gave a gasp of dismay. She had hoped it might be with Aunt Laura. Sleeping with Aunt Elizabeth seemed a very formidable thing. But she dared not protest. They went up to Aunt Elizabeth's big, sombre bedroom where there was dark, grim wallpaper that could never be transformed into a fairy curtain, a high black bureau, topped with a tiny swing-mirror, so far above her that there could be no Emily-in-the-glass, tightly closed windows with dark-green curtains, a high bedstead with a dark-green canopy, and a huge, fat, smothering featherbed, with high, hard pillows.

Emily stood still, gazing about her.

"Why don't you get undressed?" asked Aunt Elizabeth.

"I—I don't like to undress before you," faltered Emily.

Aunt Elizabeth looked at Emily through her cold, spectacled eyes.

"Take off your clothes, *at once*," she said.

Emily obeyed, tingling with anger and shame. It was abominable—taking off her clothes while Aunt Elizabeth stood and watched her. The outrage of it was unspeakable. It was even harder to say her prayers before Aunt Elizabeth. Emily felt that it was not much good to pray under such circumstances. Father's God seemed very far away and she suspected that Aunt Elizabeth's was too much like Ellen Greene's.

"Get into bed," said Aunt Elizabeth, turning down the clothes.

Emily glanced at the shrouded window.

"Aren't you going to open the window, Aunt Elizabeth?"

Aunt Elizabeth looked at Emily as if the latter had suggested removing the roof.

"Open the window—and let in the night air!" she exclaimed. "Certainly not!"

"Father and I always had our window open," cried Emily.

"No wonder he died of consumption," said Aunt Elizabeth. "Night air is poison."

"What air is there at night but night air?" asked Emily.

"Emily," said Aunt Elizabeth icily, "get—into—bed."

Emily got in.

But it was utterly impossible to sleep, lying there in that engulfing bed that seemed to swallow her up, with that cloud of blackness above her and not a gleam of light anywhere—and Aunt Elizabeth lying beside her, long and stiff and bony.

"I feel as if I was in bed with a griffin," thought Emily. "Oh—oh—oh—I'm going to cry—I know I am."

Desperately and vainly she strove to keep the tears back—they *would* come. She felt utterly alone and lonely—there in that darkness, with an alien, hostile world all around her—for it seemed hostile now. And there was such a strange, mysterious, mournful sound in the air—far away, yet clear. It was the murmur of the sea, but Emily did not know that and it frightened her. Oh, for her little bed at home—oh, for Father's soft breathing in the room—oh, for the dancing friendliness of well-known stars shining down through her open window! She *must* go back—she couldn't stay here—she would never be happy here! But there wasn't any "back" to go to—no home—no father—. A great sob burst from her—another followed and then another. It was no use to clench her hands and set her teeth—and chew the inside of her cheeks—nature conquered pride and determination and had her way.

"What are you crying for?" asked Aunt Elizabeth.

To tell the truth Aunt Elizabeth felt quite as uncomfortable and disjointed as Emily did. She was not used to a bedfellow; she didn't want to sleep with Emily any more than Emily wanted to sleep with her. But she considered it quite impossible that the child should be put off by herself in one of the big, lonely New Moon rooms; and Laura was a poor sleeper, easily disturbed; children always kicked, Elizabeth Murray had heard. So there was nothing to do but take Emily in with her; and when she had sacrificed comfort and inclination to do her unwelcome duty this ungrateful and unsatisfactory child was not contented.

"I asked you what you were crying for, Emily?" she repeated.

"I'm—homesick, I guess," sobbed Emily.

Aunt Elizabeth was annoyed.

"A nice home you had to be homesick for," she said sharply.

"It—it wasn't as elegant—as New Moon," sobbed Emily, "but—*Father* was there. I guess I'm Father-sick, Aunt Elizabeth. Didn't you feel awfully lonely when *your* father died?"

Elizabeth Murray involuntarily remembered the ashamed, smothered feeling of relief when old Archibald Murray had died—the handsome, intolerant, autocratic old man who had ruled his family with a rod of iron all his life and had made existence at New Moon miserable with the petulant tyranny of the five years of invalidism that had closed his career. The surviving Murrays had behaved impeccably, and wept decorously, and printed a long and flattering obituary. But had one genuine feeling of regret followed Archibald Murray to his tomb? Elizabeth did not like the memory and was angry with Emily for evoking it.

"I was resigned to the will of Providence," she said coldly. "Emily, you must understand right now that you are to be grateful and obedient and show your appreciation of what is being done for you. I won't have tears and repining. What would you have done if you had no friends to take you in? Answer me that."

"I suppose I would have starved to death," admitted Emily—instantly beholding a dramatic vision of herself lying dead, looking exactly like the pictures she had seen in one of Ellen Greene's missionary magazines depicting the victims of an Indian famine.

"Not exactly—but you would have been sent to some orphanage where you would have been half-starved, probably. You little know what you have escaped. You have come to a good home where you will be cared for and educated properly."

Emily did not altogether like the sound of being "educated properly." But she said humbly,

"I know it was very good of you to bring me to New Moon, Aunt Elizabeth. And I won't bother you long, you know. I'll soon be grown-up and able to earn my own living. What do you think is the earliest age a person can be called grown-up, Aunt Elizabeth?"

"You needn't think about that," said Aunt Elizabeth shortly. "The Murray women have never been under any necessity for earning their own living. All we require of you is to be a good and contented child and to conduct yourself with becoming prudence and modesty."

This sounded terrible hard.

"I *will* be," said Emily, suddenly determining to be heroic, like the girl in the stories she had read. "Perhaps it won't be so very hard after all, Aunt Elizabeth,"—Emily happened at this point to recall a speech she had heard her father use once, and thought this a good opportunity to work it in—"because, you know, God is good and the devil might be worse."

Poor Aunt Elizabeth! To have a speech like that fired at her in the darkness of the night from that unwelcome little interloper into her orderly life and peaceful bed! Was it any wonder that for a moment or so she was too paralyzed to reply! Then she exclaimed in tones of horror,

"Emily, *never* say that again."

"All right," said Emily meekly. "But," she added defiantly under her breath, "I'll go on thinking it."

"And now," said Aunt Elizabeth, "I want to say that I am not in the habit of talking all night if you are. I tell you to go to sleep, and I *expect* you to obey me. Good night."

The tone of Aunt Elizabeth's good-night would have spoiled the best night in the world. But Emily lay very still and sobbed no more, though the noiseless tears trickled down her cheeks in the darkness for some time. She lay so still that Aunt Elizabeth imagined she was asleep and went to sleep herself.

"I wonder if anybody in the world is awake but me," thought Emily, feeling a sickening loneliness. "If I only had Saucy Sal here! She isn't so cuddly as Mike but she'd be better than nothing. I wonder where she is. I wonder if they gave her any supper."

Aunt Elizabeth had handed Sal's basket to Cousin Jimmy with an impatient, "Here—look to this cat," and Jimmy had carried it off. Where had he put it? Perhaps Saucy Sal would get out and go home—Emily had heard cats always went back home. She wished *she* could get out and go home—she pictured herself and her cat running eagerly along the dark, starlit roads to the little house in the hollow—back to the birches and Adam-and-Eve and Mike, and the old wing-chair and her dear little cot and the open window where the Wind Woman sang to her and at dawn one could see the blue of the mist on the homeland hills.

"Will it ever be morning?" thought Emily. "Perhaps things won't be so bad in the morning."

And then—she heard the Wind Woman at the window—she heard the little, low, whispering murmur of the June night breeze—cooing, friendly, lovesome.

"Oh, you're out there, are you, dearest one?" she whispered, stretching out her arms. "Oh, I'm so glad to hear you. You're such company, Wind Woman. I'm not lonesome any more. And the flash came, too! I was afraid it might never come at New Moon."

Her soul suddenly escaped from the bondage of Aunt Elizabeth's stuffy feather-bed and gloomy canopy and sealed windows. She was out in the open with the Wind Woman and the other gipsies of the night—the fireflies, the moths, the brooks, the clouds. Far and wide she wandered in enchanted reverie until she coasted the shore of dreams and fell soundly asleep on the fat, hard pillow, while the Wind Woman sang softly and luringly in the vines that clustered over New Moon.

* * *

That first Saturday and Sunday at New Moon always stood out in Emily's memory as a very wonderful time, so crowded was it with new and generally delightful impressions. If it be true that we "count time by heart throbs" Emily lived two years in it instead of two days. Everything was fascinating from the moment she came down the long, polished staircase into the square hall that was filled with a soft, rosy light coming through the red glass panes of the front door. Emily gazed through the panes delightedly. What a strange, fascinating, red world she beheld, with a weird red sky that looked, she thought, as if it belonged to the Day of Judgment.

There was a certain charm about the old house which Emily felt keenly and responded to, although she was too young to understand it. It was a house which aforetime had had vivid brides and mothers and wives, and the atmosphere of their loves and lives still hung around it, not yet banished by the old maidishness of the régime of Elizabeth and Laura.

"Why—I'm going to *love* New Moon," thought Emily, quite amazed at the idea.

Aunt Laura was setting the breakfast table in the kitchen, which seemed quite bright and jolly in the glow of morning sunshine. Even the black hole in the ceiling had ceased to be spookish and become only a commonplace entrance to the kitchen loft. And on the red-sandstone doorstep Saucy Sal was sitting, preening her fur as contentedly as if she had lived at New Moon all her life. Emily did not know it, but Sal had already drunk deep the delight of battle with her peers that morning and taught the barn cats their place once and for all. Cousin Jimmy's big yellow Tom had got a fearful drubbing, and was minus several bits of his anatomy, while a stuck-up, black lady-cat, who fancied herself considerably, had made up her mind that if that grey-and-white, narrow-faced interloper from goodness knew where was going to stay at New Moon, *she* was not.

Emily gathered Sal up in her arms and kissed her joyously, to the horror of Aunt Elizabeth, who was coming across the platform from the cookhouse with a plate of sizzling bacon in her hands.

"Don't ever let me see you kissing a cat again," she ordered.

"Oh, all right," agreed Emily cheerfully. "I'll only kiss her when you don't see me after this."

"I don't want any of your pertness, miss. You are not to kiss cats at all."

"But, Aunt Elizabeth, I didn't kiss her on her mouth, *of course.*

I just kissed her between her ears. It's nice—won't you just try it for once and see for yourself?"

"That will do, Emily. You have said quite enough." And Aunt Elizabeth sailed on into the kitchen majestically, leaving Emily momentarily wretched. She felt that she had offended Aunt Elizabeth, and she hadn't the least notion why or how.

But the scene before her was too interesting to worry long over Aunt Elizabeth. Delicious smells were coming from the cookhouse—a little, slant-roofed building at the corner where the big cooking-stove was placed in summer. It was thickly overgrown with hop vines, as most of the New Moon buildings were. To the right was the "new" orchard, very wonderful now in blossom, but a rather commonplace spot after all, since Cousin Jimmy cultivated it in most up-to-date fashion and had grain growing in the wide spaces between the straight rows of trees that looked all alike. But on the other side of the barn lane, just behind the well, was the "old orchard," where Cousin Jimmy said the columbines grew and which seemed to be a delightful place where trees had come up at their own sweet will, and grown into individual shapes and sizes, where blue-eyed ivy twined about their roots and wild-briar roses rioted over the grey paling fence. Straight ahead, closing the vista between the orchards, was a little slope covered with huge white birches, among which were the big New Moon barns, and beyond the new orchard a little, lovable red road looped lightly up and up, over a hill, until it seemed to touch the vivid blue of the sky.

Cousin Jimmy came down from the barns, carrying brimming pails of milk, and Emily ran with him to the dairy behind the cookhouse. Such a delightful spot she had never seen or imagined. It was a snow-white little building in a clump of tall balm-ofgileads. Its grey roof was dotted over with cushions of moss like fat green-velvet mice. You went down six sandstone steps, with ferns crowding about them, and opened a white door with a glass panel in it, and went down three more steps. And then you were in a clean, earthy-smelling, damp, cool place with an earthen floor and windows screened by the delicate emerald of young hop-vines, and broad wooden shelves all around, whereon stood wide, shallow pans of glossy brown ware, full of milk coated over with cream so rich that it was positively yellow.

Aunt Laura was waiting for them and she strained the milk into empty pans and then skimmed some of the full ones. Emily thought skimming was a lovely occupation and longed to try her hand at it. She also longed to sit right down and write a description of that dear dairy; but alas, there was no account book; still, she could write it in her head. She squatted down on a little three-legged stool in a dim corner and proceeded to do it, sitting so still that Jimmy and Laura forgot her and went away and later had to hunt for her a quarter of an hour. This delayed breakfast and made Aunt Elizabeth very cross. But Emily had found just the right sentence to define the clear yet dim green light that filled the dairy and was so happy over it that she didn't mind Aunt Elizabeth's black looks a bit.

After breakfast Aunt Elizabeth informed Emily that henceforth it would be one of her duties to drive the cows to pasture every morning.

"Jimmy has no hired man just now and it will save him a few minutes."

"And don't be afraid," added Aunt Laura, "the cows know the way so well they'll go of themselves. You have only to follow and shut the gates."

"I'm not afraid," said Emily.

But she was. She knew nothing about cows; still, she was determined that the Murrays should not suspect a Starr was scared. So, her heart beating like a trip-hammer, she sallied valiantly forth and found that what Aunt Laura had said was true and cows were not such ferocious animals after all. They went gravely on ahead and she had only to follow, through the old orchard and then through the scrub maple growth beyond, along a twisted ferny path where the Wind Woman was purring and peeping around the maple clumps.

Emily loitered by the pasture gate until her eager eyes had taken in all the geography of the landscape. The old pasture ran before her in a succession of little green bosoms right down to the famous Blair Water—an almost perfectly round pond, with grassy, sloping, treeless margins. Beyond it was the Blair Water valley, filled with homesteads, and further out the great sweep of the white-capped gulf. It seemed to Emily's eyes a charming land of green shadows and blue waters. Down in one corner of the pasture, walled off by an old stone dyke, was the little private graveyard where the dead-and-gone Murrays were buried. Emily wanted to go and explore it, but was afraid to trust herself in the pasture.

"I'll go as soon as I get better acquainted with the cows," she resolved.

Off to the right, on the crest of a steep little hill, covered with young birches and firs, was a house that puzzled and intrigued Emily. It was grey and weather-worn, but it didn't look old. It had never been finished; the roof was shingled but the sides were not, and the windows were boarded over. Why had it never been finished? And it was meant to be such a pretty little house—a house you could love—a house where there would be nice chairs and cozy fires and bookcases and lovely, fat, purry cats and unexpected corners; then and there she named it the Disappointed House, and many an hour thereafter did she spend finishing that house, furnishing it as it should be furnished, and inventing the proper people and animals to live in it.

To the left of the pasture field was another house of a quite different type—a big, old house, tangled over with vines, flatroofed, with mansard windows, and a general air of indifference and neglect about it. A large, untidy lawn, overgrown with unpruned shrubs and trees, straggled right down to the pond, where enormous willows drooped over the water. Emily decided that she would ask Cousin Jimmy about these houses when she got a good chance.

She felt that, before she went back, she must slip along the pasture fence and explore a certain path which she saw entering the grove of spruce and maple further down. She did—and found that it led straight into Fairyland—along the bank of a wide, lovely brook—a wild, dear, little path with lady-ferns beckoning and blowing along it, the shyest of elfin June-bells under the firs, and little whims of loveliness at every curve. She breathed in the tang of fir-balsam and saw the shimmer of gossamers high up in the boughs, and everywhere the frolic of elfin lights and shadows. Here and there the young maple branches interlaced as if to make a screen for dryad faces—Emily knew all about dryads, thanks to her father—and the great sheets of moss under the trees were meet for Titania's couch.

"This is one of the places where dreams grow," said Emily happily.

She wished the path might go on forever, but presently it veered away from the brook, and when she had scrambled over a mossy, old board fence she found herself in the "front-garden" of New Moon, where Cousin Jimmy was pruning some spirea bushes.

"Oh, Cousin Jimmy, I've found the dearest little road," said Emily breathlessly.

"Coming up through Lofty John's bush?"

"Isn't it our bush?" asked Emily, rather disappointed.

"No, but it ought to be. Fifty years ago Uncle Archibald sold that jog of land to Lofty John's father—old Mike Sullivan. He built a little house down near the pond and lived there till he quarrelled with Uncle Archibald—which wasn't long, of course. Then he moved his house across the road—and Lofty John lives there now. Elizabeth has tried to buy the land back from him— she's offered him far more than it's worth—but Lofty John won't sell—just for spite, seeing that he has a good farm of his own and this piece isn't much good to him. He only pastures a few young cattle on it through the summer, and what was cleared is all growing up with scrub maple. It's a thorn in Elizabeth's side and likely to be as long as Lofty John nurses his spite."

"Why is he called Lofty John?"

"Because he's a high and lofty fellow. But never mind him. I want to show you round my garden, Emily. It's mine. Elizabeth bosses the farm; but she lets me run the garden—to make up for pushing me into the well."

"*Did* she do that?"

"Yes. She didn't mean to, of course. We were just children— I was here on a visit—and the men were putting a new hood on the well and cleaning it. It was open—and we were playing tag around it. I made Elizabeth mad—forget what I said—'twasn't *hard* to make her mad, you understand—and she made to give me a bang on the head. I saw it coming—and stepped back to get out of the way—and down I went, head first. Don't remember anything more about it. There was nothing but mud at the bottom—but my head struck the stones at the side. I was took up for dead—my head all cut up. Poor Elizabeth was—" Cousin Jimmy shook his head, as if to intimate that it was impossible to describe how or what poor Elizabeth was. "I got about after a while, though—pretty near as good as new. Folks say I've never been quite right since—but they only say that because I'm a poet, and because nothing ever worries me. Poets are so scarce in Blair Water folks don't understand them, and most people worry so much, they think you're not right if you don't worry."

"Won't you recite some of your poetry to me, Cousin Jimmy?" asked Emily eagerly.

"When the spirit moves me I will. It's no use to ask me when the spirit don't move me."

"But how am I to know when the spirit moves you, Cousin Jimmy?"

"I'll begin of my own accord to recite my compositions. But I'll tell you this—the spirit generally moves me when I'm boiling the pigs' potatoes in the fall. Remember that and be around."

"Why don't you write your poetry down?"

"Paper's too scarce at New Moon. Elizabeth has some pet economies and writing paper of any kind is one of them."

"But haven't you any money of your own, Cousin Jimmy?"

"Oh, Elizabeth pays me good wages. But she puts all my money in the bank and just doles out a few dollars to me once in a while. She says I'm not fit to be trusted with money. When I came here to work for her she paid me my wages at the end of the month and I started for Shrewsbury to put it in the bank. Met a tramp on the road—a poor, forlorn creature without a cent. I gave *him* the money. Why not? *I* had a good home and a steady job and clothes enough to do me for years. I s'pose it was the foolishest thing I ever did—and the nicest. But Elizabeth never got over it. *She's* managed my money ever since. But come you now, and I'll show you my garden before I have to go and sow turnips."

The garden was a beautiful place, well worthy Cousin Jimmy's pride. It seemed like a garden where no frost could wither or rough wind blow—a garden remembering a hundred vanished summers. There was a high hedge of clipped spruce all around it, spaced at intervals by tall lombardies. The north side was closed in by a thick grove of spruce against which a long row of peonies grew, their great red blossoms splendid against its darkness. One big spruce grew in the centre of the garden and underneath it was a stone bench, made of flat shore stones worn smooth by long polish of wind and wave. In the southeast corner was an enormous clump of lilacs, trimmed into the semblance of one large drooping-boughed tree, gloried over with purple. An old summer house, covered with vines, filled the southwest corner. And in the northeast corner there was a sun-dial of grey stone, placed just where the broad red walk that was bordered with striped grass, and picked out with pink conchs, ran off into Lofty John's bush. Emily had never seen a sun-dial before and hung over it enraptured.

"Your great-great grandfather, Hugh Murray, had that brought out from the Old Country," said Cousin Jimmy. "There isn't as fine a one in the Maritime Provinces. And Uncle George Murray brought those conchs from the Indies. He was a sea-captain."

Emily looked about her with delight. The garden was lovely and the house quite splendid to her childish eyes. It had a big front porch with Grecian columns. These were thought very elegant in Blair Water, and went far to justify the Murray pride.

A schoolmaster had said they gave the house a classical air. To be sure, the classical effect was just now rather smothered in hop vines that rioted over the whole porch and hung in pale-green festoons above the rows of potted scarlet geraniums that flanked the steps.

Emily's heart swelled with pride.

"It's a noble house," she said.

"And what about my garden?" demanded Cousin Jimmy jealously.

"It's fit for a queen," said Emily, gravely and sincerely.

Cousin Jimmy nodded, well pleased, and then a strange sound crept into his voice and an odd look into his eyes.

"There is a spell woven round this garden. The blight shall spare it and the green worm pass it by. Drought dares not invade it and the rain comes here gently."

Emily took an involuntary step backward—she almost felt like running away. But now Cousin Jimmy was himself again.

"Isn't this grass about the sun-dial like green velvet? I've taken some pains with it, I can tell you. You make yourself at home in this garden." Cousin Jimmy made a splendid gesture. "I confer the freedom of it upon you. Good luck to you, and may you find the Lost Diamond."

"The Lost Diamond?" said Emily wonderingly. What fascinating thing was this?

"Never hear the story? I'll tell it tomorrow—Sunday's lazy day at New Moon. I must get off to my turnips now or I'll have Elizabeth out looking at me. She won't say anything—she'll just *look*. Ever seen the real Murray look?"

"I guess I saw it when Aunt Ruth pulled me out from under the table," said Emily ruefully.

"No—no. That was the Ruth Dutton look—spite and malice

and all uncharitableness. I hate Ruth Dutton. She laughs at my poetry—not that she ever hears any of it. The spirit never moves when Ruth is around. Dunno where they got her. Elizabeth is a crank but she's sound as a nut, and Laura's a saint. But Ruth's worm-eaten. As for the Murray look, you'll know it when you see it. It's as well known as the Murray pride. We're a darn queer lot—but we're the finest people ever happened. I'll tell you all about us tomorrow."

New-
found-
LAND

from

Hold Fast

by

KEVIN MAJOR

Fourteen-year-old Michael's parents have just been killed by a drunk driver. He and his little brother Brent are staying with relatives, waiting to hear their fate.

"Mike."

"Yeah."

"Is you afraid?"

I knew it was that. "A bit afraid," I said.

"A lot?"

"Yeah . . . when I thinks about it."

I could see his eyes starting to fill up.

"I mean, they won't send us away, will they? Like to an orphanage?"

"No, they wouldn't do that."

"Cause if they do, I won't go. Aunt Flo won't send us where we don't want to go, will she?"

"You knows Aunt Flo wouldn't do that."

"She might. She might. Nobody wants us. We got no mudder or no fa—"

"Shut up!"

Then the water really started to come.

"I'm sorry. Stop it now. Com'on, stop it. Nobody is goin to take you anywhere."

"You don't know."

"Yes, I do."

"No, you don't."

"Stop your cryin. You're not that big of a baby any more. Look at ya. Like some two-year-old."

"You're someone to talk. You was bawlin too. I heard ya."

"Shut up. Everybody'll be upstairs if you keeps that up."

"I don't care."

"Shut up!"

He wouldn't stop.

"Cry baby. Cry baby. You big sook!"

"Shut up," he said.

"Cry baby! Sook!"

"Shut up."

"Make me."

"I'll hit ya."

"You might try, sook."

"I said shut up or I'll hit ya good and hard."

"Hit me. Com'on and hit me."

"I really will. Hard."

"Cry baby!"

"Shut up!"

He wrung up his fist.

"Sook!"

And I let him hit me really hard. As hard as he darn well liked.

The next morning the sunlight came pouring in through the bedroom window. The heat spread all over us across the bed. I was already hot and sticky with sweat, stuck and twisted in my clothes. Not so much as a draft all during the night because I never had the mind to get up and open a window. Brent was next to me, sweaty the same way. The poor kid. He cried till I gave up trying to make him stop.

All that night I had tried like crazy to sleep. I had turned in the bed a thousand times. It came back to me, back and back and back to me all night. I got stomach sick. But if I had throwed up my guts it wouldn't a made me any better.

I looked at Brent. "You think it's going to be easy," I said, waking him up. "The hell with you buddy, it's not. Get outa bed. Go get some clean clothes on. Go on."

When Aunt Flo came and looked in the doorway to see if we was awake, she got an awful surprise. I never gave her so much as a chance to say anything. I just told her we'd soon be down to breakfast. Then I hauled on a clean pair of jeans and a red and white T-shirt. One with leaves on it. It was the best one I had. And I made sure that Brent had himself washed good and dressed like I told him to.

See, I'm pig-headed. Dad always said I was pig-headed. No more than he was. Well, I was trying to take all that had happened square in the face. I was trying. They both would a told me to do it that way. They would a said see what you can make of yourself.

It wasn't going to be that easy. Downstairs, me and Brent walked in on a kitchenful of miserable silence. Aunt Flo, Uncle Ted and Aunt Ellen, even Grandfather, neither one of them was saying a word.

"Whas we havin for breakfast?" I said right away. Loud, like a dish smashing across the middle of the floor.

They sat there dumb. Probably they expected me to bawl for them.

"Any eggs fried?" Loud again.

"Michael, I didn't think you'd want eggs this morning," Aunt Flo said, almost stuttering it out. "I made you some pancakes, just like you likes them. But you wait a minute. If you wants eggs, I'll fry you some. You'll have some too, won't you, Brent?"

"Sure he will," I told her, and looked at Brent as much as to say that he better not say no, if he knew what was good for him.

Aunt Ellen and Uncle Ted on the daybed—they both started to come alive as if I had yanked on their strings. Like me talking was a signal for them to have something to say.

All kinds of brilliant stuff. "It's a great day on the water, Michael. I daresay there's a few fish on the go this morning."

"That's what we should have for dinner, boys—a good meal of fish." Right full of being normal.

"No odds to us what we haves," I said. "What we wants to know is if we gotta get outa this house and where you got in mind for us to go if we do."

That loused up their fish talk pretty quick. I could a struck the kitchen with a bulldozer and they wouldn't a got any more of a shock. I wasn't about to try to be extra nice about it. No sense himmin and awin all morning when we all knew it had to come down to that sometime.

You could just about see their nerves twitching. Aunt Flo almost dropped the frying pan. The two on the daybed could barely keep hold of the cigarettes they had nipped between their fingers. Ashes flying all over the place. It even got Grandfather upset. The rocking chair he was in went off stride.

"We'll talk about that after breakfast, Michael," Aunt Flo said, trying to smooth it all over.

"No sir. We wants to know right now." As simple as that. I wasn't being brazen about it if that's the way it looked. I just wanted to get it straight right then and there.

"It's better you boys had your breakfast first." That was Uncle Ted. Coming on strong like he was the voice of experience or some big deal.

"What, is it so bad that you can't tell us?"

"Michael," Aunt Flo said, "it's only been one day."

"You mean you haven't talked about it yet?"

"No, I didn't say that."

"Then tell us. I was awake all last night thinkin about it. Brent too."

Then Brent, who hadn't opened his mouth the whole time, said to Aunt Flo, "Is we goin to an orphanage?"

When she heard that she just about broke down crying right there. She came over to the table, stood up by him and squeezed him into her dress. She could hardly keep it in.

"Brentie my love, you knows better than that." Then, in a few seconds, after she got a hold on herself, she said, "Brentie, how would you like to come and live with me and your Grandfather?" She looked at him and pushed his hair back from his forehead.

"OK," he said right away. A big relief.

And what about me? The other one. The one who is not going to ask. Where does he fit into all this? I was waiting. Feeling stupid, because I didn't want it to look like I was waiting.

"Mike too?" Brent said then.

Nobody answered. Until Aunt Ellen spoke up, all full of life, but not laying her eyes on me atall. "Michael is going to come to live with us in St. Albert."

So that was it. That was what they had in their minds. St. Albert. The least she could a done was look at me when she said it.

"You're going to like it in St. Albert, Michael," Uncle Ted said. Again like he was positive that what he said had to be right.

"Maybe I will."

"I know you will."

"I said maybe I will."

And then a long silence, everybody waiting. Until I said, "I'll give it a try." I said it like I meant it.

*　　*　　*

I had a whole two months before I would be packing up and getting myself shipped off to St. Albert to start school there. Aunt Flo said I could stay with her until then. Maybe she thought that by the end of August I'd have no problem to face on a move.

But I was definitely going. That was understood and there wasn't much more said about it. I knew both of us, me and Brent, living with her was a lot to expect from Aunt Flo. And she had Grandfather, too, to take care of. It would be hard enough on her to cook and wash and spend money on them, let alone me too. So I wasn't about to ask her to change her mind.

It was just that Marten was the best darn place I knew to live. God, what was I talking about, it was the only place I ever did live. Of course, you can almost count the number of people on one hand. Not really, but going by some places in Newfoundland, Marten is pretty small. Probably no more than seven hundred people all together. But that didn't matter. In fact, I liked it that way cause it gave us all kinds of room to be roaming around. I could put on the boots and leave the back of the house and in no more than two minutes I'd be up in the country, out of sight of any house in the place. Go on all day then, if I wanted, and not see a single soul.

You might think a person would get bored silly with nothing to do in a place that small, but no sir, not me. I can hardly think of a morning when I woke up and there wouldn't be something on my mind that I'd have to look forward to. If it wasn't going in the woods to check my snares after school, it might be riding around on skidoo. Or setting lobster traps. There was times when I bloody near went nuts trying to get some sleep, I'd be planning that much for the next day.

And now my whole life was going to be changed. I just kept thinking to myself that St. Albert better not be as bad as the picture of it I had in my mind.

I got carried away a lot that summer, all the time thinking about things that was gone past and what I would be leaving behind. I should a been planning ahead for when I got to St. Albert instead of moping around in a daydream half the time. I did spend some time out and around with the fellows. Not very much though. Nothing like other summers. In fact, except for some of the times me and Brent spent together, it was the rottenest summer I ever had. Even all the extra baking and stuff Aunt Flo did for us didn't seem to make it any better.

Over the years Aunt Flo and me always got along fairly good, I spose, all things considered. Although for as long as I could remember, she was always the kind of person who fussed over you too much. For one thing, any time I ever went over there, say after school to see Grandfather and maybe have something to eat, she always had to see that I was stuffed right to the gills. No such a thing as one piece of cake. It had to be two or three or she'd figure you didn't like it. And I wouldn't get outside the door but I had my pockets stogged full with oranges or bananas or something.

And sometimes the questions she'd put me through would get right clean on my nerves. I spose it only showed she was worrying about me. I spose that was it. Like if it was either bit cold atall, the first question she'd be sure to put to me was did I have on long underwear. Now, is that any kind of question to get asked you by your aunt? I always said yes, whether I did or not. Lots of times I'd have plenty of things on the tip of my tongue to say to her to cure her of that little habit. But if I ever did and what I said got back to Mom, then I'd a been hung.

After, though, when I moved over and started to live in her house, all that stuff about her I didn't notice so much. She was different. She left me alone a lot. And when I got it in my mind to, I done my part to help her out around the house.

For the two months before I left, I spent most of the time to myself or with Brent. For me, getting along with Brent as good as I done was even stranger than Aunt Flo and me finally seeing eye to eye. Before that the two of us could hardly look at each other sideways but a fight started. It mightn't a been as bad as that, but we sure got into some vicious arguments. Like a lot of younger brothers, he could be a real pain in the neck when he wanted to be. What use to bug me more than anything was when he'd come home to Mom with these stun stories about me. Wherever he got them I don't know. He'd try to make her believe that he seen me smoking or he'd say he heard me curse so bad he couldn't repeat it. Or if he seen me with some girl. That was another thing. Cripes, I warned him about that so many times my tongue had blisters. What he needed most was a good smack on the arse. He came darn close to getting it too, a good many times. He'd only say that stuff about me if we was all around the dinner table or something and he knew I couldn't belt him one.

But that came around to being changed too. It's odd when I thinks about it. How us two could a changed into being pretty good buddies. I spose it all started when I began to feel that I should be looking out to him more. When I knew that something just had to be done about the way he was acting.

I seen that it was even worse for him than it was for me. Being only seven he took it awful hard. Some people got the idea that a kid his age could get over something like what happened in no time. They don't know much if that's what they thinks. I couldn't let him stay like that, so dopey and not interested in doing a thing. Crying every hour almost. I wasn't any rock myself, I'll admit to that. But I was nothing like what Brent was. I was afraid he was going to stay like that all his life.

So I got him talking to me as much as I could. About everything I could think of that I knew he had either bit of interest in. Sometimes it was hard to drag so much as a word outa him. He would just sit there like a dummy and listen to me. Then gradually he started to come around.

"Take that horse Jack Coles got there. He's some animal," I'd say to him. "You like to have a horse like that?"

"Yeah," he might say.

"Now what would you do with en if you had en?"

He'd have to come up with more than just a word or two.

It worked too, enough that I could see a big difference in him. I done all I could to get Brent back to the way he should a been. I'd rather a seen him yelling and screaming at me than for him to be the way he was first.

By the end of a few weeks he looked and acted a whole lot better. Some nights we'd have a real cuffer. If Mom and Dad could a seen it they probably would a had to laugh to theirselves. There we was, carrying on what you could call a sensible conversation. Neither one of us stretching our lungs the least bit.

What we was talking about this one night was squids. It wasn't quite the right time of the year for them then, but we was on to talking about them anyway. A good evening of squid jigging in September or October is one of the best bits of fun you can have out on the salt water. I've been at it a good many times and I knows a fair bit about it. But Brent, he only ever been out once. Lucky for him though they was jigging good that evening and he had the real time of it.

Most everybody knows I guess what a squid looks like. It's like a pouch with suckers on their arms coming out at one end. Arms like an octopus, only smaller. If anything grabs hold of them, they shoots out this black inky stuff—squid shit.

Now all the fun is in being out jigging them. Around dark in the evening or early in the morning is the best time. A small red squid jigger with a bit of line is all you needs. You don't have to go out very far, only just off the cove. All the boats generally anchors around about in the same spot.

Talk about your fun, old man, when the jiggin's good. We've been out, me and Dad and Grandfather, some evenings when we could a filled the boat. Squid shit going everywhere then, cause as soon as they comes up outa the water, they lets fly. That's half the fun of it—getting squirt, or better still seeing someone else getting their face full.

That's what we was talking about mostly—squids. When Grandfather came in on the two of us cuffering away there in the bedroom, it must a been ten o'clock or later. All the time I was sorta half expecting to see him. It seemed Grandfather was the right one to be in with us all along.

It might seem odd about me and Grandfather, the way we

always got along so good. I guess he was a lot of the reason that it would a been at Aunt Flo's that I'd a been staying for good, if I had my own way.

Some fellows I knows haven't got no time for their grandparents. Like they figures it's not very smart to be saying much that's good about them. Or about any old people, for that matter. Like what they thinks or says is too old-fashioned for them. Or maybe it's because the grandparents they got are too contrary. I don't know. But me and Grandfather wasn't one bit like that. We got along great, better than I done with some my own age.

The trouble with a good many old people is that they thinks they was never young. But Grandfather was not that way. He had stories, my son, that'd put some of what you reads in magazines and books to shame. And I knows for a fact they're true. Now and then he might tell one to pull someone's leg, just for fun, but if you had all what happened to him put together, you'd have enough to fill ten books. No joke about it. Sure he went fishing in a sailing schooner on the Labrador every summer for twenty-two years from the time he was thirteen years old. And that was no easy job, that's for darn sure.

You had to know how to go about speaking to Grandfather, too. It was no use to say something to him and be looking out the window or fiddling with whatever was on the table or have your mind half on something else. You had to look right straight at him and talk loud. If you learned that you wouldn't have to go repeating what you was saying to him more than once.

Grandfather's hair's been white ever since I can remember. He use to keep it cut right tight to his head, but late years he took to letting it grow out, that and his sideburns. I told him once he should buy an electric guitar and practise up a bit. He'd make a few bucks. Of course, Aunt Flo was always after him to get it cut.

Just like she use to be after me. He'd always say to her, "Let en bide, let en bide if he wants it like that." He'd always stick up for me. And so then things got switched around and it was his own mop she was pestering him about.

When he strolled into the bedroom where me and Brent was that night, he looked first like he wasn't in a very good mood.

"Grandfather," I said to him, "I was just tellin Brent about the times me and you and Dad was out squiddin." I was hoping that would do something to change the serious look he had on his face.

"Told him about the time you almost put your father overboard?"

I didn't want to be getting into that. "Com'on, you knows that's not right. I didn't almost put en overboard."

"Sure I was there," he said, still not smiling.

"I knows you was. He just lost his balance and fell down in the bottom o' the boat, that was all. I wasn't really use to the motor then. I cut the boat too much when I turned to go back in the cove. Sure I was only nine."

Before I got finished his face broke into a grin. I should a known that. He was only trying to tease me.

"I remembers how your father fell down, flozzo, right on top o' the squid we caught, ass first," he laughed.

He didn't need to remind me. And how the old man got so dirty with me for being careless. Although he let me steer the boat back into the wharf just the same.

"Forget about that time," I said. "We'd always jig a nice many, wouldn't we, Grandfather?"

"Yeah, I guess we would. We'd sell some of it," he said, "and dry a bit. Some of it we'd use for bait. And we'd always bring home so many for your mother to stuff and bake."

"You should remember that good enough, Brent. Sure we'd get home and you'd still be half on the bawl cause you didn't get to go."

"I would not."

"You would so," I said. "And then as soon as ever we'd get inside the porch door, Dad'd shout out to see what was on the go for supper. It'd be after dark probably by the time we got home, and we right gone for some food."

"And it was sure to be something good. God, your mother was able to put on some pot o' soup, I can tell you that."

"Mom'd have people in off the road with their tongues hangin out, wouldn't she?"

"Right down to their bootlaces," Brent added.

"Probably your father would march straight into the kitchen then, rubber boots and all on, and plank whatever squid he had into the kitchen sink," Grandfather said.

"And sometimes, just to tease her, he'd bend down and grab Mom around the legs and hoist her up to the ceiling. That man had some strength in hes arms."

"Him trottin around the kitchen with her then. Just for the devilment, that's all he done it for. Your Mother'd have to laugh in spite of herself. All of us laughin then when she'd start, gettin a real kick out of it," Grandfather said.

We all laughed. Him and Brent and me. Just the three of us. Grandfather was the only one now who could remember it all, the times that went on before. We was able to share things that nobody else could any more. And I could see it in his face that he knew it too.

"Grandfather," I said after a while, "squiddin is a lot o' fun, idn't it?"

"Yes b'y, it is so."

"We'll have to go at it again."

"Yes, I spose."

"And me too this time," Brent said.

"You and me and Poppy."

"All right," Grandfather said. "All right."

That was all that was said about it. We knew, though, that there was no such thing as all right. There couldn't be with me gone in a few weeks to St. Albert, nowheres close to squidding, or to Grandfather or Brent. Nowheres close to anything connected to either one of them.

*   *   *

Like I said, in lots of ways it was the rottenest summer I ever had. Most summers are over before you knows it and you're back at school with hardly enough time to stop and think. But that summer dragged on and on.

And then Sunday, the second day of September, there I was at the Irving station on the highway waiting for the bus to come. The three of them came to see me off. The waiting was the part that I couldn't stand. If we could a got there just as the bus pulled in, and me got aboard and went on, it would a been OK. But, of course, Aunt Flo had to make sure we was there in plenty of time. So we ended up waiting for twenty minutes.

Perhaps it wouldn't a been so bad except for Brent. All along he hadn't been saying much. Then with about five minutes before the bus was due to come, there he was off to one side by himself, staring at the road and blinking water out of his eyes. He tried to keep from having to look at me.

I went over to him. I might a known that was going to happen. "Look," I told him, "you're not goin to mind it once I gets gone."

He still wouldn't look at me.

I tried to make a joke of it. "There'll be nobody around to bother ya. You'll be able to do just what you likes."

That was even worse. He never budged, and then when I tried to force him to look at me, he broke away and turned back on.

"Listen, what's there to worry about," I half-yelled. "I'll see ya again before long. You can write and I'll promise to write ya back every time."

"I can't write very good."

Dummy. "Then print, for frig's sake."

"Quit swearin at me!" he yelled. He started in bawling.

"OK, OK. If you're goin to cry then it's no use even trying to talk to ya. Com'on, stop it."

That made him slack up a bit. "I told ya before what it was going to be like. And buddy, you better start in gettin use to it. Sure you got Aunt Flo. And Poppy is there. What more do ya want? She's goin to be takin good care of ya."

"It won't be the same."

"Now, it's no good startin that. I didn't want for us to have to split up. You knows that. But right now it's sposed to be the best thing. And I guess we just got to go along with it. But I knows one thing—if you behaves yourself and tries to get along with Aunt Flo all ya can, then that's going to be a whole lot better for all of us. But if you stays like you are here now, with a mouth on ya all screwed up, then that's going to make it ten times worse for everybody."

He didn't say anything.

"Now you just remember what I said. And don't let me hear tell of anything from Aunt Flo about you being a nuisance to her."

"Ah, keep quiet!"

"I'll keep quiet, but you just remember that."

"You shut up and worry about yourself!"

The bus hauled into the garage and I had to leave him. I was the only one getting on and I knew the bus would be stopping only just long enough for that. The driver took the suitcases and box I had and stowed them away with the rest of the luggage.

I let Aunt Flo have her little peck on my cheek. I figured that wasn't much on my part. But, before I knew it, she had her arms wrapped around me and nearly had my chest caved in. Now *she* was the one half on the bawl.

I shook Grandfather's hand and said goodbye to him.

"Michael, take care of yourself." I was going to miss him an awful lot.

And Brent. I didn't know really what to do. Trying to shake his hand or something would a seemed too stupid.

"See ya, buddy," I said, and sorta just smiled at him.

"Yeah, see ya." His eyes red and watery.

Then Aunt Flo piped up, just as I turned to go aboard the bus, "Put on plenty o' clothes now. Keep yourself warm." All the people with the windows open and looking out at us.

Cripes, she went and done it again. Leave it to a woman to make a fellow feel like a fool in front of strangers. I took off up the steps. The driver punched my ticket and then I walked straight back without turning the head one way or the other. I planked myself down in the first vacant seat I came to.

from

The Dream Carvers

by

JOAN CLARK

*Thrand is a young Greenlander who has voyaged with his family
to Newfoundland in the year 1115. After one of the native Osweet
boys, Awadasut, is killed by the Greenlanders, Thrand is captured
by the Osweet people in retaliation.*

Ten days have passed since I bloodied myself. I still don't
know why I smeared blood on my skin, unless it was to
make myself red. Perhaps despair at my aloneness and invisibil-
ity drove me to draw attention to myself in that way. Whatever
the reason, it seems to have improved my situation with my captors, for they are now willing to include me in various ways.

It also seems that the season of mourning Awadasut's death has
passed, for my captors, who I've learned call themselves Osweet,
have stopped looking at me as if I were a ghost or an evil spirit.
Now they see me, I think, as someone who is flesh and blood
like them.

The men now encourage me to work by their side. I've been
given various cutting tools and shown how to use them on stone
and wood. I'm making myself a knife with a wide flat blade to

which I intend to tie a wooden handle. I have discovered that carving wood gives me such pleasure that this will only be one of several carving tools I intend to make. While I've been working, I've been trying to remember how iron is made. But I can't remember what I never knew. Although Nagli the ironworker was in Leifsbudir last year, I didn't take the time to inquire as to how he turned bog ore into iron. I know he used charcoal which he made by burning wood. Apart from that, I have little knowledge of what Nagli did. I suppose I didn't trouble to learn because iron ore is scarce in Gardar. Most of the iron goods in Greenland are brought in from Iceland and Norway. I regret not having learned, for if ore could be found in these parts, I could teach the Osweet to forge iron so they wouldn't have to work with stone tools to make what I regard as inferior goods.

Since my capture our main source of food has been salmon.

Now we are eating cod. Twice daily two men go out to empty the nets, usually the same two, Shawbawsut and Boasook. I don't know why this is. There are two boats after all. I can only think that one boat is used because the fish supply is dwindling and only two men are required. I've watched Shawbawsut and Boasook mending the skin nets. It's the only time I've seen men using a bone awl which they store inside a hollow caribou bone.

One morning I awaken to find a bow, four arrows and a spear have been set beside my sleeping place along with a caribou skin sheath and fur-lined boots. Imamasduit and Bogodorasook are sitting near the fire. I can see they have been waiting patiently for me to waken and notice the goods they've made. Because these gifts are unexpected, I am surprised by the pleasure they bring. To give a captive gifts seems an unlikely thing. In Greenland thralls are given little but cast-off clothes. I don't know of any thrall who's been given gifts his owners have made for him.

I am overwhelmed by the kindness of these two old people. I examine the arrow and spearheads which are light brown in colour. The spear and two of the arrows have been sharpened to very fine points. The other two arrowheads are blunt; they are for bringing down birds. I fit an arrow into the sheath and put it over my shoulder to show Bogodorasook that I know what it's for. Imamasduit gestures for me to try on the boots. The caribou fur is thick and soft against my skin. Since the weather's turned cool, my feet have often been cold. Now they'll be warm and dry.

It snows again, more heavily this time. Because of my warm boots, the snow no longer bothers me. Imamasduit has given me a caribou fur and bid me wear it over my shoulders as a robe, as she and Bogodorasook do. These robes have been inside our tent all along where they've been folded to make sitting places for us. Now that it's grown colder, all the people are wearing robes.

Several days later, I take my calendar stick and cut a line through my second month of captivity. The same morning we begin breaking camp.

For the last two days, we have had to go without eating fish. Instead the men have gone into the forest to hunt small game. I myself went into the woods with Bogodorasook. I attempted to kill a large gull but my arrows fell short. Bogodorasook shot two black-backed gulls and these, along with four ptarmigan the other men have brought in, were roasted for our meal that night. It's been clear to me that once fishing stopped, we would have to leave this place or starve. Lacking cattle and other livestock, the Oswect must move to where there is a supply of food.

The sleeping furs and skins are rolled up and tied, our tools and utensils bundled up. The tents are taken down and packed. The tent poles are lashed together at one end as well as halfway down to make a sling for carrying goods. The birch-bark the women have harvested is tied together, wrapped in caribou skin and placed on a platform of boards lashed together with caribou ties. One end of the boards is curved for easier pulling through heavy snow. Watching this, I think how useful it would be to have a sled to carry goods. The platform could be made into a sled by mounting it on skis. Later on, when there's time, maybe I'll try making skis.

These preparations take the morning. By early afternoon our goods are ready for carrying. When the next snowfall comes, the only sign a camp-site has been here will be fire-blackened rocks, the drying racks and the sticks and poles we have used. I remove the stake where I once was tied and toss it into the woods. I expect to be harnessed to the sling of poles since two men will be needed to haul that load.

Bogodorasook gestures for me to follow him to the water's edge. Zathrasook is already there. Two boats, two men. So this is what my work will be. Bogodorasook leans down, grips two crossbeams and hoists them up so that a crossbeam rests on his shoulders. Then he walks a few paces with the boat and sets it down. He gestures for me to pick it up and I do, though not as easily as he. The boat is amazingly light, so different from Norse boats, which can't be easily carried. Of course if Norsemen want to travel far, they use ships, not boats. Now I know why the Osweet haven't made wooden boats. It's not that they lack the skill, but that a heavy wooden boat wouldn't suit them half so well. The boat on my shoulders, which they call a canoe, was built to be carried. The fact that we are taking the canoes with us means that we will be travelling through places where canoes can't be paddled, to a destination where boats will be needed.

Bogodorasook and Imamasduit lead the way, each carrying a bundle of skins on their backs. Shawbawsut and Boasook come next hauling the pole sling; their wives, Thoowidith and Woasut, follow, pulling the curved boards. The others fall in behind carrying an assortment of bundles and sacks. We boat-carriers bring up the rear, Zathrasook first, then me.

The snow is well below our ankles except where it's wind-drifted here and there. By the time we boat-carriers reach the drifts, they have been trampled down by those ahead and are easily crossed. We are following the shore of the lake that joins the river flowing into the bay. Both sides of the lake are thickly forested but there's a trail of some sort between the trees.

It's cool but far from cold. Dressed in my robe and fur-lined boots I'm pleasantly warm. Fortunately the air is windless. I can see that a strong wind could make carrying a canoe difficult for it would push the canoe from side to side. I am carrying the canoe on my shoulders, not my back. To keep my neck from being bent, I hold my head inside the canoe, which smells of spruce and something else, seal oil I think. Every so often, I tilt the canoe up so that I can see Zathrasook ahead. I don't want to get too close to him lest we collide. On the other hand, I wouldn't put it past him to go ahead so quickly that I'm left far behind. Since I'm following his tracks, he could lead me astray. It's hard to say what he would do to me if he got me alone, away from the others. I continue to expect the worst until it occurs to me that as long as I'm a carrier, Zathrasook won't hurt me for he knows I'm needed to carry the canoe.

We come to a small lake. Here we stop to rest and I have a chance to look around. The lake has begun to freeze from the outside in. The river flows from the end of the lake, toward the sea we are leaving behind. Untying the bark cup Imamasduit gave me before we left, I make my way to the river to fetch a drink. I keep a wary eye out for Zathrasook, but he's run ahead to visit the others and I'm left alone.

It's not long before we're on our way again. Soon we reach the end of the lake where we again pick up the river that gradually narrows into a smaller stream. We follow it along until we come to a second lake. On the south side of the lake we stop beside a round cleared area now filled with snow. This is a tent-site very like the ones we left behind, only three times their size. I expect us to begin making a tent, but no one makes a move to do this. Instead the women and children collect firewood and the men take their weapons and go off to hunt.

By now it's late afternoon and the trees cast long blue shadows across the snow. I'm reluctant to enter the woods alone. At the same time, I don't want to stay with the women. I take up my bow and arrows and follow the men into the forest. I notice their tracks go off in different directions, in pairs. All except one. I follow these. It occurs to me that I could continue walking away and escape. But this is only a passing thought. Escaping in snow would be a futile exercise since the Osweet could easily follow my tracks and bring me back. I would be staked all over again. In any case, where would I go? This land is so vast that without a boat I would be swallowed by its size. I have learned the hard way that if I am to make a successful escape, I will have to plan it well ahead.

I see ptarmigan tracks and follow these. All the while the shadows deepen and merge. The air grows darker. I must remember to follow my footprints back to the camp while it's light enough. But my empty belly pushes me forward after the ptarmigan. I try to walk softly as the Osweet do.

I come upon the ptarmigan suddenly in an open space. Leaning against a tree to steady myself, I fit an arrow and lift my bow. Slow and sure, I say to myself, don't rush and fumble. I pull the arrow far back, farther still. I let it go. Amazingly the arrow hits its mark, piercing the bird through the throat.

Before I can retrieve my kill, an arrow comes from behind me, enters my tunic cloth above the elbow and pins me to the tree. Quickly I duck then look around but no one's in sight. I reach over, across my pinioned arm and wrest the arrow free. It comes away easily. I poke my finger through the tunic hole. There's no hole in my body, not even a scratch on my skin. Even so, blood rushes between my ears. Anyone who can hit so precise a mark can easily pierce my throat or heart. Of course, the ptarmigan has vanished from the clearing along with my arrow.

By the time I reach the encampment, a large fire is blazing and several ptarmigan are being cleaned. I hold the offending arrow up to the firelight so that I can see how it differs from mine. I notice the arrowhead is dark grey whereas my arrowheads are light brown. I intend to look at the other men's arrowheads to see if I can find out whose are dark grey. This proves to be unnecessary for soon Zathrasook appears with a ptarmigan, *my* ptarmigan, which he gives to his mother to clean. Then he comes up to me, takes his arrow from my hand and gives me mine. He does this silently, never looking me in the face.

That night, we sleep sitting in a circle around the fire. I am positioned between Imamasduit and Tisewsut's wife and baby. Zathrasook sits opposite. As usual, he pays me no mind. In the distance, one wolf then another begins to howl. I think about the trick Zathrasook played on me. I ask myself why he wanted me to know it was *his* arrow that pinned me to the tree while he took my ptarmigan. As I sit listening to the wolves, the answer to this question comes to me. By tracking me as he did, Zathrasook was telling me that though the Osweet no longer shun me, as far as he's concerned, I am an enemy. He is reminding me that as a stranger and an outsider, I am at a disadvantage, and that he can kill me any time he likes.

*   *   *

We are now in our winter camp which is a day's walk past the second lake. This is a flat area with grassy clearings between the trees. We've camped here because of the caribou. When we first arrived seven days ago, the caribou were all around us, grazing in the clearings. Since then they have moved away. They're still close but have put some distance between themselves and us.

Our tent has been set up near a large round lake. I have learned that the Osweet call this tent a "mamateek." The mamateek has been built in the same way as the other tents, with poles and birch-bark but it's much bigger, being large enough to hold us all. It has caribou skins on top of the bark to make it warmer inside. We all sleep with our toes toward the fire, bodies touching on either side. Now husbands and wives sleep together, and young children double up. There are eight sleeping places, most of them large enough to hold two or more. Three of us sleep alone: Abidith, Zathrasook and myself. I have been placed between Imamasduit and Abidith.

I am slowly learning to understand what my captors say. I can't put exact meanings to words but I'm often able to sense what's being said. The Osweet don't talk at length. They speak slowly in a measured way which makes what they say easier to understand. I think they speak less than Greenlanders because they talk to one another in other ways. Now that the whole family lives inside one mamateek, I notice that someone will know another's thoughts without a word being said. This is because movements and gestures speak instead. Just as a tilt of the head or a softening of the lips carry meaning, so too do the eyes. Now that I know the Osweet somewhat better, they also speak to me through these gestures and looks.

Only Abidith speaks inside my head. Usually this is at night before I sleep, or in the morning before I wake. Always when Abidith speaks to me, she's angry and scolding.

"You have much to learn, Wobee, before you can become one of us. You were captured by my people to take my brother's place. I don't think you can do that but Grandmother says it's possible you will become one of us some day. Since Grandmother holds the wisdom of our family, I will try to think as she does even though in this case, it goes against my will. It is not for you that I speak inside your head but for her."

Whenever Abidith enters my thoughts like this, I try to answer her back. I try to tell her that I would prefer Imamasduit speak to my thoughts herself, rather than someone who never lets me forget that I ran down her brother. I want to tell Abidith that in her place I too would be angry. If someone killed Magnus or Erling, I would go after him with an axe. I want to tell her that she might feel better if I had been killed. But I wasn't killed, I was taken captive, and there's nothing I can do to change those events. All of this I say to her inside my head. I have no way of knowing if she hears what I say. She never looks at me or gives any sign that she does. And I have no reason to think I have the power to enter her thoughts the way she can mine.

Now we are eating caribou, killing them one at a time, mainly strays the wolves have missed. We hear the wolves day and night. From them we know exactly where the caribou are. It's Bogodorasook's wish that before we have a caribou run, we should strengthen ourselves with meat. We set up racks for drying the caribou. We collect firewood. When this has been done, we prepare ourselves for the hunt and wait until the caribou position themselves where Bogodorasook wants. He says we must lure the caribou into our dreams to keep them close.

In Greenland men hunt deer which are much the same as caribou though slightly shorter in the legs. These deer are hunted on the island of Hreinsey which is a long way from our farm. My father's brother, who is a far better hunter than my father, was going to take me to Hreinsey this year. Probably he's there now.

Bogodorasook wants the caribou to follow a passageway we'll make beside the stream. This is the tail end of the river we've been following and which has now become a brook. It's narrow enough for the caribou to cross and escape into the woods. For this reason Bogodorasook bids us fell trees in such a way that they overlap each other to make a fence that will prevent the caribou from crossing the stream. Opposite the fence but on the same side of the stream, he has us stick poles into the ground in a line that follows the same turns as the fence. On top of the poles Bogodorasook ties tassels made from birch-bark. I don't know why he does this, but I assume the tassels serve a useful purpose. I have learned that the Osweet never do anything without good reason. When we're finished, there's a passageway between the fence and the line of poles all the way to the lake.

The morning of the hunt, we arm ourselves with bows and spears. There are seven of us altogether. Bogodorasook, Tisewsut and I take one of the canoes to the lake while Shawbawsut, Hathasut, Boasook and Zathrasook go into the woods and position themselves behind the caribou so that they can drive the animals through the passageway and into the lake where we will begin the slaughter.

We break the shore ice with our paddles, put the canoe into the water and paddle a short distance into the lake to wait. After a time, we hear yelling and shouting. I imagine the men behind the caribou jumping up and down in an effort to drive the animals through the passageway. Then we hear the caribou themselves, snorting and huffing. They are coming along the passageway, eight or nine caribou pounding over the snow toward the lake. At the water's edge, the caribou stop. In the distance Shawbawsut shouts that the main herd is coming this way. The caribou on the shore of the lake plunge into the water and begin swimming to the opposite shore. With skilful paddling, Bogodorasook steers the canoe to intercept the swimming caribou. He's already told me that the way to hunt caribou from a boat is to plunge my spear into an animal's neck and hold its head under until it drowns.

Tisewsut is already doing this. He plunges the spear deep, forcing the animal's head underwater. As soon as the caribou ceases to struggle, Tisewsut removes the spear.

A second caribou swims close by. Bogodorasook positions the canoe so that I can spear it, which I do. The spearing itself isn't difficult but it requires all my strength to keep the animal's head underwater.

Tisewsut and I kill another caribou before the other hunters reach the shore. I have been far too occupied to count the number of caribou which have gained the opposite shore but I know most of them have escaped. Zathrasook and Shawbawsut now have the other canoe in the water. They are trying to head off the caribou we miss. Hathasut and Boasook remain on shore to prevent the animals from retreating along the passageway. They use their bows as well as spears to bring down animals close to shore. Bogodorasook tells us to begin towing the carcasses ashore where we will remove the antlers and feet. The caribou float on the water which makes towing them easy work. Soon the shore water seethes with blood.

While we are moving carcasses ashore, I look up and see a large stag enter the lake. Without any forethought at all, I run after the stag and plunge my spear into his neck. Bogodorasook is saying something to me but I can't make out what it is above the animal's loud snort. With no thought of the consequences, I leap onto the animal's back, stretch forward and push its head under. The stag rears up and plunges toward deeper water. I hold on and rock his antlers back and forth while the stag swims toward the other side of the lake. The caribou twists its body and I'm thrown off. Before I can swim free, I feel myself being pushed below the surface of the lake by the weight of the caribou. A hoof pounds my head and I lose sight of everything, the water, the caribou, the sky.

When my eyes open, I am near the bottom of the lake. I can see nothing except the huge dark body far above me on top of the water. My chest burns for want of air. I try to hold my breath. Water seeps into my nose and mouth. I choke and gasp. I know I have to get to the surface of the water but I don't have the strength to lift myself up.

Now a strange thing happens. My mind begins to separate itself from my body. It seems to be floating up and up, out of the lake, while my body is sinking lower and lower. My mind has reached the surface of the lake. It goes higher and higher, into the air. Now I am looking down on myself. Below me in the murky water is the body of a young man drowning in the lake.

THE North

Baseball Bats
for Christmas

by

MICHAEL KUSUGAK

This is the text of a picture-book based on the author's childhood in Repulse Bay. The original is illustrated by Vladyana Krykorka.

It was a glorious time, even for a very asthmatic boy. Arvaarluk was seven years old, and Arvaarluk was very asthmatic. He struggled when he walked and struggled to catch his breath when he sat down. And Arvaarluk loved Christmas.

In 1955 Arvaarluk lived in Repulse Bay.

Let me tell you a thing or two about Repulse Bay. There is a brass plate on a rock outcrop that was put there when Arvaarluk was just a baby. And no matter how many times you hit it with another rock, it would not come off.

Arvaarluk's mother would say, "If you knock that brass plate off that rock, the whole world will come to a terrible end." Arvaarluk imagined the brass plate coming off and the whole world blowing air out through the hole like a giant seal float bouncing around and around, all over space. So he hit it time and again, but to no avail. It still sits there, declaring for all the world that Repulse Bay is way up at the north end of Hudson Bay—smack dab on the Arctic Circle. Less than one hundred people lived there in 1955 and, in winter, they all lived in igloos and sod huts.

Another thing about Repulse Bay is that there are no "standing-ups." Or, as Peter, Jack, Yvo and Arvaarluk later found out, things commonly known as trees. There is not one single tree to be seen anywhere. The land is as bald as the belly of a dog with puppies.

In 1955, though, trees arrived in Repulse Bay.

They came in by aeroplane. As usual, the Union Jack had been hoisted up the flagpole just before they arrived. The Union Jack always went up before an aeroplane came. Then Rocky Parsons flew his trusty Norseman aeroplane over the Arctic Circle—and ran out of gas. His engine went, "PUTT, PUTT," and quit, way up there in the sky. His propeller stopped going around, but he glided his aeroplane, ever so gracefully, and plunked it down in front of the Hudson's Bay Company store. The trees were brought out of the aeroplane and dumped on the snowbank in front of Arvaarluk's hut. And there they sat.

Rocky Parsons was our hero. When people were sick, he always brought us a doctor. And when we needed some stuff he always came. He appeared in fair weather and foul. All the manager of the Hudson's Bay Store had to do was hoist up the Union Jack and Rocky Parsons would come. But we could not talk to Rocky Parsons because we did not understand any English at all. We just smiled at him a lot and dreamed of, some day, flying his aeroplane with him.

Rocky Parsons smiled back as he pumped gas into his aeroplane from a 45-gallon drum. He pushed and pulled the lever on his pump back and forth, back and forth, going, "Squish-chuck, squish-chuck, squish-chuck . . ." Then he jumped back into his pilot's seat. The Norseman spit out a lot of thick smoke, then the propeller started going around with such a big "BANG!!!" that it made your ears dizzy.

He went way out on the ice with the skis bouncing over the snow drifts going, "Flop, flop, flop, flop . . ." Then, turning around, he took off with a deafening, "Rooaaarrrr!!!!," just over their heads. He would not come back until the Union Jack went up the flagpole again.

But there were the things he had brought sitting on the snow-bank in front of Arvaarluk's hut. They were green and had spindly branches all over.

"What are they?" Jack asked.

"Standing-ups," Peter said, confidently. "I have seen them in books at the church. Father Didier showed them to us."

"What are they for?" Yvo asked.

Peter shrugged his shoulders and replied, "I don't know."

They did not have too long to wonder about them, of course. Christmas was coming. There were things to be done. There was church to go to at midnight.

Everyone gathered at the little mission. The older people sat on benches against the walls. The younger men and women stood. And the kids played on the floor in the middle. It was warm and there were electric lights; the only electric lights in all of Repulse Bay. On the walls were pictures of the Pope, the Bishop and Queen Elizabeth. Also on one wall hung a giant pendulum clock.

Father Didier, a tall thin man in a black robe, stood with the men and women, smoking his pipe. Around his neck he carried, by a string, a silver cross with Jesus nailed to it. He was a kind man who enjoyed a good laugh. He was our priest, he was our teacher and, when we were sick, he was our nurse.

When the clock chimed midnight, the curtains in front of the church were opened, the benches were rearranged to face the altar and the people sat; women and girls on the left, men and boys on the right. Arvaarluk sat with his mother. Father Didier donned a white, pleated robe and, over that, a fancy vestment with a cross on the back of it. Peter, who was the altar boy, put on a white robe with white lace on the hems. And the service began.

There was a big organ in the church with giant foot pedals and lots of buttons. Father Didier adjusted the buttons, pumped the pedals and played, swaying back and forth as he moved his fingers over the keys. The music filled the small church and people sang:

O come all ye faithful
Joyful and triumphant
O come ye, o come ye
To Bethlehem.

And so Christmas came.

Christmas was a time when you took your most favourite thing in the world and gave it to your very best friend. Arvaarluk trudged into Peter's igloo with his toy gun (the one with the bullets that looked like real bullets) behind his back. He said, "Happy Nuuya," gave the gun to Peter and left. Peter "Happy Nuuyaed" him a pair of caribou-skin mitts which he wore until the palms had no fur at all left on them—and they were still warm.

Arvaarluk's father gave his only telescope and got a wild dog in return. The dog ran away for a whole year, then came back the following Christmas. But no matter how hard they tried, they could not catch her. When all else failed, Arvaarluk's father lay on his belly on the roof of their hut with a lasso in his hand and waited. When the dog approached the bait he had set, he rose and, twirling the lasso around his head, he threw it.

The lasso flew way out and landed right around the dog's head. The hours and hours Arvaarluk's father had spent playing cowboy had paid off. When they finally tamed it, that dog became the best lead dog they ever had.

That Christmas the manager of the Hudson's Bay Company store gave Arvaarluk a blue and red rubber ball with a white stripe around the middle. We loved to play ball. We would set up four bases, try to find a stick to use for a bat and play. If you had a good stick you could hit the ball a long way. Yvo was the best hitter. He was always the biggest and strongest.

But there are no trees in Repulse Bay and when there are no trees, there are hardly ever any sticks to use for bats. At Christmas in 1955, though, there were trees in Repulse Bay. There were six of them.

Yvo (who was also the smartest) looked at those spindly trees with a twinkle in his eye and said, "I know what those things are for!"

"What?" we all asked.

"Baseball bats," he replied. "Rocky Parsons brought us baseball bats for Christmas."

He got an axe. He took one of the spindly trees and chopped off all spindly branches. Then he fashioned a bat, a real round bat. After much hacking and swinging of the bat to see how it felt, it was ready.

When the kids in Repulse Bay found out about our bat, they all came to play. Yvo batted first with Peter pitching and Arvaarluk playing catcher. Arvaarluk always played catcher since he could not run as much as the other kids. When Yvo hit the ball, it went up far, far away.

"Yay, yay, yay, yay!!!" Everyone cheered, jumping up and down.

Sometimes, when he hit the ball just right, even Arvaarluk could run all the way around and touch all four bases before Jack had time to get the ball and hit him with it to take him out. He would then sit on the fourth base and puff and cough and try to catch his breath. And he would smile and laugh and laugh.

We played ball all that spring and all that summer, making more bats with the spindly trees when they broke. And, in autumn, we could hardly wait for Christmas when, again, the Union Jack would go up the flagpole and Rocky Parsons would, once again, bring us baseball bats for Christmas.

Taima!

from

Tikta'liktak

by

JAMES HOUSTON

While hunting to save his starving family, Tikta'liktak becomes marooned on an ice floe. Finally he struggles to land. The book is illustrated by the author.

As his breath returned to him, Tikta'liktak could scarcely believe that he had reached solid ice and was still alive. Slowly he walked toward the sheltering hills of the great barren island that rose before him, grateful to be on land once more.

He chose a valley that formed a long sheltered passage leading upward to the top of the island. In this valley, under the protecting hills, he built a small strong snowhouse and slept he knew not how long. After this, he lost all track of time.

Tikta'liktak awoke with raging pangs of hunger and hurried out to see what treasures his new island might provide. Weak as he was from lack of food, it took a full day to walk the length of the island. Although Sakkiak was fairly narrow, it also took him a day to cross it because of the steep rocky spine of hills that ran its whole length.

The beaches were blown almost clear. Snow had been driven against the hills in hard wind-packed drifts many times the height of a man. Tikta'liktak walked along the frozen beaches, searching them for any kind of food and peering out hopefully over the shore ice for seals.

Nothing did he see but snow and rock and sometimes bleached white bones or hard dry scraps of bird skins eaten out a season before by foxes. The lemmings, small rodents without tails, seemed not to be on the island, for he saw no tracks. The fat eider ducks had left evidence everywhere, in the form of old nesting places, of their summer occupation of the island. But by the time they returned to lay their eggs, he would surely be dead of hunger.

Often he gazed out across the straits, where the white ice floes churned past in the dangerous rip tides. He could see the mainland hanging blue and serene like a dream of some far-off place. There was his home, his family, his friends. All of them must think that he was dead. The mainland seemed near, and yet to Tikta'liktak, without food or materials or a boat, it was an impossible distance.

Staggering from hunger and fatigue, he returned to the snowhouse that evening and had terrible dreams until he awoke in the morning in the cold grey igloo scarcely knowing whether he was truly awake or still in some dark nightmare.

When he climbed the hill the next day, Tikta'liktak used his harpoon for support, like an old man. He had to tell himself again and again that he had lived fewer than twenty summers.

From the top of the rocky hill, Tikta'liktak saw far out on the drifting ice many walrus, fat, sleek, and brown, lying together motionless like great stones, their tusks showing white in the sunlight. The wind was carrying them away, out to sea, and he could never hope to take one.

Sitting there in the cold wind, with no help, he said aloud, over and over again, "This island is my grave. This island is my grave. I shall never leave this place. I shall never leave this place." The idea obsessed him, and at last, in fright, he hurriedly stumbled downward, falling many times, until he came to the snowhouse and slept again for a very long while.

When he awoke, Tikta'liktak cut small strips from the tops of his boots and chewed them to ease his hunger. This seemed to give him some strength. Then, slowly, as if drawn by magic, he started again up the long hill.

It was warmer now. True spring was coming to the land. But it helped him not at all, for there was nothing living on the island, nor would there be until the birds came to nest again, and that would be too late for him.

On top of the hill once more, Tikta'liktak scanned the sea and saw nothing but water and glaring ice. Again a distant voice seemed to say, "This island is your grave." He stood up slowly and looked around. There were many great flat rocks, and Tikta'liktak decided they would be his final resting place. Two of the largest ones lay near each other, offering him a sheltered bed, and with his failing strength, he dragged two more large stones to make the ends, at head and foot. Another large one placed on top covered the lower half. The stones now formed a rough coffin.

He searched until he found a large flat piece to cover his head. Half laughing and half crying, he climbed into his stony grave. After one last look at the wide blue sky and the sea around him, he lay down with his harpoon, knife, and bow arranged neatly by his side. He hoped that his relatives would someday find his bones and know him by his weapons and know what had happened to him.

Tikta'liktak did not know how long he slept. When he awoke, he was numb with cold. Slowly, a new idea started to form in his mind. "I will not die, I will not die, I will not die." With a great effort, he pushed away the stone that formed the top half of the coffin. Painfully, he arose and staggered out of that self-made grave.

Holding himself as straight as he could with the aid of his harpoon, Tikta'liktak staggered down the side of the hill to the beach. He lay there to rest and again fell asleep. This time he dreamed of many strange things: skin boats rising up from their moorings, haunches of fat year-old caribou, rich dark walrus meat, young ducks with delicious yellow fat, juicy seals, and the warm eggs of a snow owl.

He could not tell if he was asleep or awake, but again and again the head of a seal appeared. It seemed so real in the dream that he took up his harpoon and cast it blindly before him. He felt a great jerk that fully awakened him, and, behold, he had a true seal firmly harpooned. He lay back with his feet against a rock and held onto the harpoon line until the seal's spirit left him.

With his last strength, Tikta'liktak drew the seal out of the water and across the edge of the ice until he had all this richness in his hands. He knew that the seal had been sent to him by the sea spirit and that this gift would give him back his life.

After some food and sleep, and more food and sleep again, he soon felt well. Using his bow, he whirled an arrow swiftly into a hollow scrap of driftwood and dried shavings until they grew hot, smoked, and burst into flames. The seal fat burned nicely in a hollow stone in his snowhouse, making it warm and bright. The spring sun helped to restore his health and strength, and Tikta'liktak remembered once more that he was young.

He kept the meat of the seal in the igloo and prepared the

fat for use in the stone lamp. The sealskin he turned inside out without splitting it open and scraped it with a flattened bone in the special way that he had seen his mother teach his sister.

One day, he found the tracks of a white fox that had come to the island. After that, the fox came to visit his dwelling every day. It always came along the same way, and that was its mistake. Tikta'liktak built a falling-stone trap across its path, baited with a scrap of seal meat.

The next morning, the fox was in the trap, and after skinning it, Tikta'liktak drew from the tail long strong sinews that make the finest thread. That evening he ate the fox meat and placed the fine white skin above his oil lamp to dry. Tikta'liktak also made a good needle by sharpening a thin splinter of bone on a rock, and with this, he mended his clothes.

After his work was done, he stepped out through the entrance of the small igloo to look at the great night sky. It was filled with stars beyond counting that formed patterns familiar to all his people, who used them for guidance when travelling.

Off to the north, great green and yellow lights soared up, slowly faded, then soared again in their magic way. Tikta'liktak's people knew that these were caused by the night spirits playing the kicking game in the sky. In the way his father had taught him, he whistled and pushed his hands up to the sky, marvelling as the lights ebbed and flowed with his movements as though he controlled them.

Life on the island was better now, but still Tikta'liktak longed to return home to his own people.

Half of another moon passed, and now the spring sun hung just below the horizon each night and would not let the sky grow dark. Two seals appeared in the open waters of the bay in front of the snowhouse, and by good fortune, Tikta'liktak managed to harpoon first one and then the other. This gave him an abundance of food and of oil to heat his igloo. He again carefully drew the meat out of the seals, without cutting them open in the usual method, and scraped and dried the skins.

Tikta'liktak sat before his small house thinking and making plans. An idea for building a kind of boat without any tools or driftwood for the frame had finally come to him.

He began to prepare one of the three sealskins. First, he tied the skin tightly and carefully where the back flippers had been so that no water could enter. Then where the seal's neck had been, he bound in a piece of bone, hollow through the middle. When he had finished, he put his mouth to the hole and, with many strong breaths, blew the skin up so that it looked again like a fat seal. Next, he fitted a small piece of driftwood in the bone to act as a plug and hold in the air.

The sun was warm on his back as he worked with his floats on that bright spring morning. His stomach was full, his clothes were mended, and he began to make a song inside himself, hoping that someday he might return to his people on the mainland. The song had magic in it. It spoke of fear and wonder and of life and hope. The words came well. There was joy in Tikta'liktak and yet a warning of danger, too.

He looked up from his work as a huge shadow loomed over him. Tikta'liktak threw himself sideways, rolling toward his harpoon, which he caught hold of as he sprang to his feet. Before him, between his small house and the sea, stood a huge white bear. The bear's mouth was half open, and its blue-black tongue lolled between its strong teeth. Its little eyes were watching him warily as it decided how best to kill him.

Fear stirred the hair on the back of Tikta'liktak's neck and reached down into his stomach. His harpoon was small for a beast such as this one, and although he had often heard of encounters with bears, Tikta'liktak had never met one face to face.

Remembering the wise words of his father, Tikta'liktak carefully studied every movement of the bear. He tried to think like a bear to understand what the great beast would do next. He slowly knelt down and felt with the chisel end of the harpoon for a crack between two rocks. Finding this, he wedged it in firmly and levelled the pointed end at the bear's throat. He had not long to wait for the attack.

The bear lunged forward, and the harpoon pierced the white fur and went deep into its throat. Tikta'liktak held the harpoon as long as he could, then rolled away, but not before he felt the bear's great claws rake the side of his face. He scrambled to his feet and ran uphill.

The huge beast tried to follow, but the harpoon caught and caught again in the rocks, forcing the point more deeply inward. The harpoon found its life, and with a great sigh, the bear's spirit rushed out and it was dead.

Tikta'liktak's face was numb at first. Then it started to throb with pain. He made his way slowly to a small hillside stream that flowed from the melting snow down to the sea. There he washed his face in the clear icy water.

Returning to his snowhouse, he took a patch of foxskin the size of his hand, scraped and scrubbed it clean, and set it squarely over the terrible wound. As it dried, the clean patch of foxskin tightened and grew smaller. It drew the open wounds together almost forming a new skin on his face.

Tikta'liktak was weak after his fight with the bear and nervous of every shadow. Also, he feared that his wound might fester, so he washed the foxskin dressing often. In time, his face showed signs of healing, and the pain ceased to bother him.

Then Tikta'liktak set about making a little stone and sod house for the summer like the ancient houses of his forefathers. He had no material to make the kind of sealskin tent now used by his people.

Inside the new house, it was warm and comfortable, and the light from his small lamp glowed brightly. The new bearskin was warm to sleep on and the meat good to eat. At this time, another seal came to him one evening in the half dark of spring before the moon had fully risen. It did not see Tikta'liktak until his harpoon reached it.

Cutting this seal open in the usual way, from the rear flippers to the throat, Tikta'liktak then scraped and stretched the skin. With the skin, he made new hip-length boot tops to sew above his own. These bound with drawstrings and packed with dried moss were quite waterproof.

He had placed the two shoulder blades of the white bear under a stone in the water so that the sea lice would pick them clean as snow. He now bound them firmly with seal thongs to each end of his harpoon. In this way, he made a strong double-bladed paddle.

On a windless day, he tied the three blown-up sealskins together and placed them in the shallow water. Sitting astride them, he balanced himself and floated. It took some practice before he was able to hold steady and paddle and control this strange craft, but a boat of any kind seemed his only chance of reaching the mainland again.

By day, Tikta'liktak would look out over the great expanse of water with its treacherous tides and wonder if he had lived through this terrible spring only to drown. At night, he would dream of his mother, his father, and his sisters. He wondered if they had starved or had found food as he had and were still alive.

He must try to make the crossing. First, he gathered a small parcel of meat, which he wrapped in seal fat so it would float and covered with sealskin so that it would be protected from the salt of the sea. Tikta'liktak tied the package to his waist with a thong, and it floated nicely behind him like a small duck. He filled two seal bladder pouches with fresh water, and these he hung around his neck.

The next morning was grey with fog, but the wind was down, and he decided this would be the day to start the dangerous journey. Pushing the inflated sealskin floats into the water, Tikta'liktak carefully climbed onto the strange watercraft. Then he started out, with only one glance back at his island home and upward to his open grave on top of the hill.

Cautiously, he began to use the bone paddle to steer out into the current, which swirled away from the island and carried him into the open water of the strait. With alarm, he noticed the great strength of the tide as it swept him eastward instead of north to the mainland as he had hoped. Tikta'liktak paddled very gently, careful not to upset his frail craft, learning as he went to guide it with his feet, which hung down awkwardly like those of a young snow goose trying to swim for the first time.

Tikta'liktak tried not to look down, for he could see far below him in the clear grey water great fronds of seaweed waving mysteriously, moved by powerful underwater currents. A light breeze rippled over the surface of the water, sending him out toward the centre of the strait. He could see the rip-tides now pressing down or swelling upward in a smooth icy rush. His feet and legs began to feel the freezing grip of the water, although they stayed dry. The chill of the sea drove through his boots, moss packing, and heavy fur socks, leaving him numb with cold.

Slowly, the hills of Sakkiak grew smaller and turned blue in the distance. Tikta'liktak judged himself to be halfway to the mainland. He paddled gently to give himself direction in the fast-moving current and was carried on the tide through grey patches of mist that hung over the water. Now stiff with cold and thirsty, he managed to drink a little of the fresh water from one of the pouches that hung around his neck and paddled on through the eerie silence.

Suddenly, Tikta'liktak heard a familiar sound, a sound he feared. It boomed across the water again and again, the great grunting roar of a huge bull walrus. The tide was carrying him straight into the herd the walrus was jealously protecting.

Dark heads appeared as the large herd grouped together, peering weak-eyed at this new intruder. Almost all of them showed the long thin tusks of female walrus.

The old bull separated from the herd, ready for combat. It started to rear up in the water, trying to see and also to frighten the new enemy, while working itself into a fury. Tikta'liktak knew that to the poor eyesight of the beast he would look like another walrus trying to enter the herd.

With a roaring bellow, the great bull, flashing its white tusks, dove beneath the surface and went straight at Tikta'liktak. He braced himself, expecting to be lifted from the water, when to his surprise the old bull rose up before him locked in combat with a powerful young male walrus.

Tikta'liktak watched them struggle, their tusks ripping and locking, their eyes rolling. The water around them frothed white and then turned red with blood.

By good fortune, helped by the tide and steady paddling, Tikta'liktak was carried safely away. The huge struggling beasts thrashed in the sea, never noticing that he had drifted onward.

Seabirds screamed around him, and he felt the welcome pull

of the tide as it drew him at last toward the shores of the mainland. The dark granite cliffs seemed to tower over him when he
drifted into their shadows. Delicate lacings of snow on the cliffs
glowed in the long rays of the evening sun.

Suddenly, with a bump that almost upset him, Tikta'liktak felt
solid rock beneath his feet. He stumbled ashore, scarcely able to
stand on his numb, nearly frozen legs. Looking back over the
waters he had crossed, he was filled with gratitude that the spirits who guard the land and sea and sky had allowed him to make
his dangerous journey.

Dragging behind him the three inflated sealskins, Tikta'liktak
struggled over the rocky beach while the first shower of summer
rain beat against his face. With his knife, he cut the thongs that
held the bone paddle blades to his harpoon, and it again became
his weapon. He then cut the three skin floats open from end to
end, and placing the dry inside of one beneath himself, he
stretched the other two over himself and fell deeply asleep.

He was awakened by the damp cold the next morning. The
mists of early summer hung down everywhere, obscuring the
cliffs and the seabirds that cried above him.

Joyful at the thought of being once again on the mainland after
so many moons, he jumped up, ate some of the meat in his small
package, drank some fresh water from a nearby stream, and set
out along the coast toward the west. Although Tikta'liktak had
never travelled in this part of the country before, he knew it
would be easier and safer to stay on the coast than to risk a
straighter path across the mountains. Climbing would use up his
strength, and perhaps he would lose his way.

Tikta'liktak walked for two long days and slept at night under
rock ledges like a wild animal. Then he came to a narrow inlet
that he had never seen before, but he recognized it from his

grandfather's description as the bay called "The Place of Beautiful Stones."

Walking fearfully along the edge of the small half-hidden cove, it did indeed seem like a place from another world. The grey rock cliffs that stood above him had the weird forms of ancient giants. At the end of the small bay, a well-worn path led up to the mouth of a dark cave in the crumbling rock wall.

Tikta'liktak stood before it in the gloom of the late afternoon listening for some sound, almost afraid to enter, yet eager to see for himself the inside of this strange place.

Hearing nothing save the dripping of water, he bent down and stepped quickly into the cave. Its entrance was small, but the cave was large inside and rose to a great height. When his eyes grew accustomed to the half darkness, he knelt down and examined the floor of the cave.

It was covered with smooth round white pebbles, and among them lay a number of shining red stones. These were so sharply cut that Tikta'liktak's people believed they could only have been shaped by strange men or spirits. There were also other stones cut in this wondrous way, and as clear as water, they glowed like the waning moon even in the half darkness.

Tikta'liktak looked to the wall on his left, and there, just as his grandfather had said, were two neat rows of holes, exactly as many as he had fingers and toes, each containing a fox skull bleached white with age. Near these, embedded in the walls, were more red stones that seemed to wink like eyes in the fading light.

Some said that this was an ancient secret place of the little people who used to rule the land. It was here they came to collect and cut the precious stones they loved to have and to trade sometimes with other people.

Tikta'liktak gathered a few stones and would have taken more, but he heard a tapping sound deep in the cave and hurried out. He walked quickly all of that night, glad to be away from the strange place.

Throughout the next day, he slept peacefully on a moss-covered ledge above the sea. Before he fell asleep, he watched a rough-legged hawk circling high above him and heard brown female eider ducks cooing below as they plucked the soft down from their breasts to line the warm nests they were building for their young.

That evening as Tikta'liktak strode along the coast in the soft twilight of the Arctic summer, he saw the rugged coastal mountains sloping gently into the great inland plain. Crossing the foothills, he finally reached the immense plain that stood before his homeland. Now his feet welcome every step forward in the soft tundra.

The warm sun the next morning followed its course through the eastern sky, and small bright flowers burst into bloom everywhere. The edge of each pond was made beautiful by patches of white Arctic cotton that swayed in the light breeze. Best of all, his namesake, the butterfly, travelled in a straight line before him and seemed to guide him on the long journey homeward.

Now he saw many caribou lying on the hillside with their brown backs blending into the land itself, their antlers covered in thick summer velvet. Tikta'liktak ran for joy to think that he was once again in a place of plenty.

He waded straight across wide shallow lakes, whose water came no higher than his knees, and through streams where every step sent fat sea trout darting away like silver arrows. As he travelled, he crossed high sandy beaches covered with shells, where the sea had washed in ancient times.

At last, he looked across the valley and recognized the three familiar hills that stood before his home—Telik, Egalalik, and Ashivak. Soon he would be among his own people. Were they alive? He was almost afraid to know.

He hurried down the gravel slope, across the boulder-strewn floor of the valley that had once been the bed of an immense river, up through the mossy pass between Egalalik and Ashivak, and up the rise past the small lake where his family took their water for drinking. There lay his sister's sealskin water bucket beside a freshly worn path. They must be living still.

Tikta'liktak sat down beside the path and thought. "If I appear before them quickly, they will think I am a ghost or spirit, for they must surely believe I am dead."

Getting up, he peered around a large rock down into that beloved valley. There was the big sealskin tent of his family, and beyond it the tent of his uncle, and a little father up the valley, the family tents of Tauki and Kungo. Tikta'liktak saw his mother bending over at the entrance to their tent with her head deep in her hood, as was the custom of his people when sad. He saw his sister Sharni carrying something that looked like clothing. She took this to her mother, who placed it on a small pile before her. A moment later, Tikta'liktak saw his father step out of their tent and gaze toward the sea.

In the long shadows of early morning, he saw Kungo and his family, soon followed by the others, walk down toward his father's tent. Although it was not cold, they all had their hoods drawn over their heads in sadness and wore their oldest clothes. Tikta'-liktak wondered how he could let them know he had returned without frightening them.

He walked back until he reached the edge of the hill behind the camp, where he knew his figure would be seen easily against the morning sky. Now he moved slowly. Kungo's sharp eyes saw him first. Tikta'liktak watched him point and call to the others in a low hunter's voice. In a moment, they were all looking at him on the skyline.

"Who is that?" said Kungo's daughter.

"Can it be?" asked his sister.

"That person has the shape of Tikta'liktak and his way of walking," said Tauki.

Tikta'liktak coughed twice, and they all said, "That is his cough. He coughs in that way."

Then someone said, "Ghost," and another said, "Spirit," and he could see they were all about to run away.

"Relatives," he called in a soft, ordinary voice. "I have returned. I am glad to see you all again." And he sat down on a rock and started to chant and sing a funny little song his mother had taught them as children.

Sharni, his sister, called, "Brother of mine, that must be the real you singing that song and no ghost!"

Tikta'liktak answered, "Sister of mine, it is really me. May I come down to you and visit?"

They all began to talk at once. Then Tikta'liktak's father called to him, "Come forward," and he walked out bravely, alone, to meet this ghost, or perhaps his returning son, halfway between the hill and camp.

Tikta'liktak's father looked frightened and suspicious. But coming up to his son, he reached out timidly, touched his arm, and tenderly ran his hand over the great new scars on his son's face. He then passed his hand over his eyes, and feeling tears in them, he leaned forward and gave Tikta'liktak a hug that nearly broke his bones.

In a voice ringing with joy, his father called to his wife and daughters and all the others, saying that this was no ghost but a real person and that, on the very day that they were to give his clothes away, their son at long last had returned home to them.

Tikta'liktak's mother and sisters led him gently into the dark skin tent and seated him on their wide bed made of sweet-smelling summer heather covered with soft, thick winter caribou skins.

They drew off the long worn-out sealskin boots that he had made and replaced them with warm fur slippers. Slowly, they fed him many of the good things he had dreamed of during his long adventure.

When Tikta'liktak could eat no more, he lay back on the rich warm skins, feeling full of food and contentment. His family was well, and he was overjoyed to be alive and once again in the tent of his father. He closed his eyes and drifted peacefully toward sleep.

In his mind's eye, there arose a shining vision of his island home. Sakkiak now seemed to him a warm and friendly place, for it had become a part of his life, a part of himself.

Tikta'liktak's song floated down to him from the sky. Each word had found its proper place. He could feel himself swaying to the rhythm of the big drum that beat inside him, and he heard the long answering chorus of women's voices in some distant dance house. His mind, knowing the words, started singing softly:

Ayii, yaii,
Ayii, yaii,
The great sea
Has set me in motion,
Set me adrift,
And I moved

As a weed moves
In the river.

The arch of the sky
And mightiness of storms
Encompassed me,
And I am left
Trembling with joy,
Ayii, yaii,
Ayii, yaii.

About the
Contributors

MARGARET BUFFIE lives in Winnipeg, Manitoba. She is the author of five young adult novels, including *The Guardian Circle, My Mother's Ghost* and *The Dark Garden*. In 1996, she received the Vicky Metcalf Award for her body of work. *Who Is Frances Rain?* won the C.L.A. Young Adult Book Award. Margaret Buffie's latest novel is *Angels Turn Their Backs*.

ROCH CARRIER's novels and short stories are well known both in French and English. Many of his stories are as beloved by children as by adults, especially "The Hockey Sweater," which has become a Canadian classic. *Prayers of a Very Wise Child* received the Stephen Leacock Award for Humour. An officer of the Order of Canada, Roch Carrier recently finished a term as head of the Canada Council. He lives in Montreal, Quebec.

JOAN CLARK has written novels and short stories for adults as well as six children's books, including *The Hand of Robin Squires* and *The Moons of Madeleine*. She received the Marian Engel Award and was chosen for the Canada–Scotland Writer Exchange. *The Dream Carvers*—a younger reader's version of her adult novel, *Eriksdottir*—received Mr. Christie's Book Award and the Geoffrey Bilson Award for Historical Fiction for Young People. Joan Clark lives in St. John's, Newfoundland.

GEORGE CHARLES CLUTESI (1905–88), was a member of the Tse-Shaht Nation and lived in Port Alberni, Vancouver Island. He was an artist, actor and lecturer who recorded and taught the stories, songs, dances and art of the Nootka people. His other books are *Potlatch* and *Stand Tall, My Son* (unpublished).

MARY ALICE DOWNIE is an editor and reviewer and the author of more than twenty children's novels, picture books and retold folk tales, including *Honor Bound, The Wind Has Wings: Poems from Canada* and *Snow Paws*. She lives in Kingston, Ontario, where she is helping to produce a musical version of two of her adapted French-Canadian folk tales, including "The Witch Canoe."

BRIAN DOYLE has won numerous awards for his many novels for young people: the C.L.A. Book-of-the-Year for Children Award for *Up to Low, Easy Avenue* and *Uncle Ronald*, Mr. Christie's Book Award for *Covered Bridge* and *Uncle Ronald* and, in 1991, the Vicky Metcalf Award for his body of work. He was named Canada's entry for the international Hans Christian Andersen Medal in 1998. Brian Doyle lives in Ottawa, Ontario.

JAMES HOUSTON was made an officer of the Order of Canada for his many contributions to Canadian culture, including being the prime force in the promotion of Inuit art. A renowned artist and a Master Designer for Steuben Glass, he is also the author of many books for adults and children. He won the C.L.A. Book-of-the-Year for Children Award for *Tikta'liktak*, *The White Archer* and *River Runners*, and the Vicky Metcalf Award for his body of work. He lived in the Arctic for many years and now divides his time between New England and the Queen Charlotte Islands in British Columbia.

MICHAEL ARVAARLUK KUSUGAK spent his first eleven years in Repulse Bay, at the northern tip of the Hudson Bay, and lived many years in other parts of the eastern Arctic. He has written six picture books, all reflecting his Inuit background. They include *A Promise Is a Promise* (co-authored with Robert Munsch), *My Arctic 123* and his latest, *Arctic Stories*. *Northern Lights: The Soccer Trails* won the Ruth Schwartz Award. Michael Kusugak lives in Winnipeg, Manitoba.

JULIE LAWSON lives in Sooke on Vancouver Island, B.C. She writes both novels and picture books for children, including *A Morning to Polish and Keep, Fires Burning, Cougar Cove* and *Whatever You Do, Don't Go Near That Canoe!* *The Dragon's Pearl* won the NAPPA Award for Folklore in the U.S., and *White Jade Tiger* won the Sheila Egoff Award. Her latest book is *Goldstone*.

CELIA BARKER LOTTRIDGE based *Ticket to Curlew* and its sequel, *Wings to Fly*, on stories her father told her about his early years in Alberta. She lives in Toronto where she is a storyteller and the director of the Parent–Child Mother Goose program. Her writing for children includes novels, picture books and retold folk tales. *Ten Small Tales* won the Storytellers Choice Award and the Toronto I.O.D.E. Award; *Ticket to Curlew* won the C.L.A. Book-of-the-Year for Children Award, the Geoffrey Bilson Award and was an IBBY Honour Book for Canada. Her latest book is *Music for the Tsar of the Sea*.

JANET LUNN has written picture books, non-fiction and historical novels for children. *The Root Cellar* and *Shadow in Hawthorn Bay* won the C.L.A. Book-of-the-Year for Children Award. *Shadow in Hawthorn Bay* also won the Canada Council Children's Literature Prize, the I.O.D.E. Violet Downey Award and the C.L.A. Young Adult Book Award. *Amos's Sweater* won the Ruth Schwartz Award and *The Story of Canada* (co-authored with Christopher Moore) won Mr. Christie's Book Award and the Information Book Award. Janet Lunn has received the Vicky Metcalf Award for her body of work and was recently appointed a member of the Order of Canada. Her newest novel is *The Hollow Tree*. She lives in the country near Hillier, Ontario, where many of the characters in her novels first settled.

JANET MCNAUGHTON lives in St. John's, Newfoundland. Her first novel, *Catch Me Once, Catch Me Twice,* and her latest, *Make or Break Spring*, are both set in St. John's during World War Two. *To Dance at the Palais Royale* is based on stories of when her mother and aunts came to Canada. It won the I.O.D.E. Violet Downey Book Award, the Ann Conner Brimer Award for Children's Literature in Atlantic Canada and the Geoffrey Bilson Award.

KEVIN MAJOR has written young adult and adult novels, plays and, most recently, an illustrated book, *The House of Wooden Santas*. *Hold Fast* and *Eating between the Lines* both won the C.L.A. Book-of-the-Year for Children Award; *Hold Fast* also won the Canada Council Children's Literature Prize, the Ruth Schwartz

Award and was recently chosen second on a list of the best Canadian kids' books of all time. *Far from Shore* received the C.L.A. Young Adult Award, and *Eating between the Lines* won the Ann Connor Brimer Award. In 1992, Kevin Major received the Vicky Metcalf Award for his body of work. He lives in St. John's, Newfoundland.

LUCY MAUD MONTGOMERY (1874 1942) grew up in Cavendish, Prince Edward Island, and later moved to Ontario. Her first novel, *Anne of Green Gables*, still draws visitors to Prince Edward Island from all over the world. She wrote twenty-two books of fiction, hundreds of poems and short stories, and ten volumes of journals. *Emily of New Moon* has recently been adapted for television.

FARLEY MOWAT has written over twenty books of non-fiction and fiction for adults and children, many of them evoking his passion for the natural world. He has won the C.L.A. Book-of-the-Year for Children Award for *Lost in the Barrens* and the Vicky Metcalf Award for his body of work. An officer of the Order of Canada, Farley Mowat lives in Ontario and Cape Breton Island.

KIT PEARSON has written six novels for children and retold a folk tale, *The Singing Basket*. She has won the C.L.A. Book-of-the-Year for Children Award for *A Handful of Time* and *The Sky Is Falling*; the Geoffrey Bilson Award for *The Sky Is Falling* and *The Lights Go On Again*; Mr. Christie's Book Award for *The Sky Is Falling*; the Manitoba Young Reader's Choice Award for *Looking at the Moon*; the I.O.D.E. Violet Downey Book Award for *The Lights Go On Again*; and the Ruth Schwartz Award and the Governor General's Award for her latest book, *Awake and Dreaming*.

SIR CHARLES G.D. ROBERTS (1860–1943) was an influential poet, a popular lecturer and the author of over a dozen volumes of animal stories, which were based on his boyhood in rural New Brunswick. His books include *Red Fox*, *The Kindred of the Wild* and *The Feet of the Furtive*. He was knighted in 1935.

SHIRLEY STERLING, a member of the interior Salish Nation, grew up on a ranch near Merritt, B.C. *My Name Is Seepeetza*, her first novel, is based on her experiences at an Indian residential school in Kamloops. It won the Sheila Egoff Award. Shirley Sterling lives in Vancouver and in Nanaimo, where she teaches First Nations Studies at Malaspina College.

JAN TRUSS writes short stories, plays, poetry and novels for adults and children, including *Summer Goes Riding* and *A Very Small Rebellion*. *Bird At the Window* won the Alberta Search for a New Novel Award. She lives in Water Valley, Alberta, where *Jasmin* is set. It won the Ruth Schwartz Award.

BUDGE WILSON has written twenty novels, books of short stories and picture books for children, young adults and adults. *The Leaving* won the C.L.A. Young Adult Award and the City of Dartmouth Book Award; the title story from it won first prize in the CBC Literary Competition in 1981. *Oliver's Wars* won the Ann Connor Brimer Award and *Lorinda's Diary* won the Marianna Dempster Award. Budge Wilson lives in North West Cove, Nova Scotia. Her latest young adult novel is *Sharla*.

TIM WYNNE-JONES, who lives near Perth, Ontario, has written adult and young people's novels and short stories, picture books, radio plays, musical lyrics, a libretto and songs. He was the children's book columnist for *The Globe and Mail* and an editor for Red Deer College Press. *Some of the Kinder Planets* and *The Maestro* both won the Governor General's Award, and *Planets* was the first Canadian book to win the *Boston Globe*-Horn Book Award. In 1997, Tim Wynne-Jones won the Vicky Metcalf Award for his body of work. His latest young adult novel is *Stephen Fair*.

PAUL YEE grew up in Vancouver and now lives in Toronto. His books include adult non-fiction, young people's novels and short stories, and folk tales. *Tales from Gold Mountain* won the Sheila Egoff Award and the I.O.D.E. Violet Downey Book Award. *Roses Sing on New Snow* and *Ghost Train* both won the Ruth Schwartz Award; the latter book also won the Governor General's Award.